THE HEROES' WELCOME

LOUISA YOUNG

LARGE PRINT

Oxford

First published in Great Britain 2014
by
The Borough Press
an imprint of HarperCollins*Publishers*

Published in Large Print 2015 by ISIS Publishing Ltd.,
7 Centremead, Osney Mead, Oxford OX2 0ES
by arrangement with
HarperCollins*Publishers*

03|16

The moral right of the author has been asserted

CIP data is available for this title from the British Library

ISBN 978–1–4450–9948–4 (hb)
ISBN 978–1–4450–9949–1 (pb)

Printed and bound in Great Britain by
T. J. International Ltd., Padstow, Cornwall

THE HEROES' WELCOME

RJL
RIP

"Joy, warm as the joy that shipwrecked sailors feel when they catch sight of the land ... only a few escape, swimming and struggling out of the frothing surf to reach the shore, their bodies crusted with salt but buoyed up with joy as they plant their feet on solid ground again, spared a deadly fate. So joyous now to her the sight of her husband, vivid in her gaze, that her white arms, embracing his neck, would never for a moment let him go ..."

from *The Odyssey*,
trs Fagles

"I knew that I was more than the something which had been looking out all that day upon the visible earth and thinking and speaking and tasting friendship. Somewhere — close at hand in that rosy thicket or far off beyond the ribs of sunset — I was gathered up with an immortal company, where I and poet and lover and flower and cloud and star were equals, as all the little leaves were equal ruffling before the gusts, or sleeping and carved out of the silentness. And in that company I learned that I am something which no fortune can touch, whether I be soon to die or long years away. Things will happen which will trample and pierce, but I shall go on, something that is here and there like the wind, something unconquerable, something not to be separated from the dark earth and the light sky, a strong citizen of infinity and eternity. The confidence and ease had become a deep joy; I knew that I could not do without the Infinite, nor the Infinite without me."

"The Stile"
from *Light and Twilight*,
by Edward Thomas

"It has taken some ten years for my blood to recover."

from *Goodbye to All That*
by Robert Graves

Part One

1919

CHAPTER
ONE

London, March 1919

Riley Purefoy did not think very much about the war. He didn't have to. It was part of him. If others mentioned it . . .

. . . but then they didn't: neither the other old soldiers, who had, most of them, realised very quickly that nobody wanted to hear what they might have to say, nor the civilians, who drifted away at the same rate as the soldiers fell silent.

Phrases and scraps, from time to time, slithered back at him. There was a taste in his throat sometimes, unidentified. There was an insistent image of bits of coughed-up gassed lung on the floor of an ambulance, which brought with it the necessity of standing still for a moment. There were moments still, a year and a half after he had stumbled off the battlefield, when the silence confused him as dry land confuses a sailor's legs. There was Peter Locke's voice, saying: "Then you're in charge, old boy." This last stuck with him, because he knew that however unlikely it seemed, this remained largely true. He was in charge.

Despite his physical damage, Riley was well equipped: a sturdy young man, clear-eyed. So as the months went by, when he did think of war, he thought more of future war, and how to prevent it; of the future children, and how to keep them safe from it, or of the future of his fellow wounded; and how to improve it. He saw people look at him with pity and doubt. He registered the small (or large) involuntary gasps that his scarred face provoked. When a taxi driver drove off because he couldn't understand what Riley was saying, Riley did his best to conjure sympathy for the man's embarrassment over natural fucking anger at this continued humiliation.

He was quite aware that not many people thought he'd add up to much, poor fellow. But if he learnt anything from being shot to bits and patched up again, it was this: now is a good time to do what you want.

Riley Purefoy and Nadine Waveney married under a daftly beautiful wave of London blossom cresting over a city that had been at war for so long that it didn't know what to do with itself. On the wall of the register office a sign read: "No Confetti — Defence of the Realm Act". The flying blossom storm took no notice of that, dizzying eddies of it on the spring breeze, and mad sugar-pink drifts accumulating against the damp Chelsea kerbstones. Nadine, still so skinny she wasn't having her monthlies, wore Riley's vest under Julia Locke's utterly out-of-date wedding dress from before the war, taken in. Riley was in uniform. Peter Locke, Riley's former CO, tall, courteous and almost sober, was best man. Peter's cousin Rose was maid of honour, in white gloves, and his son Tom, flaxen-haired symbol

4

of innocence and possibility, was the pageboy. No one else was there. Tom's mother, Julia, had picked early white lilac and given it to Rose to bring up from Locke Hill, but she didn't come herself. She was not well enough, or perhaps just embarrassed. It had only been a few months since her own crisis. It had only been a few months since everything.

Afterwards, they went to the pub across the road where, it turned out, Peter had earlier deposited two bottles of Krug '04, acquired he didn't care to say how. Rose was in the dark green tweed suit that she'd worn to Peter and Julia's wedding (though she thought she wouldn't mention that), and confessed to a small thrill of shame to be in a pub. It was a beautiful ceremony and a happy day. Any fear that anyone might have had for the future of the marriage, its precipitous start, the battered souls of the bride and groom, lay unmentioned. It was a great time for not mentioning. No one wanted to remind anyone of anything. As though anyone had forgotten.

The bride and groom were to spend the wedding night at Peter's mother's house in Chester Square, where the tall handsome rooms were still draped with dustsheets and the chandeliers swathed in pale holland, because the old lady still didn't dare come down from Scotland.

They had not kissed. How could they? Through the long quiet winter of 1918-19 at Locke Hill, Nadine (so jumpy and tender, crop-headed) and he (damaged) had taken long walks with their arms around each other, spent long days curled up together on the chintz sofa, and failed over and over to go to bed at all, because they could not go to bed together, and did not want to part. They had paused, like bulbs underground in winter, immobilised, and reverted to a kind of reinvented virginity, as if their tumultuous romance had never been consummated during the unfettered years of war.

That the war was over, and things were to be different, was the largest truth in the house. The next was that nobody — apart from Rose — had much idea of what happened now. But for Riley and Nadine, one immediate shift was that the sexual liberties allowed by the possibility of imminent death had disappeared like a midsummer night's dream. Their reborn chastity happened passively and without comment between them. This had seemed to each of them at the time a form of safety, but by their wedding night Riley had become hideously aware of it, and also of the fact that he did not know what his new wife was thinking on the subject. He recalled the letter she had sent him in 1915: "Riley, don't you ever ever ever again not tell me what is going on with you . . ." But saintly woman though she was — in fact *because* of her saintliness — he could not — and he was aware of the irony here — find the words.

Riley brought with him to Chester Square various accoutrements: his etched brass drinking straw made from a shell casing, a gift from Jarvis at the Queen's Hospital Facial Injuries Unit; a rubber thing with a bulb, for squirting and rinsing; small sponges on sticks, for cleaning; mouthwashes of alcohol and peppermint.

6

His pellets of morphine, carried with him in a little yellow tin which used to hold record-player needles, everywhere, always, just in case. In case of what? he thought. In case someone shoots my jaw off again?

Riley's mouth had for so long been the territory first of bloody destruction, then of its complex rebuilding by surgery and medical men, that he had trouble seeing it as his at all. Eating was still difficult, and took a long time. Trying to chew was difficult, trying to swallow, trying not to choke, trying not to dribble, even though he couldn't always tell that he was dribbling because his nerve endings could not be relied on to know where they were. Trying to cough, or stop coughing. Learning to live with somewhat undisciplined saliva and phlegm — though that had improved a lot, thank Christ — and to accept that even when he had learnt to live with it, other people would always find it disgusting. Learning to accept when Nadine passed him a handkerchief. Learning to accept endless generosity and inventiveness with soups and coddled eggs and milk puddings, fools and mousses and shape from Mrs Joyce, the cook: baby food, he'd thought, then get over it, and he was getting over it. He still did not care to eat with others. The embarrassment of some strangers, the inappropriate concern of others, Nadine's careful developed calmness, all exhausted him, but worse in its way was his own requirement of himself that he calmly ignore the food that started bit by bit to reappear as the privations of rationing faded away — fragrant Sunday joints, the clean crunchy salads, the chokable pies, the sweet smells of potatoes frying in butter, chicken roasting,

7

bread baking. At times he was afraid of his own breath, of stagnant saliva, of deadened unresponsive lips, of his medicalised mouth in the normal world. He would clean it fanatically; and he would lapse into silence, sometimes, for several days, knowing that speaking was exercising, and he should do it, as he should eat. At times, during the winter, after their reunion and before their wedding, he had not known what he had to offer her.

The rooms at Chester Square were graceful and quiet. Rose, tall kind Rose who had nursed him at the Queen's, had set up a decanter of whisky and some cold supper in the drawing room.

"Have a sandwich," he said to Nadine. Egg and cress, he thought. Rose made them specially because they're soft. He knew it was courtesy and affection, but in his longing for normality he couldn't help feeling it as controlling, as singling him out . . . Oh it's not the kindness of Rose's response that singles you out, Riley. It's the damage itself. He was so grateful. He was getting tired of being grateful. But he was grateful.

Nadine, perched on the corner of a sofa half unfurled from its covering, took a little white triangle. He knew she didn't like eating in front of him either, though he pretended he didn't, hoping that she would get over it. It was another thing he had to be gracious about. They each drank a little whisky, and were silent. He was terribly happy. Look at her! With her yellow eyes and her sideways smile. But —

It is our wedding night. But —

8

He couldn't — didn't want to — put it into words. Oh the irony! If he could speak clearly, there would be no need to say anything! If my mouth was normal, I wouldn't have to speak, I could just . . . act . . . He looked at her, and in his mind his look became a caress, a touch, an invitation, a demand . . . how could he follow up such a look? How could she respond to it? He looked away.

Nadine, as nervous as him, stood suddenly, and said, "Well!" cheerfully, smiled at him, and started for the door. He stood too, wondering whether he would follow, or wait. He didn't know. He went out into the hall and as she reached the landing she looked back at him, and said, briskly, "It doesn't matter, you know."

He, who knew her so well, did not know what she meant by it. It doesn't matter? Of course it bloody matters.

She was off, almost scurrying, into the bedroom. So he went up, and stood in the doorway. She was further round, out of view, putting on a nightgown — a new one.

Then he was in the bathroom, trying to clean his mouth without disgusting illustrative noise, and his thoughts flooded in: We should have talked of it. I should have kissed her before this. I should have prepared — myself — her . . . But how could he kiss her? He had tried it out, on his own arm, like a youth. His lips had lain there, incompetent. He could not kiss her — not her mouth, her breast, nor any part of her. He could remember kissing her. It tormented him.

When he came back she was in bed, so he undressed. The previous times — before, during the war — they had blushed and fumbled and laughed and burned up and torn each other's clothes off: the first time, in the field; the miraculous interlude in Victoria. He had never seen her in a nightgown before, in bed. His wife. Safe and sweet. Her hair had grown back a little over the winter, the wild dark curls starting to coil again. She'd brushed it.

She was smiling up at him — nervously? He didn't want to make her nervous.

It was pretty clear to him that she couldn't want him that way. Damaged as he was. How could she?

She was thinking: Why did I say that, on the landing? "It doesn't matter?" What doesn't matter?

She'd felt foolish even before the words came out. She thought: I'm sure he would want me, if he was physically, um . . . She was thinking: I must not pressurise him . . . but he hasn't — since — and he's had so much morphine, over the past years . . . She didn't know, actually, if he was still taking it. There were areas of his life where his independence and his privacy were so important to him, which was quite right. Quite right. She had been watching him, cautiously. He did not seem to see himself as a patient, or a cripple, and she was not going to tell him that he was. She didn't know if he was or not. Even if she had an opinion, it was not her decision.

She had been thinking about this moment for weeks. Something would change, now they were married. The most important thing (which she had borne in mind all winter, and was, she felt, doing well at integrating) was

10

that, specially as she *had* been a nurse, she absolutely must not become *his* nurse. But this vital consideration made it difficult for her to, for example, enquire about whether the morphine had affected his . . . Hm.

To be blunt . . .

She didn't know if he would be physically capable. She didn't know how to ask. Or if she wanted to ask. She hadn't wanted to spoil anything by asking. They had always been so magically immediate with each other, understanding, catching eyes. Since they were children they'd had that! Apart from the one great stupid error, his attack of spurious honour, of over-gentlemanliness, when he'd told her he had a girl in France, when in fact there was no girl, it was that he hadn't wanted to inflict his wounds on her — oh, Lord, the kindness he had meant by that, and the *arrogance* . . . Apart from that, *that little thing*, they'd never really had to ask, or explain, about anything. She didn't want to ask now. She wanted the romantic. She wanted them to be magical, not to have to ask or explain. They *had* to be romantic. Because if they weren't romantic, what were they? She was aware how their union could be seen. She was damned if she was going to be seen as his nurse, and him as some pathetic, incapacitated . . .

Stop it. Nobody thinks that. And who cares if they do?

And a woman is not meant to want it anyway . . .

Yes, but I'm not that kind of squashed, repressed Victorian woman — and I bet they did want it, they just didn't dare say . . .

And . . .

11

He came back in his pyjama bottoms. His face, so extraordinary. His mouth. The beautiful upper lip, the battlefield below. The skin above smoothed ivory by morphine, the scars below carefully shaven, not hidden, not displayed, only the moustache worn a little long, like the hair of his head, so as not to frighten people too much. His beautiful grey eyes. Twenty-three years old, looking a hundred. She watched his arm reaching in the shadow to turn out the lamp: the long scar from the Somme streaked across the muscle, shining. The glow from the streetlight outside fell on his strong back, the shape of his shoulders, the curve of his spine. He reached for his pyjama top and she said, "Don't." And saw him misunderstand it.

He pulled it up over his shoulders.

"No," she said. "I didn't mean . . ." and as he came to lie by her she slid her arms inside the shirt, and he sighed.

And one thin layer of tension flew off him — but . . .

But what about my mouth? he thought. I don't . . . She can't . . .

They didn't kiss. They lay entwined on the cool sheet. Awake. Unconsummated.

She doesn't want it, he thought. I mustn't.

He's not . . . He can't, she thought. And I can't —

Well.

If that's it . . .

I must respect that.

12

The proximity of flesh was irresistible. Riley bit his tongue, natural upper teeth to false lower, and rolled over, so his back was to her, so she would not notice.

Oh, she thought.

After quite a long time, they went to sleep.

The day after the wedding, they went to Nadine's parents' house on Bayswater Road. She had not been home since the end of the war. Not for Christmas. Not at all. She had written bland letters to her mother saying she was all right, and less bland ones to her father saying she would come soon, but the fog of shock and exhaustion in which they had been dwelling at that time had prevented her from properly recognising the cruelty of staying away. Neither she nor Riley had even told their parents where they were living. It had been part of the silent arrangement. Nothing, till spring. Just a suspension between past and present which allowed them to attend to neither.

They stood on the steps in the front garden, their backs to Kensington Gardens, the door shiny before them, and each gave the other a brave look as Riley rang the bell. Nadine took Riley's hand, and he felt the flow of feeling shared and supported by the physical union: two bodies stronger than one, two hearts more capacious. Being — becoming — more than the sum of their parts.

A maid answered, and he wondered what had become of Barnes: perhaps he joined up after all. Perhaps he got killed. Or perhaps he got that guesthouse with Mrs Barnes. Let's hope so. It's been six months since the end.

Lady Waveney was home, and Sir Robert too, the maid said, Who could she say was calling?

"I'm Nadine," said Nadine, and the girl blinked, and said: "Oh! She's in there, Miss . . .", and stared: the prodigal daughter returning, and with a wounded officer . . .

Riley knew the look, and what it meant: Oh my word, oh poor thing, such nice eyes, and it's not right to stare, but how can she bear him? He didn't stare back at the maid. And when he and his bride went into the beautiful, unchanged, unforgotten drawing room, all velvets and spring light and rather good paintings, he allowed his new mother-in-law a few moments, too, to look at his face, before he looked up at hers. His determination and habit was to wear his scars without apology but with kindness. The last time they had met (Jacqueline, Lady Waveney, what was he meant to call her?), he had had only his scar from Loos, the little dashing cut on his cheekbone, the clean, romantic, officer-in-a-duel-of-honour scar. So he would be a shock, with his reconstructed jaw, his twisted mouth, his slightly too-long hair lying only slightly effectively over the scars where the skin flaps had been taken from his scalp and brought down to cover his new chin. He was beginning to realise that he did not know what he looked like to anyone else. People said his surgeon, Major Gillies, had done a good job, and Major Gillies himself said it had healed well, and Riley chose to believe this was true. It would have been unhelpful to

14

do otherwise. However. He had learnt that he had to be patient, and allow everyone who saw him their own response, and if necessary lead them through their shock and doubt to the fact that he had accepted his lot. This despite the fact that his speech was not entirely clear. Oh, and he had to let them understand that unclear speech did not equate to an unclear mind. This too was turning out to be part of his responsibility, every time he spoke to someone new. Or, indeed, someone from before. He hadn't on the whole been meeting new people.

Jacqueline, wearing a luxurious old-fashioned kind of house-gown, her red hair piled up, was doing something with a plant by the long window at the back of the drawing room. She turned, and blinked three times. Once to see her daughter. Once to see her with Riley Purefoy. Once to see Riley Purefoy's face. Then she lifted her hands — to open her arms? For an embrace? Riley couldn't tell. It turned somehow into a shrug, which was visibly not what she had meant. She put down her secateurs.

"Oh my dear," she said. "Oh my dear."

"Hello, Mother," said Nadine.

Neither of them advanced across the blocked-out distance between them. They seemed to him to be suspended. So he stepped forward, held out his hand to Jacqueline, and said, in his odd, quiet, bold voice, mangled a little through the straitened mouth: "Lady Waveney — I am pleased to see you. You look well."

"Captain Purefoy," she said, nothing more than another blink betraying any response. He was impressed.

"Mr, I think, by now," he said.

"Oh no," she said, with a little passion in her voice. "Always Captain. Always. Will you have tea?"

"Thank you, Mother," said Nadine. "We will."

The "we" stopped Jacqueline in her movement towards the bell. She turned, looked, saw: gold ring.

"Is Sir Robert at home?" Riley said gently. "I need to speak to him. I have left it rather late already . . ."

"So you have," said Jacqueline. She raised her eyes to stare at him, at her daughter, at him again. No one dropped from anyone else's look.

"Well, I . . ." said Jacqueline.

Riley observed: Jacqueline covering shock with bred-in-the-bone manners, the calmly beautiful half-smile she wore whenever she didn't know what to do. Nadine, still in her mother's presence feeling thirteen years old, naughty, resentful and blank. He saw the careful breath with which Nadine prepared to start the speech she had for her mother.

"I'll just call your father," Jacqueline interrupted, undercutting her daughter at just the most effective moment. She crossed to ring the bell. The maid, standing agog in the hall, stepped into the room. "Call Sir Robert, Mary."

And Nadine instead burst out: "I do hope, Mother, that you're not going to make some stupid fuss about this, because it's done, it's right, and with or without your blessing Riley and I are —"

My brave fighting girl, he thought.

"Oh no," said Jacqueline faintly. "My dear. No."

16

Nadine fell silent. Her mother looked, in a way, as if she was thinking about something else entirely. Silence drifted round the lovely room; the pale panelling, the dark velvets, the sea colours, the windows full of leaves and light.

What does she mean by that? No, what?

"So, have we your blessing?" Riley asked, cautiously. He was fairly sure that was not what she had meant.

Jacqueline looked up. "I invited you in here, Riley, all those years ago. Me. I thought you were sweet. I thought you needed drying off and feeding, and you responded, and look at you now. Look what you have made of being knocked into the Round Pond."

He said nothing. It was not clear whether this was sneering or admiration. Or both.

"You are an astonishing boy."

He hadn't been called a boy in a long time. Ah — it makes her feel better about me. As if I'm not a man, and I haven't — ah —

Well, madam, you're closer than you know.

Sir Robert came down the stairs: a clattering, hurrying step, and a figure at the door.

"What's going on, my dear?" he said, before he saw: and when he did the joy in his face was heart-melting, immediate, irresistible. There was no difficulty here. Riley wondered how much it hurt Jacqueline to see the bare-faced love Nadine gave her father, running to him, burying herself in him, visibly radiating the joy she took in the fatherly smell of him; his inky fingers, greyer hair, familiar voice. He held her away to look at her, held her back to his chest to embrace her, held her away again to admire her — and noticed Riley.

"Purefoy!" he exclaimed. "You cuckoo! Where've you been? Good Lord — excuse me, darling — my word." He stared, for a moment only, at the face, then gave a tiny sigh and a shake of the head. "Well, Purefoy —" he said, and he strode over, attempted to shake hands, and couldn't stop himself from embracing.

"It seems —" said Jacqueline, with a slightly twisted smile, but Riley broke in and said: "Might I have a word with you, sir? In private?" So little had been correctly done. He *would* do it correctly. As far as possible.

Sir Robert couldn't make out what Riley was saying. Riley repeated it.

"Modern world, Purefoy," said Sir Robert, getting the words, but not the purpose of them. "No secrets here . . ." But he sensed there was something, so he allowed himself to be manoeuvred out of the room, into the hall. The maid skittered from under their feet, and there they foundered for a moment. Riley did not know where to go. The library, he felt, from novels, was the correct location. There was no library.

"What is it?" Sir Robert said. "What's on your mind that the ladies can't hear?"

Riley grinned his sideways grin. No excuses. No avoidance. No modifying his vocabulary even. Get it done.

He wanted to say that he had a *post facto* request, but he knew he would not be able to get it out clearly.

"The horse has bolted, sir," he said. "I. I. I. Wanted to ask."

18

This was hard. All right. Pretend he's a senior officer. All right. Robert was looking curious, and civil.

"For Nadine's hand. To marry her, sir. But. We're married already." Pause. All right. Off we go. Long sentence coming up. "Yesterday, sir, without your permission, because if anything had prevented our marrying now, we might not have been able to bear it, sir."

Sir Robert was concentrating to make out the words, and utterly taken aback — silent — and then: "You cheeky little . . ." he said. "You — it's not even wartime! Explain yourself, man. Does Jacqueline know about this?"

"Only just," said Riley.

Sir Robert stared at him. "Oh, good God," he said. "What on earth? What am I meant to — have you any money?" he said. "To marry on?"

"No, sir."

"Prospects?"

"Far from it, sir, as you know."

"Dependants?"

"I hope to have, in due course."

"And, er, this?" Robert gestured to Riley's face. "What about this? I mean — oh, good God." The ramifications were filtering through. Wounded, disfigured, penniless, war hero, *fait accompli*, cheeky sod, bright though, common as muck, his family — good people though, decent working people — and that face, that voice. Oh, good God. What a bloody cocktail.

"She doesn't mind it, sir. So I can hardly complain."

"Passchendaele, wasn't it?" Robert said.

"Yes, sir."

19

Silence.

"Hmm."

What a bloody cocktail.

"So what are you doing with yourself? What are you going to do?"

"Thinking of Parliament, sir."

"What!"

"The Labour Party, sir."

"Are you a Communist, Purefoy?"

An echo of someone else asking him that years ago passed through his mind . . . Peter. That dugout on the Salient, a conversation about music, the first human look you'd had in months — 1916?

"No sir," Riley said. "But I've become attached to notions of peace and justice. I believe they're worth working for."

"Good Lord — you didn't stand, did you?"

"The election came a bit quick."

"Good God."

Riley stared at him, waiting. Calm, strong.

Sir Robert stared back, ran a hand over his face, and then said: "Let's join the ladies, shall we?"

They could all see by Jacqueline's still, polite expression, that she was too surprised to know what to think.

"Riley," Sir Robert said. "Nadine. You leave us no choice. We are not the kind of people who turn their daughter away — as you should bloody well know — sorry, darling."

Relief?

He continued: "Though you could've given us the chance to, well, discuss it, and demonstrate our . . .

spontaneously, if you see what I mean . . . so we could give our blessing in a more organised fashion . . ."

"We didn't choose," Nadine said gently. "We had no choice. It was a fact . . ."

"I dare say," her father said. "Of course. And so . . ."

Jacqueline was staring. "Don't you dare," she interrupted. "Robert? This is outrageous."

"Well . . ." he was saying, and Riley could almost see the cold drifting down through Nadine's limbs.

"Outrageous," said Jacqueline. "Unforgivable."

Riley dipped his head, and took Nadine's arm into his.

Robert glanced from him to Jacqueline and back. "Oh," he said. Nadine was frozen.

"I'm sorry," said Robert.

"*They* should be sorry," Jacqueline said. "Well — they will be, won't they? A silly girl and a boy who doesn't know his place. How ridiculous."

Riley saw his new mother-in-law's short breath, and the high triangles of pink on her cheeks. Somewhere, he felt pity and it warmed him through the horrible little silence that sat on the room. Silence can mean so many things. His arm was firm under Nadine's hand as she let go of it.

"Well, never mind. Goodbye, Daddy," she said, and leant in to give him a kiss. "Goodbye, Mother" — from a safe distance. "Don't worry. As the war's over, we'll probably all survive long enough for you to indulge your little fit of pique."

"Darling girl," Robert said.

"We'll see you soon," she said, and blew him a kiss on the end of her finger.

Riley watched her: My lovely, beautiful fighting girl.

As soon as they were out of the house she took Riley's arm again, and held on to it.

"You up for the next round?" he asked, and she nodded tightly as they walked.

Walking up the street towards Paddington, his family, his childhood, a cloudy shame rose in Riley. Yes, he had every excuse under the sun, but he had neglected them. One afternoon in 1917 his mother had burst into the ward and not recognised him and shrieked and collapsed at the sight of his fellow patients; just before Christmas last year he had arrived out of the blue and stayed for fifteen minutes. Other than that, he had not seen any of them. You could have handled it better, said one little voice; you did your best, said another. Anyway. Now was the time for putting things right.

Up towards the canal, they turned into the little terrace of little houses.

As they came up to the door he could see his mother from the street, scrubbing the inside of the front windows with newspaper. She would have dipped it in vinegar. He remembered the smell. She did it every week; so near the station, things got dirty quickly. A figure moved behind her: Dad.

Riley squeezed Nadine's hand, and knocked.

A moment or two passed before Bethan opened it. He knew she had been hiding the newspaper wads and taking off her apron.

"Hello Mum," he said, apologetically, and she squeaked, and put her hand to her mouth, and called, "John! John!" And his father came, and dragged him in, and he said: "Dad — Mum —" and though his plan had been just to blurt it out, quick and straight, he found he couldn't speak at all, so he sat at the kitchen table, and Bethan put the kettle on the hob, and John came through, and looked at him, and patted his shoulders, and said, "My boy."

"There's a woman outside in the street, just standing," announced a girl, popping round the kitchen door — and, seeing the man at the table: "Oh my word, what's this?"

Riley looked up. Looked down again. Looked up, and laughed. Wispy, pert, blonde, mouthy.

"Elen?" he said.

Her face went very wobbly.

"You look exactly the same," he said.

"Well you don't," she said. "What the hell happened to you?"

"Kaiser Bill stole my jawbone," he said, and stood, and smiled, but she pushed past him saying: "Excuse me. Four-and-a-half years, Riley. Four-and-a-half years and . . . three postcards . . . and a promise of a teddy bear. The war ended last November, or didn't you notice?"

"Elen," said John. "Mind your lip."

"I'm right though, ain't I?" she said. "It's not fair on Mum. Well I suppose I'm glad you're back. You *are* back? Merry! Merry?"

Merry was in the doorway, staring. The little room was already crowded now. How am I going to fit Nadine in here? Merry was darker, heavier built, more guarded. She stared at him.

"Here's Riley!" said Bethan, encouragingly. They were all in a sudden parabola of cross-currents. So many emotions. Riley felt unsteady. He should have written. It wasn't fair on them. Sunday afternoon.

"How do you do," said Merry, and Riley flinched. She'd been eight when he left. Both girls were looking at his scars.

"Yeah, Mum said your jaw was blown off," said Elen brutally. "That a new one, then?"

"Yes," he said.

"Fancy," said Elen.

"Make the tea, Elen," said John. "You all right with tea, son?"

Riley took his brass straw from his pocket, and twirled it sadly at his father. Merry stared at it.

Elen poured the boiling water, and plonked the pot on the table. "Well, thanks for turning up, Riley. I'm back off now, Mum. See you next Sunday, same as usual."

"Elen," said Riley and Bethan.

Elen's mouth was white as she swept past. Merry hopped out of her way.

"Elen," Riley said again, and turned to follow her. Bethan put her hand on his arm. They both heard Elen say, at the front door, "You might as well go in. I don't know why he's bothering to be tactful."

Merry was still staring when Nadine appeared in the kitchen doorway, and said, "Hello," quietly.

"Miss Nadine!" cried Bethan, and John shot Riley a look, and Riley took a big breath before stepping to her side, past the chair and the coal scuttle and Merry. Quick to the kill, quick to the kill.

"Mum," he said. "Dad. Nadine and I are married."

It was Merry's face his eyes landed on. Big tears were on her young cheeks.

"Oh, Merry," he said. "Oh, Merry."

Silence drifted, pulled and swung between them all. Then Bethan said: "We would have liked to have been informed."

John held his hand out to Nadine. "Married," he said. "You married our boy? Well. Well. Good for you, Miss."

"I know it's all odd," Nadine said. "Please call me Nadine. I think that will make it less odd. Please."

Bethan gave a kind of roll back on her heels, a surveying look with a chin lift, which said, "so that's how it's going to be".

"It's all right, Ma," Riley said. "We were afraid of a fuss. That's all. We didn't even want a wedding. We just wanted to be married."

"All your worldly goods, eh, Miss?" said Bethan. "There's nice."

"I don't have much," said Nadine, and got a withering look.

"Who's going to wear the trousers, if you're to be a kept man, Riley?"

"Mum!"

"Wounded hero only lasts so long. What about when you're just a sick, ugly man with no money? Where are you going to find a job to keep her? No offence, Miss Nadine, and I've always liked you well enough."

"None taken, Mrs Purefoy," said Nadine, mortified. "I like you well enough too. Riley, should we give them a little time to get used to it, perhaps?"

Bethan was grinning. Riley saw her waiting for him to agree to Nadine's suggestion. She has cast it now that any time I agree with my wife, I am less than a man. And any time I disagree with my wife, she can say, "I told you so."

"Mum," he said. "Don't be foolish over this. Had to happen one day, eh? Dad?"

"Come round for Sunday lunch next week," John said. "They'll calm down. Congratulations, son."

Riley thanked him. It was all so quick.

Merry was still crying. Riley said to her: "I'm sorry for being such a bad brother. I'll be a better one."

Merry said: "Are you my brother?"

They crossed into Kensington Gardens, holding hands, walking into the green. Up the Broad Walk, beyond the Orangery, the pleated new leaves of the arcaded hornbeams gleamed in the sunlight like Venetian glass. Through the observation windows in the hedge they caught sight of the Sunken Garden, terracing down geometrically, with its long pond and lead planters.

"Our mothers are afraid for us," he said. "That's all." He could understand the fear without feeling any obligation either to adopt it himself, or to try to make the situation more acceptable to them.

Nadine said: "If they haven't the sense and courage to look at us and give us every bit of loving support in the world, then they can go to the devil." She glanced up, as if to check. "I shall feel nothing but relief," she said, "that I don't have to deal with them." She was wearing that green wool dress of Julia's, too hot for the day, but she had been living in uniform for so long she had no clothes of her own, and during the long, quiet hibernation at Locke Hill, she had made none nor bought any. With Julia still hardly leaving her bedroom it made sense for Nadine to borrow her clothes. She was still wearing the high lace-up boots, and the cap. Riley had a surging feeling of freedom at the idea that she might now acquire some clothes. He wanted to kiss her. Will my desire for her fade? he wondered. How long am I to live with this?

They stayed in the gardens late, wandering, sitting on benches, talking mildly.

The irony was that what Jacqueline and Bethan were scared of was true. The surface of society had been blown around by the war, but had the architecture changed? Were things going to be different now? Where would a Riley, married to a Nadine, fit in? If Nadine were straightforwardly posh, and he straightforwardly a working man, might it be simpler — if only simply more impossible? But she is half-foreign and artistic, he thought, and I am a semi-educated semi-adopted cuckoo in the nest. And my face reminds everyone every moment of what I have given for them, and of what they want to forget about now. And don't we all . . .

They had arranged for two rooms in Chelsea, and they would work. They had considered education: they both half felt they wanted more of it, and concluded that at twenty-three they were too old, and then doubted their conclusion. Certainly, no one was "going back" to anything. They weren't mourning some pre-war Utopia, the golden years before the *Titanic* sank and Captain Scott died on the ice and the Empire and Ireland started to bite back. For Riley and for Nadine, looking back would involve unbearable regret about what might have been. Unbearable. So there was nothing to go back to.

And the war was still over.

Nadine said, as they wandered over to the Round Pond: "We'll have to take ourselves outside all that and create our own new world. Chelsea will be the start . . ."

She said, as well, "You seem to feel you need to justify your existence, but you don't." And he replied: "Yes, I do. I don't know why, but I do."

And she said: "Take your time. We have time now . . ."

"I don't want to take time. I want — I want —!" He'd been stuck for too long, resting, recovering, receiving, disengaged. "We're not going to be living off your parents, at twenty-four. I'll be doing something."

"It does seem ridiculous that just because your wound is in your head, you get no pension for it . . ." she said. "When if it had been a toe, even —" She stopped. They'd said this before. It annoyed him. And it was his territory.

28

"It makes sense," he said. "They only needed our bodies to follow orders. They didn't value our heads then; why should they value them now?"

She laughed.

By the time the keeper called for closing, the damp, growing, evening smell of the park was rising around them: moss, tubers, lilac, hyacinths. At Locke Hill, during the half-paralysed, shattered, Rip-Van-Winkled winter, Nadine had marked the days of emergence from hibernation by drawing each flower as it appeared from black earth and mossy branches, marking the way to spring: snowdrops, aconites, crocuses, scylla, stars of Bethlehem, grape hyacinths, daffodils; camellias, almond blossom, cherry blossom, pear and apple blossom. Harker, the silent, ancient gardener, would quietly nudge her towards each new arrival. It seemed like progress, of a sort.

They were restless. The marriage rooted them to each other, but everything else was still nebulous and reverberating.

"Perhaps our brains are still shaking," she said. "I still feel jumpy. It's too soon to settle."

"I've heard that it takes as long to get over something as you spent in the something you're trying to get over," he said. "Makes a kind of sense."

She smiled at his beautiful face. "That's good," she said. "So we've got till, say, 1923. Barring future crises."

"1923! Where will we be then?"

"One thing at a time," she said. "Honeymoon first."

Honeymoon.

And that night, rattling in the separate couchettes, which gave an excuse for not thinking about *that*, for the moment, on the train to Paris, he couldn't stop thinking about decisions, and the future, about how strange it was to be able to think about those things. There was going to be a future. He looked towards it, consciously, turning his mind away from the past the way a car's lamps turn at a junction: illuminating possibilities, the road ahead, with beams of light that do not, cannot, show everything. As the car turns the lights are only ever shining straight on, out over — what? Another path, a path you won't take and can't know, that you glimpse in passing. It's the future, it's forward, but what forward entails, you can't know. It's shocking enough for now, after those years of orders and terror and imminent death, that forward even exists. He and Nadine had a forward to go into. They had choices. They had decisions to make. They had a degree of power. It was quite peculiar.

He was hideously aware of her, lying beneath him, separated by the padded wooden shelf he lay on, rattled and thrown around by the train.

CHAPTER
TWO

Locke Hill, Sidcup, March — April 1919
After the wedding Peter, Tom and Rose returned to
Locke Hill. Max the red setter ran up, tail floating, and
put his nose in Tom's face. Tom stood on the drive
while his father opened the front door; then he stood in
the hall, by a jug of white jonquils, while Peter, tall,
slender, still in his overcoat, hurried through to his
study. He watched Julia, his mother, shimmy down the
stairs and across the hall.

"Darling!" she cried, to Peter's back. "It's roast beef!
What luxury! Will you eat with us? Or — I suppose
you're tired — Mrs Joyce has made Yorkshire
pudding?"

She stopped at the dark, polished door of his study,
which had fallen shut. All was silent.

"I could bring your tray," she said. She was wearing
lipstick. Tom watched her. He was nearly three years
old and had been living with his grandmother and the
nursemaid Margaret in another house; he didn't know
why. At Christmas he had been brought here; he didn't
know why. Now Eliza looked after him, and everything
he wanted and needed was in the power of this

Mummy and this Daddy, who he didn't know, but who he understood were the important ones.

He went and stood by Julia, uncertainly.

"Or if you prefer I could coddle you an egg . . ." Julia called gaily, fresh and nervous. "Or . . ." Her chalk-white face stretched immobile and expressionless, and her blue eyes shone, wide and terrified. Tom didn't know why her face didn't move the way other faces did.

The jonquils smelt beautiful. All winter Julia had been bringing up hyacinth bulbs in glass jars from the cellar — "heavenly smell, isn't it?" — or finding the first narcissi, or a sprig of early blossom from the orchard wall, and taking them in to Peter. Occasionally Tom, imitating her, would take a flower, and give it to Julia, or Nadine. They would say, "Thank you, darling."

Nadine had not come back after the wedding. Tom had not known why she and Riley were living in his father's house in the first place, any more than he knew why he had not been, or why Nadine and Riley had not come back. He did not know what the war was, nor how even if people had a home they did not always feel capable of going there. Of the webs that had bound these adults together over the past years he knew nothing. That his father had been Riley's commanding officer; that Riley had carried his father back from No Man's Land; that Rose had nursed Riley; that Riley had deserted Nadine; that Julia had comforted Nadine and offered her a home. He knew that they were tangled up with each other, but he knew only with a child's aeonic instincts, not as information.

And he knew that though Julia was called Mummy and smelt right, she behaved wrong, and so it was best to go and sit with whoever was consistently kind. That was Nadine. He had liked to sit curled up against her, and when Riley came to sit there too, he didn't make Tom go away.

Riley's face had something in common with Julia's, this much Tom saw, in that neither face moved with ease. But few faces were easy to read. His father's eyes were pale and rich, grey-shadowed, with most to give and most to lose. They switched on and off like a lamp; you wanted their kind look, but you couldn't trust it at all. Mrs Joyce, the cook-housekeeper, had an occasional expression of concentration it would be foolhardy to approach. Eliza, his nursemaid, had a sleepy, empty face. But his mother's eyes lied like the tiny waves on the beach washing in four different directions, her skin made no sense, and her eyebrows were not made of hair but of tiny painted strokes which did not come off. He'd tried, once, with a hanky and lick, like his grandmother used to do to his cheeks when they were going somewhere. His mother had brushed him off. Nadine's face was easiest: it had a warmth which Tom liked looking at. And so he was sad that she had not returned.

Julia's sufferings during the war had been extreme, and exacerbated by the fact that from the outside they seemed the result of folly and vanity. Throughout those years she had tried to maintain her marriage by investing in the only thing about herself which had ever been valued by others: her blonde and luxuriant beauty. During that time Julia's mother had taken Tom away, "for his own good". By the end, lonely, neurotic, deserted, Julia had become unbalanced, and had inflicted on herself a misconceived chemical facial treatment, which she had deluded herself into believing would ensure her husband's happiness. This had stripped and flayed her complexion into a scarlet fury, making it frightening and unreadable to a child — to her child, when he was brought back. He was scared of her, and she was scared of him. Now, by spring, her face had faded to a streaked waxy pallor. It was not unlike the make-up the girls in town were wearing, and the ghost of beauty appeared unreliably in her bones and in the smoothness. Meanwhile her painted mouth uttered the over-emphasised banalities with which she tried to make up for . . . everything. Her blue eyes shone wide and terrified. She had spent four years of war preparing for her husband's return; four years of concentrated compacted nervous obsession with loveliness, comfort and order, for his benefit. She had utterly failed.

Even now she tried to give him treats all the time, like a cat dragging in dead bird after dead bird, laying them at the feet of an indifferent Caesar. The flowers. Dressing too smart for dinner at home. Snatching cushions out from behind his head to plump them up and make him "more comfortable". He was not comfortable.

There was a fire in the sitting room. Tom went in there, and sat on the edge of the pale sofa where Riley and

Nadine had usually sat. By habit he did not go on it, because he wanted it to be free for either of them. But they were gone now.

Until Christmas, when Riley and Peter had turned up unannounced in the middle of the night, Tom had not known any men. He was unaccustomed to affection, and at his grandmother's house had sat quiet and dull with a wooden horse or a train, as instructed by whichever woman was in charge of him. When the grandmother had brought him to this house, and this father had appeared, at Christmas, Tom had felt a great and important slippage of relief inside himself: here it was, what had been missing. That the father periodically disappeared again, into the study, was not ideal, but Tom was a patient boy. The father was there. And Riley. Tom had lined up with these new people, the men, and Nadine, and Cousin Rose, as if they must be more reliable, kinder and stronger than the women he'd known so far. In this full house, he hoped he would find what had been missing.

Julia came in and held out her hand. Tom stood as he had been taught, and took it. She whispered down to him: "Come on, darling, let's go and see if Daddy will come out and eat with us."

Tom did not want to go. Daddy did not want anyone. That was why he had gone into his study. He didn't know why Mummy didn't understand something so simple. He wished Mummy would go behind *her* polished door, so that he, in the absence of Riley and Nadine, could go and sit in Max's basket with him.

They approached the study. Julia smiled down at Tom as she knocked on the door. There was no response.

"Well!" she said and, almost shamed, she opened it.

Peter was sitting in his armchair, an old leathery thing, shiny with the polishing of ancestral buttocks in ancient tweed. He'd lit the lamp and was reading the paper, his long fingers holding the pages up and open. There was no fire, and the whisky glass beside him was already smeared.

"Darling?" she said.

"Which darling?" he said, not looking up.

"You!" she said. "Of course."

"Oh! I couldn't tell. You call everybody darling." He moved the paper half an inch and glanced at her. "Well?" he said, glittering.

She dropped Tom's hand, and went away. The door swung shut behind her and so Tom stood there until Peter called him over, ruffled his white-blond hair and, finally, said, "Run along, old chap."

Most days Julia worked herself up to try again.

"Peter?"

A grunt.

"There's one thing I've been wondering about."

A further, more defensive grunt.

"It's —" from Julia, and at the same time from Peter: "Well, whatever it is, I'm sure it's my fault."

"I wasn't thinking about anything being . . . fault," she said.

Silence.

He had not looked up. It wasn't the paper now, it was Homer. What might that mean? Why would he prefer to sit and read all day instead of being with us? Or going to the office like a proper man? It's not as if he hasn't read the Odyssey before . . .

His hair is looking thin.

He's only thirty-three.

She let out a quick, exasperated sigh.

"Peter darling, please listen to me."

He turned, put down his book, looked up, and said, coldly and politely, with no tone of query in his voice, "What."

Oh Peter!

"I just want to know what happened!" she burst out. "What happened to you?"

"What happened?" he said. He gave a little laugh of surprise. "Why, my dear, the Great War happened. Have you not heard about it? You might look it up. The Great War. The clue's in the name. Now go away."

She swallowed.

She still tuned his cello most days. He hadn't looked at it since he'd been back. But he might.

He used to sing and make up little songs all the time. All the time! It was so sweet.

A few days later Julia knocked on Peter's door again.

Go away, he thought. Go away.

"What I was wondering," she said, loitering in his doorway, neither in nor out, "no, don't say anything, please — I just . . . wanted to know what you thought."

"About?" Peter said. He didn't look up. Not out of unkindness, or lack of concern, but out of inability. Julia's desperate goodwill tormented him — these constant interruptions — and then he was so foul to her — and her face — expressionless, taut, inhuman almost with those terribly human eyes glowing out — her face was a perpetual reproach. Look at her, he thought, though he couldn't look at her.

"I was wondering," she was saying, "about before the war . . ."

He raised his head and stared at her like a hyena about to howl.

"Why on earth would you do that?" he said.

"I'm trying to remember whether we were ever happy."

You want to remember happiness? Jesus Christ, woman, if one remembers happiness —

"And whether my love for you is based on anything. I can't remember. It's been so long. I want to know. Because I think perhaps we were."

Oh, God.

"So what?" he said, bewildered. "That's the past. It's dead." And — Ha! What a great big lie that is! he thought. If only it were dead. But it's not even past. The past visited him most nights. Wandering about the wide gates and the hall of death, like Patroclus . . . She is no doubt thinking about some other past.

"We *were* happy," she said, stubbornly. "We were happy in Venice, and we were happy that night at the Marsham-Townsends', when we walked by the tennis court . . . my twenty-fifth birthday. And I was happy when you proposed to me . . ."

He lifted his mind. He had been thinking about the Trojan War; specifically about when mighty Achilles' beloved friend Patroclus was killed in battle; about Achilles' grief, how he locked himself away in his tent, went rather mad really, seeing ghosts and so on. He cut all his hair off, even though he'd promised it to a river god in exchange for a safe return home after the war. He'd refused to fight, though he was the greatest of the Greek heroes, and without him to lead them, the entire army lost faith, and every man in it was at risk. It was as if he no longer cared for his country, or for his leaders, or for his fellow soldiers — he only cared for his one friend. Peter had been thinking, is there an inherent contradiction in hating war and honouring soldiers? And then his mind had flung him back into thinking about soldiers. Dead ones. Loos and the Somme.

So with considerable effort, and for her sake, he lifted his mind from all that, and manoeuvred it round to Venice, and that night at the Marsham-Townsends', and when he proposed to her. He remembered, for a moment, speaking to her appalling mother, and wondering what her father had been like. He tried to remember why he had proposed to her. Because we danced so well together — was that all? No. Because she was so beautiful? Yes — and . . . because she was so nice. She was soft, and gave kind advice. I was always pleased to see her when I turned up somewhere, and she was there. She was kind when my father died. All very straightforward, really. And I felt very tall with her on my arm.

All right, then. Yes, back in Arcadia, we were happy.

And at the thought of happiness, remembered happiness, his mind panicked and scattered: pure fear. He closed his eyes, clenched his mind, to hold on.

Hold on to your mind, he whispered to himself. Hold on. You're tied to the mast. All right.

All right.

Now say something nice to the poor woman. Go on.

He couldn't.

Julia tried to remember herself before she knew him. Desperate to please, obedient, bossed and squashed by her mother at every turn, her dear dad only a memory. She had realised the game early: the sweeter and prettier she was, the nicer people were to her.

And then there was Peter. How glad she had been to run to him, his amusement, his kindness.

To her, that night at the Marsham-Townsends' sprang out, glistening with verisimilitude. She smelt the orange-flower water, saw the sheen of starch on the gentlemen's shirt fronts, heard the waltz, felt the brush even of the palm-frond against her bare white shoulder and her skirts swirling at her ankles, as Peter wheeled her out on to the terrace, whispering — what had he whispered? Something mischievous.

Her mother had been delighted to give her to a man with a big house.

After they were married he'd said: "Let's not have children immediately. Let's run around and have some fun first." She had no idea there could be any choice — she'd known nothing about anything loving, about being on the same side with someone, and being happy together. Then suddenly there it was: she and Peter, together. Yes, happy!

He caught sight of her by the mirror in the hall. She was glancing at herself as he glanced at her. Her eyes fell away from her own taut reflection.

She did that, he thought, to her own face, to be more beautiful, because she thought I loved her for her beauty. She thought it would help. She thought that I, while fighting the bloody war, losing men, Atkins Lovall Bloom Jones oh stop it STOP IT — was most bothered by some idea that my beautiful wife was not beautiful enough. Somehow, apparently, evidently, I let her think that. Though, dear God, I do not understand why anybody would think that washing their face in carbolic acid was going to help anything. But — bad husband — I failed to protect her from this bizarre idiocy of her own. Just as I failed — bad soldier — to protect my men. Both at home and at the Front, I failed. And I wonder if anybody else on this earth can see that she is a casualty of that war just as much as Riley, or me . . .

The next time she came to lean against his door jamb, he got in first. He pulled his jacket around him, pursed his mouth against the shallow pattering of his heart, and said: "None of this is your fault."

Think about her. Hold on to that. Poor Julia. Really. Poor tiresome bloody woman. "I don't know why you put up with me," he said. And I don't. You don't have the first idea why I behave so bloody badly. "You've always done everything you should."

He looked at her — eyes only, not turning his head — and he saw that she was, with a hopeless inevitability, taking these unexpected kind words at face value and investing them with huge meaning.

Oh, God.

She burst into tears.

Say something.

Not "fuck off". Don't say that.

"Oh, Julia," he said, trying to buy time, to hold his mind, to make it all go away. "I think it's probably too late for us. I'm an awful crock. But," — and here, desperate, he said the only thing which ever stopped her from looking so bloody tragic all the time — "I could perhaps not drink so much."

"I would like that," she said, and he saw the sudden whirling desperate hope erupting inside her. It filled him with despair.

Jesus Christ, Julia, he thought. I will never make you happy. You never will be happy! You've ruined your famous beauty, for me — poor fool! I'm a lush and no one else will want you. There is no chance for you now, shackled to me. And yet look at you, all hopeful — dear God, what a woman — let's make you smile. Perhaps I can make you smile . . .

"Well, I'll give it a go," he said. "Perhaps I might — should I? Go to one of those places." I could do that. Could I? His heart was still going in that sick-making way — too quick and light, and all over the place.

"Oh, please!" she cried, too keenly. Clearly she had been about to say, "Oh no, of course not!" when she thought: Yes! Grab the chance!

42

She's awfully keen to be rid of me, he thought. And who can blame her?

And I've overdone it. I can't do that.

But she was smiling at him, limp and tearful. "Oh, darling," she said, and corrected herself, quickly: "Oh, Peter."

She looks happy. Dear God, I've made her happy! It's so easy. But I can only do it by lying.

So lie. You owe her that.

Anyway, you lie to yourself all the time.

She was saying she would find someone, she would ask Rose, she was certain things could be better, she was so glad. She jumped up and went off to get on with it all.

Oh, Jesus.

In the course of the rest of the day he drank almost half a bottle of whisky and two bottles of wine. "Final fling," he said cheerfully. Julia beamed at him, the tight smile of her skin lit from within by a genuine if bewildered hope.

Keep away from me, he thought. Just keep away from me.

CHAPTER
THREE

Locke Hill, March — April 1919

To Rose it looked nothing like a fling. It looked like desperate unhappiness, i.e. business as usual.

The newlyweds heading off into eternal nuptial joy meant that Rose was now on her own with the two ghouls, the two fluttering, ragged banners gloriously emblazoned, in Rose's eyes, with her failure to save them. Peter and Julia lurched through her days and tagged across her mind, united in bitterness, loss and the seeming impossibility of redemption. Frankly, Rose preferred being at work with Major Gillies at the Queen's Hospital, looking after the facial injury patients. There at least the men were getting better, and moving on, or they were dying — but at least they were not stuck on a ghastly merry-go-round of their own making, with so little idea how they got on, and no idea how to get off. Not that I know any better, Rose thought. It's just that I can see their every mistake — the ones they've made and the ones they're still making.

Peter did not go somewhere. The idea of "going somewhere" dissolved with the daylight: he would not go somewhere because, it turned out, the places he might go required him not to drink at all. He seemed to think alcohol was a balanced diet — untouched trays went in and out of the study, where he sat with the blind half down, reading his Homer. Rose would stick her head in, calling him old bean, trying to tempt him out with walnut cake (they had to chase every scrap of food into him), and minding so much that he didn't seem to mind when she treated him like a schoolboy. And equally untouched trays went up and down the stairs to Julia, who went up to bed and stayed there, "resting", later and later in the mornings, longer and longer hours, the room over-warm and the curtains half open, promising that she would really try, about the getting up. Oh the curtains — Millie the housemaid trying to open them, in the interests of fresh air and health and doing as Rose had instructed her, and Julia telling her not to, and Millie, disgruntled, leaving them hanging as nobody wanted them: half open, limp, unconvincing, unconvinced. Slatternly. Millie had been a pest ever since having to come back into service, after being sacked from Elliman's for flirting with the foreman. It wasn't Rose's job to hire and fire, any more than it was to look after Peter and Julia — but when a vacuum develops in a household, someone like Rose, with her strong hands and her clear eyes, cannot help but fill it.

And into this dim stuffy room Eliza would take Tom, where Julia would cry on him, and make him lie down beside her, and stroke his head, and say: "Oh Tom, Tom, what is to become of you?"

Was it just that socks needed pulling up? Was it some kind of shock, some nerve condition? Were they ill, or not? Dr Tayle said rest, exercise, exercise, rest, fresh air, good food, rest . . . Dr Tayle seemed to think if Peter could be made to walk Max every day, everything would be all right. But Peter didn't care for Max any more, and anyway Max was always curled up on Julia's bed, adding to the fetid smell up there of hormones and old Malmaison, and leaving silky red hairs all over the silky orange cushions. Of course Peter was unhappy, but he wasn't wounded — the limp from his leg wound from the Somme was hardly perceptible — and he didn't seem to be sick. There were no particular signs of shell shock — so what was it?

He needs to see a proper doctor! she thought. But he refused to see even Dr Tayle.

And anyway, Rose had her own work. Today had been particularly demanding: two skin flaps had failed, one fellow — borderline already — had had a full-on attack of hysteria, in front of the entire ward, and another had moved from what had been a small infection into life-threatening sepsis, and Major Gillies had actually shouted at Sister Black about hygiene — unimaginable! the idea that he would shout, or that Sister Black would let standards slip. While there were no new patients as such, *thank God*, there were still men coming through from other hospitals with badly healed facial injuries, or badly done sew-ups or attempts at reconstruction — which were worse, because of having to tell them they need to go through it all again — or worse still, that they can't — and the men's disappointment . . . But they were getting there. If the end wasn't in sight, at least there were no more new beginnings.

46

She was pushing her bicycle up the lane and into the shed, wishing that Nadine was there to talk to about it. Or Riley. She missed their good sense and their humour — it was all so bloody tragic round here! But she would hardly write to them while they were on honeymoon: "Sorry to tear you from your bliss; can I moan on a bit more about my cousin and his wife?" If they think of us at all it would be to give thanks to the Lord above that they're not still stuck here with us, she thought. They've escaped. They're not really anything to us any more. Or perhaps they are. But they're not family. They're not responsible like I am. She realised she didn't know what wartime friendship meant, now that war was gone. Would we even have met, without the war?

It all brought up again a question that had been bothering Rose for a while. Her big question. Should she leave Locke Hill? She'd stayed — had special permission, even, to move out from the nurses' residence at the Queen's Hospital — in order to help them all. Her former patient, Riley; exhausted Nadine, back from nursing in France; poor sick Julia; shattered Peter . . . But now that Riley and Nadine were married and gone, and order — well — order was *meant* to be being restored to the world, did Peter and Julia need their own house back just for themselves and Tom? Because ideas had been emerging even in reliable Rose, over the dark winter, and — not that she could think of mentioning it — she very much wanted to leave. Throughout the war she'd given her donkey work to the hospital, and her affection to Peter and Julia, Riley and Nadine, Tom. Now, her intellect was dragging its nails down the walls of her captivity, demanding its turn. Thirty-two years old, a virgin, an old maid, and likely to remain so.

In other words, free.

She pictured Riley and Nadine — or tried to — but as she had never been to the south of France she didn't have much to go on. Their one postcard (Nadine's writing: "Missing you! (well, not really!)") showed slender palm trees along a curving road and a curving beach. It was apparently a corniche. She remembered eating cornichons once or twice in France: same shape! Someone had told her — Peter, it must have been — that the word came from "horn" . . . She pictured Riley and Nadine on a curving beach, eating tiny gherkins, with tiny horns growing out from their foreheads through their curly black hair. They would be wet and happy from the sea, young and beautiful —

She found herself suddenly blushing. She knew perfectly well what Riley's body looked like, from nursing him. But he was a married man, not a patient, and she was no longer his nurse.

Rose spoke to Julia about Peter. "I do think," said Rose, "that he might see a more . . . sophisticated doctor."

"Is he ill?" said Julia. "Do you really think so?" She perked up at the idea. Of course she would, thought Rose. Illness is something you could do something about. Illness is a reason.

"Worth checking," said Rose, and, nourished by this new possibility, Julia agreed to get up after all. Rose's constant concern was whether Peter was sticking to the new rule — Dubonnet instead of whisky, and not until six o'clock — and how one could civilly find out, without provoking a small English furore.

"You don't trust me, Rosie darling, do you?" he'd say, politely, glittering, and she'd say, "Oh Peter, it's not that . . ."

And then one morning he interrupted the regular cycle of this dull and dangerous conversation to shout at her, suddenly, ferociously: "Then what is it? I tell you what it is — it's a pretty sorry state of affairs, Cousin Rose, if a man can't have a glass of whisky in his own study, in his own house . . ." — and Rose stood, pinioned, shocked — "without some bloody woman —" And he stopped as suddenly as he had started, and cocked his head, and then turned and looked at her as if he had no idea where he was.

Rose had a secret.

She and Nadine had talked, during the winter, about how a nurse could be, when returned to her family. For Nadine, who had only been a nurse at all because of the war, who hadn't been one for very long, who had hardly seen her wounded hero during her nursing days, and who would never be a nurse again if she could help it, the issue was how to avoid nurseyness in marriage to a physically damaged man. Nurse and patient was not a model of marriage to which she aspired, and she believed they could avoid it.

For Rose, it was quite different. Nursing was taking her in more and more. It had given her a function where she had had none, an outlet for the natural love she carried but for which she had had no object — no man, no child, no art or passion beyond her deep affection for her once-glamorous cousin Peter, with his clever brain and the sweetness he'd always shown her, and his mild, elegant manners. And of course she was fond of Tom. It had turned out to be easy enough for her to be competent in caring for both of them, and Julia. Looking after people was going to be her life now. She accepted it and was looking forward to it. But not domestic. Healing, not tending. Science, not soup. She wanted more. She wanted, among other things, to know what was wrong with Peter. She had plans.

In February, Rose had received a letter from Lady Ampthill of the Voluntary Aid Detachment Committee.

Devonshire House, London W1

Dear Madam,

On behalf of the Joint Committee of the British Red Cross and the Order of St John of Jerusalem, I have the honour to ask you to fill up the enclosed "Scholarship Scheme Form" if you wish to train for definite work after demobilisation. The Joint Societies have decided to give a sum of money for scholarships and training, as a tribute to the magnificent work so generously given by VAD Members during the War.

Training will be given for those professions for which the work done by members would make them particularly suitable, such as the Health Services or Domestic Science. A preliminary list is appended, with the approximate period of training and probable salary to be gained when fully trained.

A limited number of scholarships to cover the fee and cost of living will be given to those who pass the qualifying examinations with special proficiency, but in other cases it is hoped to assist materially those members who wish to be trained for their various professions in centres all over the country.

The work of VAD Members is beyond all praise, and we very much hope that they will again be leaders in important patriotic work, which equally demands the best of British womanhood.

Yours faithfully
MARGARET AMPTHILL
Chairman, Joint Women's VAD Committee.

Rose read it carefully. A woman — Lady Ampthill — was writing to her, a woman, offering money, training and support. She read the final sentence three times: the words leader, important, best, work, and womanhood in the same sentence. This, Rose thought, was the most beautiful letter she had ever received. (Not the most beautiful she had ever read — those were Nadine's letters to Riley while he was in hospital, which Rose had had to read to him — my gosh, they had been something.) But no — this was about a future in which she could see herself. This was like Madame Curie setting up x-ray labs in the Belgian field hospitals, and fixing the wiring while she was at it, and rigging up field telephones. This was potentially . . .

There would be a catch.

She didn't want to study domestic science! But health services? What did that cover?

The list of requirements was enclosed. Breathing steadily, Rose unfolded it and sat down to read it.

1) *Length of Service.* — Members must have worked officially in a recognised British Unit prior to January 1917, and have continued working until their services were no longer required. *Well, that's all right.*

2) *Recommendations.* — Applications for Scholarships must be forwarded with a recommendation from: (a) The Matron . . . . For Nursing Members working in Military Hospitals. *Well that should be all right too. They will probably be sad to see me go. I think.*

3) *A new Medical Certificate* will be necessary. *Again, all right.*

4) *Age Limit.* — 20-40. *Unfair on the older ladies. But all right.*

5) *Standard of Education.* — Certain Scholarships will require a high and definite standard of education, which will be taken into consideration. *Ah. High and definite. That could mean anything. Will my plain old girl's education count? Or will they want a degree or something?*

6) *Applications.* — Applications should be made before 31 March 1919.

7) *Further Correspondence.* — When a form has been filled up by a Candidate, forwarded by her Officers, and approved, further correspondence will be carried on confidentially with the Member with regard to the amount of financial assistance required and other matters.

And on the other side was the nub of it: "Scholarships may be awarded for the following types of work . . ."

First on the list: "Medicine".

Rose read no further. Fascinating though Midwives, X-Ray Assistants, Hospital Almoners and Instructors of the Mentally Defective might find their work, she read no further.

It wasn't just that they would pay the fees. It was the idea of it. That she, Rose, could study medicine! That she could be a doctor! That all she had to do was work bloody hard — as if that wasn't second nature to her — and she, Rose Locke, could walk out into the world fully equipped with the abilities, the duties, the dignities of a doctor . . . This isn't just permission — this is an invitation. This is tantamount to an order . . .

She *had* believed, when she failed to get anyone to marry her, that she had let everyone down, and been, in fact, a failure. She had, quietly, felt the fact that some of the nurses were definitely quicker off the mark than some of the doctors, and could have made better medics than those in authority over them. And now — Lady A. might as well have written to me personally, saying

Rose, yes, we have seen you, we have noticed you, we want YOU to step up.

Dr Rose Locke.

She found herself grinning. This isn't vanity, it's not arrogance. It's possible. They want me to do this! Think how sad they would be if nobody applied!

And of course the money made the vital difference. She would not have to ask Peter, or be beholden, and nothing anybody thought about it would matter. My work is beyond all praise, and this is my reward.

She was so happy she almost skipped.

So she had filled in the form, got the new medical certificate, dug out her old school reports and certificates and birth certificate and service record, and given it all to Matron, who *had*, most gratifyingly, said she'd be sorry to lose her, and it was up to Major Gillies.

And Major Gillies had wondered why on earth a nice girl like her would . . .

And she had looked at him straight and said, "Major Gillies, sir, ignore the fact that I'm a nice girl, and think about my brain."

"Oh dear," he said. "Have you got one?"

"Have you never noticed it?"

"Tried not to," he said. "A bit of brain in a nurse is just the ticket, but not too much. It only makes them sad."

"No longer," she said. "It's about, I hope, with your blessing, to make me very happy."

"Well," he said. "If we have to have lady doctors, I'm glad it'll be you."

54

"Thank you," she said. "Sir."

Since then, Further Correspondence had been large in her mind.

But when Peter had shouted at her, her response was not scientific or nursely at all. It was purely and deeply emotional.

It wasn't so much the shouting. So he had become a man who shouted: it was very unpleasant, but men could be like that, she knew, she'd seen enough of it on the wards, and though it made it harder to love him as she had when he was a boy, he had been to war and therefore she accepted it. What upset her was the phrase "in his own house". Rose had lived and stayed at Locke Hill since before the war, and throughout the uncertainties of the war years she had taken comfort in calling it home. But now the underlying message lay there like a crushed snail underfoot: she was the poor relation — which was sort of true — and she'd better mind her step. He had never said, or implied, any such thing before, *ever* — he had always been the kindest man, the funniest companion, most loving cousin . . .

When he said that — "in his own house" and "some bloody woman" — Rose felt slapped. She left the room, and went upstairs with her feet odd on the steps, and an aerated feeling in her arms. Peter, her generous sweet cousin, friend of her youth, companion of her heart — he would not — but he just had. He had. Hadn't he?

And then she sat on her bed for a while, wondering if she was overreacting, and why she didn't understand

Peter at all any more, and what she could do to make things easier for him, and whether perhaps it was, well, not her *fault*, of course she was not responsible for what had happened at Loos, which seemed, really to be the beginning of where he started going wrong, not that he'd talked about it, but she'd seen the lists of the dead, and how many had been his men.

We cannot ever know, but that doesn't mean we can't help, she told herself. Don't mind one thoughtless comment.

What was he thinking, to say that?

Oh, he wasn't thinking. It was the drink talking.

But a man chooses to get drunk. Doesn't he?

At least, he could choose not to. Couldn't he?

But alongside her hurt impatience, she felt a deep, naked sympathy. There had been such suffering. And there was Tom, little white-haired, milk-skinned Tom with his furious eyes and his great silences, wandering the house, lurking in the hall by the elephant-foot umbrella stand, watching, growing, needing . . . He misses Nadine. She was so sweet with him.

Rose recalled, suddenly, a day when Tom had called Nadine "Mummy". Julia had tried to laugh it off, and Nadine had been mortified, and Tom had not known what he had done wrong . . . Later Julia had said, "Well, it's all in the genes, isn't it? Clearly I'm going to be as foul a mother as my mother was. Girls like me shouldn't have children," and Rose had wanted to slap her, and Julia had noticed and wept and gone and got Tom and carried him off into her dim bedroom and hugged him nearly to death when he had already forgotten all about it and just wanted to play with his ball.

Time is flying by and they are all suffering. There has been so much silence, and it is so hard to tell if it is the silence of healing rest, of peace and contemplation, or the silence of fear and loneliness, emptiness and pretending . . . Are they dying there behind their closed doors? Or dealing with it all in their own way, taking the time it takes?

Should I be doing something? Something else?

In a way, Peter being foul gives me permission to leave, if I get the scholarship. But in another way, it's another reason why I have to stay with him. He's so helpless he can't even be nice.

But I want to go. I want to live my own life.

But —

Is it pride and nothing else, to want to stand around with the men, with my notes and my professional judgement, and have other people act on my instructions, when my family needs me here?

Then she told herself that this was their own storm, and would work itself out its own way, no matter how much she threw herself at the stone walls surrounding it. Then she told herself that it was selfish of her to want to leave — if she got the chance — when they were all so helpless. Then she told herself it was arrogant to think she could help by staying. Then she thought of Tom again, and asked herself, if I leave, I will create a vacuum, and who's to say if either of them will be able to expand to fill it? And finally she said: Go to sleep, Rose. It's not your fault. He's not your husband. She's not your wife. He's not your son.

It was not, in the end, Peter's outburst that made up her mind. It was the sight of a plucked, untrussed chicken on the kitchen table a few days later. Headless, footless, wing-tipless, pink and naked, it looked alarmingly like a dead baby, arms out, knees pulled up, splayed. Flesh and skin and bone. I know about flesh and skin and bone. I know how they work. I would rather work with them.

Bugger Peter, and bugger Julia, she thought, enjoying the language she'd picked up — only for mental use — from the men she'd been caring for. When the Further Correspondence comes, if I get the chance, I will be off. I will be off.

CHAPTER
FOUR

Locke Hill, April 1919
What Peter had been thinking was what he was always thinking, one way or another: the phrases and repetitions that garlanded his dance with whisky, excusing and justifying on the one hand, denying and defying on the other.

He might have been thinking: Locke, you bastard. What a bastardly horrible thing to say to Rose, who has never done a thing wrong to you, who only cares about you, who has always looked after you. You really are a selfish nasty uncontrolled man. Why would she trust you? You're not to be trusted by anyone. Just ask (and here the string of names and faces began again, and the tight gulpy feeling would start up in his chest as he slipped into the familiar routine) Burdock . . . Knightley . . . Atkins . . . Jones . . . Bloom, Bruce, Lovall . . . Hall, Green, Wester . . . Johnson, Taylor, Moles, Twyford . . . and Merritt . . . Half of them unburied . . . loss upon bitter loss. An armful of Atkins; Bloom's head on his shoulder and Bloom's arm round his neck, resting like a woman's or a tired child's. His own long-fingered hand white against Bloom's hair, embracing the dead head to keep it from flopping . . . The warmth of the German boy's body next to his in the shell hole . . . You were a lousy officer, Peter, and now you're being a lousy civilian. It's not surprising you've turned out to be a lush. Go on, lush. Have another drink. If you're honest with yourself, Peter, don't you see that the pain you're feeling now is all you deserve? You're probably causing all this pain on purpose so you can feel worse about everything. It's all you're good for . . . all you're good for . . . makes no bloody difference . . .

Or he might have been thinking: Bloody woman! Bloody Rose, bossing me — and bloody Julia, too, upstairs in that bloody room stinking of woman, crying and blaming me for everything — some bloody Penelope she is to come home to — it's not my bloody fault! Of course I want a bloody drink. What man wouldn't want a bloody drink? You'd need a bloody drink to deal with all this — anyone would. You deserve a bloody drink . . .

Or it might have been: Rose, don't go. I'm sorry. I'm so sorry, I didn't mean that. Of course you belong in this house. You can stay here for ever. Of course you can — you must — dear Rose. Don't leave me here alone with Julia, with her dead face and her blaming eyes, and that poor child who stares at me like some kind of Cyclops. Rose, come back and have a drink with me. Come on. Sit down, come on. It'll be nice. Let's just forget about everything for a moment — for a few hours . . .

Before the war, after Oxford — where he'd managed to stay on a few years as a junior fellow, teaching and so forth, which had suited him very well — Peter had been steered into the family firm with a view to learning the business. It had not agreed with him, and the moment his father died in 1914 he had left. It was his shame and

60

his mother's good intentions that had steered him back there in January 1919. He had bowed his head and taken it on: part of his punishment. He had failed in so many ways, due to his own unworthiness as much as the idiocy of his leaders. Well, he determined, if he wasn't good enough to die with his men, and since the Army couldn't wait to be rid of him, he would at least make a go of being all that was marvellous at Locke & Locke.

He started on a dull grey morning, late January 1919. There was a meeting to welcome him, and lunch. His father had left a very practical team: they had not on the whole had to fight; they were self-perpetuating; and they respected Peter, as major shareholder, scion of the family, officer. Nobody would tell him he could not have his corner office and the lunches they assumed he would want, once he had his balance back, which everyone thought they understood would take a little while.

There was a young man there who had been instructed to update him on developments and practices, to type his letters, to, what, keep an eye on him? Peter sent him away, and settled in to catch up.

He didn't really like the look of his office. There was something oppressive about it, and the books seemed rather wrong on the shelves. The filing cabinets seemed very full, and he felt observed. He needed, he decided, to know exactly what was where. That would help him to feel at home, as it were. So he took every book and every file from the shelves and cabinets — that way he would know how far he'd got, and wouldn't miss anything out — and he stacked them on the floor, and unpacked them, and began to read.

61

Uncle Eric, wheezy, blinking, and old, who had been running the show, came in to see how Peter was getting along. He found him sitting on the floor like a grasshopper, his long legs folded, knees up by his ears.

"Not sure you really need to go through everything in every file," Uncle Eric said, mildly. There were only a couple of other men in the office who had served. Uncle Eric had not, and he was wary.

Peter looked up politely, and said, "Don't you trust me, old man? Not allowed to read my own pa's company papers, is that it?"

"Not at all, not at all," his uncle responded, looking foolish and apologetic. "Just, well — you do as you think best, and come to me with any queries."

And Peter did not press him. His uncle's concerns were transparent. I am not trusted, Peter thought. My judgement and my capacities are doubted. They know I lost men over there — do they know that those men and I were like fingers on a hand? That I held my men's lives in trust, and they mine, and they are dead, and I am not? Do these civilians have the slightest understanding of what that means? They have been told that I drink; they probably know I was dragged out of a low club by a better man than me.

I understand that.

I will prove them wrong.

In the month of his service he proved it by arriving earlier than everyone else each morning (which required the doorman to come in earlier to let him in, an extra three-and-a-half hours' pay per week); staying later (requiring the doorman to stay late, at variable cost and annoyance to his wife, depending); and by

62

refusing the lunches where he might, with the charm and intelligence they recalled from before the war, have been useful with potential customers. His main project was to refile everything in the recent archive according to a new system of his own. Putting the ledgers and legal notebooks and jute files of thin silverleaf paper into the right places seemed to him honourable work, and it made him feel safe — well, not safe. One is never safe in this world . . . But there was a small joy in it. Of course the oldest should be on the bottom and the newest on the top. It made sense! He had read about an ancient Chinese system where the position of items in a household or workplace had an effect on the fortune and spirits of the inhabitants and workers . . . he didn't go so far as to believe in it, but of course the new must lie on top of the old! It's how the planet is built, how history works, layer upon layer. It was morally and aesthetically wrong to put the new things at the back of the file. We are going forward towards Utopia after all, not harking back to Arcadia! Arcadia kills you, because it prevents you progressing into your own future. Odysseus knew that, when he made them tie him to the mast while the Sirens sang — you know what the Sirens sang of? The story of the Trojan War, of the fallen heroes whom Odysseus knew so well. Backwards looking. And the only way Odysseus and his men could get their boat to keep moving towards home was to block out those Siren songs of the past, of the war — which was its own kind of Arcadia, and love of which would keep a man from Ithaca for ever . . . and Odysseus had to listen to it all, all the corpses and the blood, and get past it.

So my filing system is right.

"Do you know what his name means?" he asked his uncle.

"Whose name?"

"Odysseus," said Peter.

"No," said his uncle.

"Sower of discord, bringer of trouble. Same root as odium. And odious."

"Ah," said his uncle.

"He was tremendously unpopular," Peter said. "After all, he lost all his men. He comes down as being wise and wily and so forth, but he lost eleven ships with all hands, and his own entire crew. Seven hundred men. Makes me seem a lightweight." He watched for some response.

"Mmm," said his uncle.

Uncle, I have just confessed to you that I let my men die — Uncle?

Uncle?

It's just as well. If they knew what was going on my mind, they'd put me away.

Sometimes he heard the barrage still, crumping away. He supposed it couldn't be real. Some trick of the ear and the brain and the nature of time. An echo. Unless it's still going on, and we're being kept in the dark, as usual.

Peter's new system did not match the one everybody else used. It was, he said, better. And he was right. But that did not seem to be the point.

"Never mind," he said. "I'll put everything back. No really, it's no trouble."

64

And he did, thinking about the Augean Stables. For weeks.

At a meeting in late February, Uncle Eric suggested that new stationery might be in order, as the old was looking rather fusty. New world, new times, and so on. That afternoon Peter, without consulting or budgeting, chose a design, approved it and ordered a large consignment.

"But why waste time?" he said. "You said it needed doing; I did it."

The next day he sacked the assistant, who was, unbeknownst to Peter, the son of Uncle Eric's mistress. "He wasn't helping me," Peter protested. "I don't need an assistant. I don't need help. I know you resent paying the doorman extra — so we can save money here. And I'm up to date on the contracts now, so I've an idea or two for this year and next . . ."

Uncle Eric suggested that Peter, with his academic and archival talents, might like to have a go at applying his new filing system to the old pre-war archive, which was kept in the Birmingham office.

Peter smiled his distant, charming smile, and felt himself drifting away, back, back, blown by winds he could not control.

Uncle Eric, without telling Peter, rehired the assistant to go through and check everything that Peter had recently refiled.

A few times during February and March, while he was trying to be civil in town, returning each night to Locke Hill or Chester Square, Peter was asked by someone or other at his club what he was up to now; or his mother would telephone from Scotland, inviting him to visit and wanting to know how he was. He actually could not say that Locke & Locke had rejected him. And of course they hadn't. They still paid him. He still had a desk, in his oppressive office. If he went in, which he didn't much, Uncle Eric would enquire mildly about the archive in Birmingham — to which Peter never went. Other than that, they didn't say anything.

"I know what's happening here," Peter told the barman at the club, politely. "I'm HMS *Iolaire*. Two hundred men after four years of war, shipwrecked and dead on the shore of their childhood home, their families waiting on shore to welcome them. Like Odysseus' last boat, when the crew let all the winds out of the sack just as they reached Ithaca, and the storms blew them away. For another ten years. Nearly home, starting to relax, and your own damn folly sends you back out there. I do understand. I really do."

The barman wiped the glasses.

Sometimes, when he caught sight of Julia from behind, in a doorway, or when the dog bounced up to him, his tail high and feathery and hopeful, Peter would be struck with a poignant scrap of . . . something . . . a little taste in his mouth of how things used to be — of how I used to be — and then he could almost see a thin skein of desire strung across some part of his being, a high wire, a cobweb, invisible except in certain lights when it might flicker, or glisten, inaccessible, and he would imagine for a moment that if he could only reach that evanescent, tiny wire, and somehow take hold of it, follow it, walk along it, even, balance on it over the void, through this chasm, then it would take him . . . somewhere . . . somewhen? No such word. There should be.

He used to like the dog so much. No more. Dirty creatures. Eating God knows what they found in the fields.

That winter he and Riley had walked out on the Downs, in the brisk wind which, as it made conversation impossible, was appropriate to their shared silence about their shared experience. Once or twice, he had felt a wild urge to tell Riley about the dreams where summer rain turned into blood, the dead men, the cheap women, the drink and the shame. He had wanted to tell him that he could not continue to sleep with his wife because the weight of her body beside his was that of the dying Hun boy in the shell crater, and he could not make love to his wife because the feeling of her body in his arms was — not even was *like*, but *was* — Bloom's corpse, which he was carrying in. Bloom, Burdock, Knightley, Atkins, Jones . . . Remember Jones? He looked like a sausage — well, he did! A big raw pink sausage. And then in the summer — '17? — he got sunburn, and he looked like a half-cooked sausage. And Burdock — was it Burdock? — joked about wanting to leave him out in the sun to cook all the way through, so they could eat him. (And Burdock had pulled Jones' corpse in, and someone had said: "He's all yours now, Birdy, cook him however you like." And the next day Burdock caught it himself. Or so we assumed, because no one ever saw him

67

again. Though Smiler Rogers saw some guts and a bit of fair hair.)

He wanted to tell Purefoy about the dying German boy.

"Captain," he murmured, on one occasion, but Riley, when he caught the military word, shot him a look, and Peter could say nothing.

He was quite certain that Riley had things he wasn't saying either. They were both able to take a bit of comfort from leaving it at that.

And in between his dreams of Loos and the Somme and the eighteen hours in the shell hole and the weight of Bloom's head on his shoulder, Peter would sometimes dream that he had gone on holiday, taken a train, and stepped off at a quiet station where the sign on the platform read, clearly, 1912, and Julia and Max were there, and they were all happy, and they came in a motorcar back to this same house, this same house where he had been a boy, and ate scones with jam.

Even in this dream he did not feel safe. He felt safe only when passed out: feeling nothing.

Sometimes when he awoke Tom would be standing by him, clear blue eyes watching.

CHAPTER
FIVE

France, April 1919
Riley was out in the world again, and Nadine was terrified for him. She was scared for him being in France again — but it was so different here in the south, he said. Even the language, they agreed, did not sound like the French they had heard in the north. He could feel as if they were in a different country: this sun, these astonishing colours. Olive trees, lizards, lavender. It was nothing like — there. And she knew that to be true.

Peter had insisted on giving Riley and Nadine the honeymoon as a wedding present (despite Riley's reluctance to accept gifts, which he maintained despite Nadine's desire that he relax about money). Peter had always been rather sentimental about his own honeymoon (probably it was the last time he and Julia were really happy, Nadine thought. Perhaps the only time). A little hotel in Bandol had been organised for them.

They arrived at night, rattling from the station under a black starless sky, and with no idea of surroundings other than smells — jasmine, pine — and sounds — rattling harness, creaking wheels, the bizarre orchestra of cicadas. In the morning, Nadine threw open the shutters of the cool dim bedroom, and when she saw the beauty that was before her — the radiant glory of blue dancing sea, green musing pines and golden glowing sunshine — she burst into tears.

Riley rolled over. "What is it?" he called, alarmed.

"I'm alive," she said. "To see this. Look at it. Look. All this was going on all the time we were so bleak."

They ate fish and fennel, smelt mimosa — what a miracle that was — and sweet broom and salt. They swam in the spring-fresh sea. Nadine bought Riley a fisherman's shirt and, it turned out, developed freckles on her nose and forehead. The hotel had a small boat in which they paddled up the calanques in search of kingfishers and turtles and flamingoes. Over and over they found themselves grinning and gasping over something lovely. The scarf that constantly lay double-coiled around Riley's chin or throat began to be left to hang in a single drape, relaxed, protecting only the back of his neck from sunburn, not his scars and his dignity from the eyes of strangers.

In the cafés, at first, she ordered for him. She explained exactly what she wanted: the *bouillabaisse*, strained, with extra cream; the *boeuf stroganoff* very tender, the chicken broth and the *oeuf en cocotte*, *crème de* this and *soufflé de* that. Her concern was visible, she knew: maddening to him and miraculous simultaneously. He let her order. But he would not let her shave him. "I'm not going to be a baby to you," he warned, and she said, "Fat chance," which she knew made him feel safer — but was that part of it? Is wanting him to feel safe another level of nurseyness and mothering? Early on, she watched him standing shirtless by the china bowl in the barely furnished room, going carefully around his scars, trying to do the folds under his chin where he could not see, nor properly feel. She could see him seeing her in the mirror sitting on her hands on the bed, wanting to help. The only time he let her, despite her tenderness she hurt him, and he flinched, and she could see that he could see that she found it hard not to weep, and he was sorry, and she was sorry, and after that she left the room while he tended himself. He's a miracle, she thought. So many things he could have died of. Flaps of skin from his scalp down under his chin, his manufactured chin. He's Frankenstein's not-monster. Sometimes she found herself shaking at the thought of what he had been through.

He grew brown in the sun. The waxen scalp skin on his jaw took it differently to the rest of his face, but even so he did not want to grow a beard. He paddled the calanque, and day by day she saw his youth and physical strength starting to flood through his body, healing him and fixing him. It transfixed her. She sketched him each day, to map the transformation as it happened, but her sketches were not good enough and she wished she could photograph him. On the third night, she was watching him sleep, wanting to look more closely at him than his manner when awake would allow, to unveil him. Moonlight was falling on his face, on the strangeness of his reconstructed mouth with its slight downward drag at the right-hand corner and the odd lift at the left, a sort of ugly Harlequin half-smile. She wondered if she feared it, if she wanted to look inside, and didn't dare. She never, ever wanted to offend him or upset him. He stirred and half woke, under the strength of my stare, she thought, and he hoicked himself up and looked at her.

"My dear," he said, and then thought for a while, and said something more — but his mouth was always clumsier after sleep, and also the moonlight was off his face now, and she could not see him to understand him. It had been interesting, academically, to learn that she needed to read his face, but it was not easy, not helpful to the confidences of the pillow and the encouraging sympathies of the dark. She shook her head, and didn't want to say, "I can't understand you," and terribly wanted to kiss him, because that would tell him . . .

Does it show, that I want to kiss him?

He smiled at her, and for a moment she thought — but then he scruffled her wild hair, and pulled her down to him, in a friendly way, an innocent way, which made it perfectly clear.

She smiled bravely in the dark. Is this it?

The trouble is, the subject only arises — think of the vulgar joke he'd make about that! — in the dark, and in the dark is just where we can't talk about it. Even if we could. Even if talking about it was what we needed to do. Which . . .

You must accept it. In sickness and in health. This is what you signed up for.

But we have never had any health, a wailing voice inside cried out, and a clammy feeling settled over her — this is what you signed up for . . .

But we're young!

72

Dear God, he'd thought. She doesn't know what she's doing. How close that was! Even as he'd tried to stop that gaze, to stop her looking at him like that . . . wanting her so much, wanting to make clear that she didn't have to worry about that from him, that he would never . . .

Oh, fuck.

By the second week Riley suggested they hungered for culture. Nadine was quick to agree, and they went back to Paris, where it was she who went to every gallery and every great building, and sought out the collections which had been put away for safety, and found the man who had the key to the closed corridor or the right to let her behind the scaffolding of the restorations. Nadine it was who stared at the light over the Seine for an hour at a time, smiling at the gold and grey.

Riley, meanwhile, read French newspapers, observed French life, watched the French responding to peace, listened to French conversations, and made Nadine talk French to him. Despite the pronunciation problems, he was rather quick to learn. "*J'aime parler français,*" he said. "*C'est nouveau pour ma bouche. Les mouvements sont bon* — exercise. *Comment on le dit? Exercise? Pour le* rehabilitation." She was proud of him. It was exhausting being with him, watching his determination.

One hot afternoon, they walked together to the elegant little street behind the Place des Vosges where Nadine's mother's family had lived. Nadine had been here a year before, in 1918, when she had been mad with grief and exhaustion.

"I don't even know where my grandparents are buried," she said. "Any of these men in hats could be my relatives, and I wouldn't know! I thought Jewish families were meant to keep close." She told him the story Jacqueline had told her, of the Pereire brothers who had built the railways and financed Haussman in building the boulevards, and how one of them had married the other's daughter. At the age of sixteen Mademoiselle Pereire had become Madame Pereire, her uncle's wife, and later there was a rose named after her.

They stood outside number seventeen and admired its red bricks and decent windows. They were good houses, prosperous and elegant.

"I don't know why it isn't my mother's still," she said.

"Will you knock, and ask?"

"No," she said. "I'll ask my mother, when we get home. It's interesting."

Interesting! She heard herself say it, and she wanted to scream. Yes, it's interesting. But. Family history is not a proper occupation on a honeymoon. I am on honeymoon in the city of lovers and I am not an old-fashioned girl. I know what I am missing . . .

It seemed to her that the balance of blessing and curse on a marriage was a strange and arbitrary thing. Here they were, together, alive, healthy — because damage is not illness. Sane, of good sense and rational optimism. Each in love with the other. And yet.

74

She knew that Europe — the world — was littered with widows — and widowers too — with shell-shocked husbands and victims of this terrible flu, with the syphilitic and those still croaking for air long after being gassed — and with couples lost to each other, or scared of each other, or who hated each other. She thought of Peter and Julia, of Sybil Ainsworth, widow to Riley's friend Jack, with her four children up in Wigan, of Rose and the thousands of women who would never now know the joys and perils of matrimony at all — though to be honest, Rose didn't seem to mind as some women did . . . oh aren't Riley and I better off than so many?

Yes, yes of course.

And yet here I am on honeymoon in the city of lovers, where couples kiss on the street, and despite all the blessings of my marriage I cannot be kissed.

Riley applied himself most thoroughly. To rowing, to admiring turtles, to improving his shaving technique, to French verbs, to newspapers, to ideas about his future, to planning who he would approach about jobs when they got home, to the names of the stars and of the streets of Paris, and most of all to not looking at Nadine too often or for too long, not catching her eye, not brushing against her.

Is this why men drink? he wondered. Is this what sends them to brothels?

But I don't want to drink, and I don't want any other girl . . .

CHAPTER
SIX

Locke Hill, April — May 1919

One night Julia, drunk on desperation, the shiftiness of spring, and the scent of magnolias on the breeze, fuelled by a faith in masculine desire and the disinhibition of her husband's perpetual inebriation, made a final, very direct attempt at reconciliation. In a way, when she entangled her negligéed body with his semi-comatose drunken one on his study couch, ignoring his whisky breath, rubbing her breasts on his stubbly face, unlatching the trousers he hadn't changed for days, murmuring, still, of love, she succeeded. Sex, of an instinctive, semi-conscious kind, was achieved, and affection was there, a sort of bewildered, ancient warmth. At the end she gazed hopefully. She was embarrassed by how inappropriate her radiance might be. And yet again, despite the fact that he was incapable of any such thing, physically, mentally, or emotionally, she allotted to him the stroke of authority and the right to decide about their marriage, their future and their love.

He did weep, which was promising. She wept too. But he had no answer for her increasingly desperate pleas for reassurance, or a declaration about the future, or something.

"I don't know," he said, over and over. And finally: "Stop asking me."

She went back up to her bed. It was not mentioned afterwards, and their eyes did not meet.

Soon after, early one morning, Peter left. He didn't tell his wife he was going, and Rose only found out because Mrs Joyce heard Max barking at the station taxi as it went down the drive.

"But where's he gone?" asked Rose, who was about to leave for the hospital.

"I don't know," said Mrs Joyce, bewildered. "Millie was about to bring him his breakfast."

They just stood by the front door, honeysuckle dangling about them from the porch, the sky clear and blue and beautiful above them.

Upstairs, a window was thrown up.

"What's going on?" cried Julia, her voice carrying down.

Rose and Mrs Joyce glanced at each other. "I'll go up," Rose said.

"What on *earth* is going on?" Julia called again, and somewhere inside the house Tom's young voice called out, "What on *earth* is going on?" (At this Rose felt her heart slip down sideways, and thought: I should have made him go to Switzerland, I should have made Dr Tayle send her on a rest cure. Mrs Joyce and I are the only sane people here. I should have sent them off, anywhere with blankets over their laps, on deckchairs. Beef tea. Chicken broth.)

Upstairs, Julia felt strange to be standing up.

"Has he gone?" she said. "Has he left?"

"Well, he's gone somewhere," Rose replied. "I —"

"Good," said Julia.

"Oh Julia —" Rose blurted, and Julia said, quite politely, "Don't you hate it Rose, when someone says, 'You don't mean that,' as if they knew better than you what you mean?"

"Yes, I do," said Rose, honestly.

Silence.

"But Julia, why . . .?" Rose blurted, and Julia snapped: "I have no idea, Rose. Who ever has any idea why Peter does or doesn't do anything? He doesn't know himself. And even if he did, I'd be the last person he'd tell." They stared at each other for a moment and then Julia said "Sorry," rather abruptly. She stood on the landing, like a lost lighthouse, her silky dressing gown pooling round her feet. "I'm trying to hate him," she said. "Obviously it's difficult, but loving him has done us no good at all and I can't think of anything else." She stared around her. "And of course it's rather undignified, you know, when one has made promises and — one's married — and so forth. It seems I'm letting the side down again after all."

Rose's eyes were full of understanding — of how Julia was by nature loving, and her love had at some stage been true and natural; of how she had loved Peter so very conciously, so much and in the face of so much provocation, during the war, that stopping now must involve a considerable wound to her dignity and the investment she had made. Her expression filled Julia with fury.

"Don't gaze at me," she snapped. "You look like some kind of large mammal."

Rose blinked.

Tom was squatting quietly behind the drawing-room door.

The next day Julia was sitting on the white iron chair on the lawn, not saying anything to Tom, who was throwing stones at the walls, the cows across the ha-ha, and finally at his mother's feet.

Rose came across, looking important. Julia glanced up. "Gosh," she said. "You've something to say, haven't you? Tommy, stop that. Is it news from my errant husband?"

"In a way," said Rose. "Blakeman rang up." Blakeman was Peter's mother's butler, currently *in situ* at Chester Square.

"Blakeman! We're honoured. No word from Peter himself, then?"

Tom wandered over and stood by them, dropping stones one by one on to his own feet.

"He's staying at Chester Square," Rose said.

"And is he all right?"

"Apparently."

Relief and disappointment curdled in Julia's breast. Relief that he was all right, disappointment that he had no good reason for his neglect. If he'd been murdered, he'd have an excuse.

"No message from him?" she asked.

"Apparently not," said Rose.

Tom was picking up the pebbles again, and suddenly threw them up into the air, like a cloud of midges, and ran into the middle of them.

"Stop that!" Julia shouted, and Tom ran away across the lawn, not even turning to look at her. The last stones fell behind him. Julia made a face, and turned back to Rose.

"No . . . news of his plans?" she said.

"No," said Rose.

Relief and disappointment retreated; fury and pity battled for a moment. Fury won.

"How charming of him," Julia said. "Ask Millie to come and help me pack, would you?"

"Where are you going?" Rose said, alarmed.

"Elsewhere," Julia said. "Else. Where." She flashed her eyes at Rose, and stood up.

"Oh," said Rose. "What about Tom?"

"Tom doesn't like me," Julia said, heading for the house. "You know that. He doesn't need me. He can go to school." She was almost marching now — through the hall, up the stairs. "Honestly, Rose — really," — calling back over her shoulder — "do you think either of his parents is the slightest good to him?"

"Julia —"

"Now . . ." she said.

"Julia —"

". . . come upstairs. Never mind Millie. *You* can help me pack."

"Julia —"

"Pass me my jewellery box, would you, darling . . ."

"Julia! Where are you going?"

"Timbuctoo," she said. "The passport office. The bank. My lawyer."

"You don't have a lawyer —"

"Istanbul," said Julia, throwing a pile of clothes on the bed. "Peru."

"Julia —"

And Julia turned and fixed her with a look. "Rose. I am not living and dying like this. In this — here . . ." She stared around. "With the herbaceous borders and the damn cushions. And the damn decanters. It's a — it's a cesspit, Rose. You know it. You should leave too. Don't stay here. Though," — and she gave a little laugh — "once we're gone, it'll probably be rather nice. Do send Millie up. I want to catch the one-twenty."

So Rose called Millie and, coming back up the stairs, she felt rising within her the combination of irritation and yearning so often felt by sensible people who long to be capable of folly. Here I am again, she thought. About to clear up after them. She made herself squash it. Still, she thought. At least Julia seems to have cast off her delusions about Peter's ability to attend to her.

"Poor Julia," Rose murmured, hardly realising she had spoken out loud, and received a quick little whiplash for it from Julia on the landing above her.

"Are you pitying me, Rose? I do wonder what you'll find to occupy your time, when we're both gone, and you have nobody to feel superior to." Julia's eyes were bright. She was not sorry. She'd spent her whole life trying to be nice and having to be grateful.

Rose thought: She does look beautiful, in a rather terrible way.

"But no matter — he'll probably divorce me and then you can marry him. You'd like that. Wouldn't you?"

Good Lord, thought Rose. I'd be the last to imagine I knew anything at all about love, but I'm fairly certain that what Julia's doing now is not it.

But actually Rose did not care what Julia said, because Rose had an interview to go to.

Rose had of course been to Devonshire House before. Its heavy rising walls held no terrors for her. She had had her initial interviews here; she had picked up items of uniform once, and her stripes: white for service, red for efficiency in a military hospital, and blue for passing the exams. She had, on occasion, made use of the little club with its library and writing room, and had liked having a place in town where there was always someone to have a chat with. Early for her interview, she was waiting there now, looking at her newspaper, checking her shoes, feeling a complete fool.

A girl called Eileen turned up, a bumptious and unstoppable girl whose path had crossed Rose's over the years, and they took each other's minds off their nervousness. Eileen had contracted pneumonia and empyema while serving in Salonika, and had been cared for at the VAD Nursing Home in Nottingham Place.

"But your singing!" cried Rose. Eileen had been a professional before the war. She had sung around the wards and made a number of young men very happy, and then very sad.

"That's why I'm here," she said. "I applied for a scholarship for training to regain my voice. Why not? I lost it to the war, in service. It's only fair. And they can say no if they want. I know it's hardly a health service, but it was my employment . . . and it is training. I have just the course in mind. With a marvellous Hungarian . . ." She had been recommended to the Finance Committee for special consideration.

"Are you here to be interviewed?" Eileen said.

Rose nodded, suddenly dumb.

"What for?"

"Medicine," Rose blurted, and whatever Matron and Major Gillies had said, she felt a fraud and a fool and an idiot, saying it out loud here to Eileen, in this place.

Eileen was gazing at her fondly. "Oh, you'll be a lovely doctor," she said. "All kind and bossy. You'll be grand. And if they'll pay for me to sing again, they'll surely pay for you to put all those men in their place."

The tiny things that help you, Rose thought as she walked in.

The Committee was Dr Janet Campbell from the Ministry of Health, Dr Janet Lane-Claypon from the Board of Education, Lady Oliver, Lady Ampthill herself, and Miss Cochrane, secretary. Lady Ampthill was in uniform. Dr Lane-Claypon was what Gillies called a doctor-doctor — she had a PhD as well as a medical degree. She had published such interesting work on breast-feeding, before the war. Five women.

Powerful intelligent educated women in charge, and not a man among them. Rose found she was smiling, though they did not smile at her.

"You seem happy, Miss Locke," said Lady Ampthill.

"I am, madam," said Rose. She actually felt rather mad. She was so excited!

"May we ask why?"

"To see a committee made up entirely of women," she said honestly.

"Are you against men?" asked Lady Oliver.

"Not in the least," said Rose. "I have worked under them and alongside them, caring for them, for some years now. I'd just rather treat them and cure them than marry one."

Eyebrows went up.

"I am glad to be judged by women," she said. "And to see women in a position to judge me."

They asked some fairly tough questions, and some very personal ones. They looked sternly over their glasses. They shuffled papers. They conferred quietly. They did everything a committee of interviewers should do, and Rose sat.

No, certainly, she had no plans to marry.

No, she had no money of her own.

No, she had no dependants.

Yes, she loved her work.

Well, that was very kind of Matron to say so. And, gosh, that was *very* kind of Major Gillies. (She feared she was blushing. He hadn't had to say anything at all!)

General practice, she felt. If she were so fortunate as to be given the opportunity. Though fascinated by surgery, she did not feel she had the steadiness of hand. Though in the course of training another specialism might emerge and she would, she hoped, if she had the opportunity, be open to any such possibility. If she had the opportunity. She was also very interested, she found herself saying, in the long-term effects of war damage on the minds of the men. Neurasthenia, shell shock and so on. What the connections are, if any, between the physical injuries and the mental disorders, and the change in character that some families were observing in returning soldiers. "A patient at the Queen's once told me," she said, "a very fearful, confused young man with a facial injury and a degree of shell shock, that he felt that the strings which held him together had been cut. That seems to me a very interesting way of putting it."

"You're not saying you believe the human body to be held together with strings, Miss Locke?" said Dr Lane-Claypon.

Rose had to look at her to see if she was joking.

"My anatomical reference was metaphorical," she said. "But I am certain that a chap's frame of mind affects his physical wellbeing. And that emotions such as fear are felt in the body. Yes."

"Lots of possibilities then, Miss Locke," said Lady Ampthill. The ladies seemed to be satisfied.

Rose came out with a tiny curl of hope inside her, feeling, not impossible. Not impossible.

CHAPTER
SEVEN

London, May — June 1919

Peter had stopped going, even occasionally, to the office. He no longer needed to display his resentment to Uncle Eric. He had been favoured by the fortune of his birth — how many men had a job to come back to? How many would have given their eye teeth in gratitude? — and he had blown the opportunity. So be it. He hadn't felt right there, anyway. Hadn't felt safe from his own inclination to smash up the office, set fire to the files and slap some kind of understanding into his uncle.

The pre-war archives in Birmingham! Is that what the past four years qualifies me for? Back in time and miles away?

The main thing now was to be undisturbed. If he put himself in the right place, in the right position, nobody would notice him, and nothing would come to trouble him. The thing was, to find that place, and that position, and to stay very still: a camouflage, a bird, a lookout, a communications mast disguised as a tree. Any motionless thing.

Last year, he had sought the stillness at the heart of the storm: the carousing and the dancing and the mad gay whirl, that tempest of jazz and idiocy with which so many held off the night and the fear and the grief. Over and over, then, he had found himself *blind with tears, staring into the dark. Cheero!* That was Sassoon — what was the poem? "To Any Dead Officer"? Something like that. You can't stare at other people's sufferings without going blind. You can't go on running around every night until you collapse in tears . . .

Then, for a while, he had found that stillness — an exquisite stillness — courtesy of Mr Brilliant Chang, or Mrs Ada Song Ping Yoo at 16 Dover Street, or on a couple of particularly squalid occasions in Limehouse. A girl he used to see at the Forty-Four, a sweet girl, Billie, had taken him to Dover Street and there had been a kind of security there in the company of the comatose. She called it Chinese Courage, though it gave him no courage at all, just the sweet dreamless sleep. But sleep's no good. You wake up, and you remember. And it seemed wrong to him. Morphine was medicinal; it was for the wounded men, for the dying and the deserving. He did not deserve it. The proper drug of the miserable was booze. And then Billie had died too, in her flat, and it had been in the press. She was some kind of actress. He hadn't known. Her brother had been killed.

There was still a special section in *The Times* death announcements headed "Died of Wounds". I would say that Billie died of wounds, but she won't be included. Nor will any of the men with syphilis who would have been at home with their wives, nor any of their syphilitic babies, nor anyone who dies of this flu, which the returning soldiers are delivering around the world so efficiently . . .

87

Oh, be quiet, mind.

Cheero!

The club, membership of which had come to Peter in his father's will, was no good. Too many acquaintances, men already memorialising their wars into anecdote, repeating their stories in a way which made Peter freeze into nausea. Restaurants could be all right, but they tended to close in the afternoons. Chester Square would have been absolutely fine, though apparently his mother had put it up for sale, but for Blakeman, who for some reason was *still* in London, despite her being in Scotland and servants being impossible to find — anyway, there was Blakeman, cleaning everything and having opinions, which made the house impossible except for sleeping in. And Blakeman's opinions, though mostly concerned with the desirability of the imminent appearance of Mrs Locke and Master Tom, included some on how much, when and where Peter slept.

For a few days, the Chester Arms answered his needs. There was a corner seat with a low table and a sheltering panel, not too far from the fire, where a man might read the paper in detail, or the *Iliad* at length, and have his whisky brought neat, with soda separate. It was close enough that returning home for a nap during afternoon closing was not too demanding. But Blakeman — apparently through some connection with the landlord — located him, and took to popping in and thinking that he should be somewhere else. So Peter moved on, across Belgravia and down towards Chelsea: the Anglesea on Onslow Gardens, the

Builders' on Britten Street, the Chelsea Potter on King's Road, the little hovel off Old Church Street. He was far from the only man moving very slowly from pub to pub, and sitting alone and silent. But wherever he went he was followed, sooner or later, if not by Blakeman then by the consciousness of duty, by fears and shames, by the memory of the expectations of others, and the ghosts of failures past, and, on occasion, the ghosts of Burdock, Knightley, Atkins, Jones, Bloom, Bruce, Lovall, Hall, Green, Wester, Johnson, Taylor, Moles, Twyford and Merritt. Patroclus. God knows, I was no Achilles, but I was betrayed . . . and I betrayed . . .

The King's Head & Eight Bells, quiet, and scruffy, down by the river on Cheyne Walk, became his favourite. The staff — such as they were — didn't bother him. It amused him that it used to be two pubs — it helped him to feel that he wasn't really anywhere. He liked how ancient it was, and to think of Tudor youths stepping on and off boats in their hose, going about their drunken Tudor business, down to Greenwich, up to Hampton Court, all of them dead now, and forgotten. This helped him to feel out of time and beyond its expectations. He could walk up to the Chelsea Physic Garden, and lie under a tree, and see if silence would come to him, and occasionally it did. Sweet dark whisky and the cold dark river matched for him: the grey muddy chill of the river, its dank wild smell, the ancient brick walls and greasy mud and the green slime clinging to its mooring posts, its inevitability; the warm honey glow of the whisky, the stone-cut flavour at its heart and the cool peaty smell, the creeping tendrils of its effect, its inevitability . . . the hidden depths of each; the capacity of each, if he just leaned forward, to rise up, and overtake him. Which to drown in?

Whisky, he felt, was Scylla — the six-headed monster guarding — or welcoming you to? — the gateway to Charybdis, the whirlpool that no one can escape. Which is death. Or, perhaps, memory — the vortex of shame and horror which drags you back, over and over — or of sweet memories — of before — of what is lost . . .

Or am I just lotos-eating? Taking off another few years on the journey home? Or turning into a pig . . .

He was leaning over Bazalgette's fine stone embankment wall, smoking, a month or so after leaving Locke Hill. His leg ached. It usually did, but he didn't think about it: background pain seemed right to him, a fair price to pay for the fact that he had been carried back when so many others stayed out there on the wire, in the sinkholes. A sort of tax. Nobody knew it hurt, and to mention it would be to ask for sympathy: *verboten*. Anyway, booze was a marvellous painkiller.

Normally in this position he would be glancing over at the Albert Bridge on the left and Battersea Bridge on the right, and musing in general terms about which would be the better to jump off so he could just be with them in the halls of death, instead of having them visit every night, but now he was distracted. Out on the river a cormorant was struggling epically with an eel, chucking it and catching it, frisking over the surface of the water, trying to get the slithery length of the creature vertical enough for long enough to swallow it down his oily black gullet — a sword swallower of a bird — astonishing patience . . .

Tom would like to see it.

Banish that thought.

He was hungover, not drunk, and if not actively pleased to find himself interested in something, aware that he should be. I wonder if I'm seeing this as a metaphor. What, that I am an eel, thrashing, desperate for my life? No. Though desperate, I am immobile, and my life — my life — there is little in my life to fight for. Nobody needs my life. Oh stop it, you self-pitying ass. I did what I could, and it was not much, and I did it badly, and I could not help, and I should be with the men I helped to kill.

Shut up, Locke. Who cares?

A skiff going by disturbed the cormorant, which dropped its prey and lifted itself, flapping slowly, heavily, from the water. Everyday life of everyday folk, he thought. A woman walked by alone in a light summer coat, a leisurely pace, a hip-swing, and a residual part of him thought, Whore? — but he didn't care. He *really* didn't care. His sins and their pleasures had long been stale to him. Anhedonia — no pleasure. Every human body was a corpse in waiting.

He dropped his cigarette end in the low-tide mud. Thoughts of Julia were coming up, so it was time for a drink. Everyone seemed to think he was allowed to hate her now, as she had bolted — Biarritz, according to the bank, not that she'd let them know — and deserted not only him but their child. But he had no interest in hating her, or blaming her. It was not, any of it, her fault. She had returned to him over and over, asking to be allowed to love him, and he had spurned her. The fact that he couldn't help it didn't prevent him from recognising it. And the time when he hadn't rejected her — physically at least — had turned into an emotional rejection more shameful, more disgusting. When she came in to him and laid her fabulous body alongside his drunken ingratitude, she told him she loved him, she forgave him, and she only wanted what was good for him. And how had he responded to this? The fleshy memory of that poor bloody boy held off just long enough for him to take her, drunk and in tears, in the most insultingly brief and animalish way — worse even than last time, in 1915 — and then he was swirling again in the mud smell, cordite and blood and sodden uniform, and that boy gasping for help . . . and forcing himself out of it, three fingers of whisky, and there she is — oh God — more brave smiles through the tears, on that terrifying face, wanting to know if he loves her, and a row, and the decanter.

How do you come back? How?

She no doubt thought that I rejected her because of her face. As if I gave a damn about that. I only wish I could give a damn about anything. I am only the more ashamed . . .

So he had left Locke Hill in order that she might justifiably leave. It had been a last burst of oddly placed chivalry. And now people blamed her anyway. And were so terribly kind to him.

What do I have to do to be punished as I deserve?

He turned to go back across the road to the pub, to settle for the afternoon and the evening. He didn't notice the other woman as he crossed the road, who stopped, and waited, and as he stepped up onto the kerb said, "Peter?" and smiled at him.

And — Oh! It was *that* woman. That non-judgemental woman, that sweet-eyed, honey-voiced, quiet, nocturnal woman . . . That woman.

"You look bad, my friend," said Mabel, the singer from the Turquoisine, from last year. The American, the black woman, the woman who lived her own life and wanted nothing from anyone. The woman who was alive. She pronounced it *baid*.

"Oh, I feel *terrible*," he said, with a little apologetic smile. He had never seen her in daylight before. How beautiful she was! Glowing . . .

She was smiling at him. Non-judgemental. He wanted to fall into her arms. She was not England. She was not Julia, or his mother, or his child, or Rose, or the men. He had not failed her. She had nothing on him.

"*You*, on the other hand, look marvellous," he said. "Marvellous. Will you have lunch? It's time, isn't it? Come! Let's go to the Savoy —"

A taxi passing — his arm flung out — his pale aquiline face aglow suddenly with a quite enchanting smile. He could feel that it was enchanting. Enchant her. Be magnificent — not terrible. Magnificent . . .

He stood tall and elegant as his arm flew into the air, and the cab drew in to them. "Come," he said, smiling. "I promise you'll be safe."

She smiled, laughed a little. Her big brown eyes looked actually happy. "No such thang as safe," she said.

★ ★ ★

In the gents at the Savoy, Peter saw a row of small brushes fixed to the wall above the basins. Two sinks down, a straight-nosed, high-foreheaded man with his right sleeve pinned up, turned on the tap, took the soap, and was musingly brushing the nails of his left and only hand along the bristles, humming quietly to himself. Washing his hand.

I am a worm. I see that chap's loss and all I can think of is that I have no such loss and yet I am helpless and how can I be so pathetic. My shame overwhelms my pity. I'm obsessed with my own suffering.

Mabel, clean my mind out for me.

For ten weeks he visited her, took her out, stayed on her sofa, lay in her bed. She made him wash and put on clean shirts.

Why does she not turn to dead flesh in my arms like every other woman has since Loos?

He didn't know. And it wasn't the sort of thing a chap could ask. He recited to her in Greek:

Man of action, no more tears now, calm these
    tides of sorrow
Well I know what pains you bore on the swarming
    sea,
what punishment you endured from hostile men
    on land.
But come now, eat your food, drink your wine
till the same courage fills your breast now as did
    then
when you first set sail from your native land.

94

★ ★ ★

And translated it for her: what Calypso said to Odysseus, what every soldier wants to hear from a woman.

Then she said, one morning: "You know, you need to drink your wine a little less, honey. And maybe talk a little more."

He gave a quiet, bitter snort.

She said: "You know it's true."

He said: "It makes no difference whatsoever, my dear, if it's true or not." Then he unfolded himself, long and angular like a parallel ruler, and said: "I'd better go, before *you* start despising me as well," to which she replied: "It's your self you want to change, Peter, not your company," and he smiled his courteous, tragic smile, and said: "I'm not fit for company."

And anyway, she's very capable. She'll be all right. She doesn't need me. Nobody needs me any more.

If she hadn't been so very accustomed to broken men and the terrible damage they do to capable women, she would have run after him and sworn to save him, but she was a grown woman and a nightclub singer, so she let him go.

CHAPTER
EIGHT

Biarritz, April — August 1919
Julia went to Biarritz. Train and ferry. France! she
thought, passing through speedily, on the way to Paris:
look, there it is. How flat. How rather dull. She looked out
the left-hand side. And all that, she thought, happened
just over there. That's where my beautiful husband lost . . .
lost his . . .

Well.

She turned her back, and looked out to the west
instead. The west seemed far more interesting. Or —
more future. That was the thing! She was so utterly fed
up with the past, with waiting for the future to begin,
with the exhaustion of trying to maintain perpetual
optimism, with waiting for Peter, with being gazed at by
Rose. For years, it had all been going to be marvellous,
as soon as the war was over. And look at us now.

How very naive I have been. Or optimistic? Where does
one finish and the other begin? I will never know, because
now they are both gone gone gone. Poor old me that I was,
useless, sad, unreliable . . . No good to anybody . . . yes,
even you, Tom . . . They will ALL be better off without me —
and I shall become a magnificent cynic, practical and safe.
Someone who does no damage. Defended.

She knew that she had done a great deal of damage. To myself, most of all. She was terribly sorry, for Peter, for Tom. She had to lift her chin at the thought of Tom, because a kind of tearfulness was coming into her eyes. Tom didn't like her. There was no route back to the few days after his birth, before her mother had taken him away, when it had been so sweet and warm and she had felt like a mother, before she started crying all the time . . . No route back. Tom would be better off without her. She could see no way of making anything better — indeed, her attempts to make things better had caused a lot of the damage in the first place.

Time to leave.

Moving fast, south and west — that felt right. She loved the speed of the train; the chuffing and rattling, the specks in the wind. She stuck her head out of the window for a moment, and wanted to shout out loud. She was Anna Karenina . . . At Paris she had a few hours before her next train. Waiting seemed impossible. What to do? New perfume! She'd been wearing Malmaison and Nuits de Chine since 1913: another from Rosine? Or — hm. Poiret was too pre-war. Something new . . . she strolled out of the great Gare du Nord — laughing at how it said NORD NORD NORD all over it — no doubt about where you're heading, and I'm not! — and looked around, but even with the spring gleaming around her nothing seemed clean enough. It was all too close to the remains of the war.

Later, she thought. I must, after all, get the right scent for my new life. New stamping grounds, new thoughts, a new way of being. The new persona.

A cab took her down to the Gare d'Orsay, across the river. All the symbolism seemed right to her. South and west. Warm and new.

Her final change was at Bayonne: Westward-ho! The train had double-decker carriages and a tremendously, humorously tall chimney. She went on the upper deck. Anna Karenina had faded away . . . Charlie Chaplin? No. Some fabulous vamp. Theda Bara! No, too tragic — Mabel Normand? Not dignified enough . . . For a moment Emma Bovary crossed her mind, but she didn't let *her* stay long. The rails spoke to her, as rails do: I tried, I tried, I tried, I tried. And in French — *j'ai essayé, j'ai essayé, j'ai essayé, j'ai essayé*.

And on through Anglet to Biarritz, where the fresh ocean air threw her backwards, and the stupendous majesty of the Hôtel du Palais, formerly Empress Eugénie's *pied à mer*, filled her with glee. She took a modest room (she wanted to be here for a while), made no excuses about being alone, and from the array of available restaurants and cafés she selected the white and gold Rotonde, a great semicircle stuck on the western face of the hotel, with a wedding-cake aesthetic and tall windows in all directions. It was slap bang on the edge of the world and at the same time in the middle of everything. She took a table at the apex of the semicircle. To her right, the Lighthouse, on its pile of rocks. To her left, the Rocher de la Vierge, with its winding walkways through the crashing surf. Behind her, the town of Biarritz, Aquitaine, the whole of France, the whole of Europe. Before her, the golden beach, the salty bright Atlantic ocean, the west spreading out — nothing but water between me and New York! It was terribly exciting. Her stomach was trilling away.

I shall take *tilleul*, linden, for its calming effect.

She felt like a queen.

New York! Well, why not New York? And what would you do in New York? I would work in a handkerchief shop. People would value me for my good manners, alluring demeanour and elegant English accent. I would live in a ladies' hotel. I would sell my jewellery. Or, I would find a lover — who would lavish me with furs and keep me at the Ritz, a railway tycoon from Pittsburgh, a Russian prince fleeing the revolution, a tall silent horse-riding man who owns half of Texas, a man — a lover . . .

A rush of blood, her spine shivered and she felt weak with sudden desire. This illicit thought, this thrilling word . . .

A new man?

Yes! If a man can be found who sees the peculiar allure of my new face, then yes, damn it, why not?

Six weeks now since that last act of union. It had not been horrible as Tom's conception had been, three years before, that nightmarish almost-attack. This had been . . . sadder. She had allowed herself to hope, and he had been incapable of hoping. It had been, really, the moment of proof of the separation between Peter and her. The act of dissolution, confirmed.

And how dissolute he is now. How dissolute we are, the pair of us. Dissolved — from each other, and in ourselves. Nothing to hold on to —

"On second thoughts," she said to the waiter, "I'd like a cocktail."

"*Bien sûr, Madame. Qu'est-ce que vous prenez?*"

Well, of course she didn't know. She'd never had a cocktail.

"You choose," she said, giving, instead of the radiant smile which used to be a mainstay of her armoury, the mysterious, vulnerable yet glamorous glance which was taking its place. Had she developed it on purpose? Ah — she didn't have to. All her life Julia had been a beautiful girl, creamy and fresh and delectable. For a while, she could see now, she had been a fading girl, a self-conscious, obsessive creature pining for what she could not have — her youth, her husband. So now? Now I am an elegant, purged, adult woman. I have suffered and I'm not ashamed of it. I am thin, and a little hard. I am not deluded. I will lie if I need to. I know what's dead, and I'm no longer in mourning. My husband is a pathetic provincial drunk — well, isn't he? And I am a free modern woman. The cliché, now, of course, would be to cut all my hair off and take up smoking. That's what a girl does, nowadays, to show what she is. But I shan't. I shall keep my beautiful hair. I shall not smoke, I am a woman of mystery, and I have brought three chequebooks. And Peter, wherever he is, probably won't even notice that I've gone.

Julia's waiter, perceiving that she was probably unused to drink, and considering her strange, unhealthy complexion, kindly chose — as some fresh oranges had come in from Morocco — to offer Madame a mimosa of champagne and orange juice; however, the head waiter, hearing the order and enquiring further, preferred that the oranges be preserved for those who a) specially asked for them and b) were known and valued customers of the hotel, rather than unknown women travelling alone. Madame should have, he suggested, a *blanc-cassis imperiale*.

Julia liked it very much. It didn't go to her head. I thought cocktails were meant to be dangerous — but it seemed not to be. She ordered another, and decided to have a lobster omelette, and watch the sun go down. Of her new books (which also included the latest Edna St Vincent Millay collection and a detective novel about a little Belgian), she had decided on the new Edith Wharton: society, marriage, love and scandal in 1870s New York. Well. The setting might be old, but she knew the approach would not be. She would sit in public alone, eating her dinner and reading. She was not lonely. She was not embarrassed. She was happy. And, though she honestly did not realise it, she was, still, waiting.

For a while Julia lay low. She slept a lot, and took walks, sheltering her white face from the sun beneath a wide-brimmed hat, and crossing the road when she saw small children.

She knew she was right to leave, and to leave Tom, *but* . . .

When the little *but* started up, she pictured it as a tiny goblin on her shoulder, whispering to her. She had had goblins all her life. They sat there, fat and squat, telling her perfectly boldly that she was not good enough, she was pathetic, and what *was* she thinking, to imagine she could do this, or that, or the other. Or anything, really. A giant version of my mother! she had realised in the end, and taken up a sort of loud singing inside her head to block it out.

Today's goblin was small, pale and mild. "You should be with your child," it murmured. Even though he can't stand me and everyone knows I'm a terrible mother and I only make things worse for him?

"You should be with your husband," it said. Even though Peter isn't even there, and when he is he's a drunk?

"What are you if you're not a wife and mother, and not even a beauty any more?" the tiny goblin whispered.

I'm a runaway, she replied. I'm a modern woman. I'm a self-sacrifice for their sake. I'm facing my responsibilities by getting out of the way of all those people who know better than me what to do, to help Peter, and Tom . . . I'm no good. I wish I were. Rose, and Mama . . . they are, well, they're better than me, aren't they? When it comes to it? They can do things, and they know that I can't.

"You weren't bright enough to be educated," the goblin said, happily repeating the old truths. "And you weren't maternal enough to be allowed to keep your baby . . . and Rose just laughed when you wanted to help with the war effort. They don't like you. You just get in the way. You're tiresome . . ."

"I'm tiresome even to myself!" Julia cried out loud on the seafront. Then, "For goodness sake, Julia, throw that goblin in the sea!" She'd unclip its nasty long nails from her shoulder and untangle it from her hair, silence its wheedling voice, and stop it from constantly turning her mind backwards. She pictured it with long tentacles reaching down through her ear into her blood, down to her heart and belly, enveloping them and growing, sinking into them like ivy round a rock; roots, feeding. A network. How painful it would be to pull them out. And how beautiful. She had an image of the goblin uprooted and surprised, blowing away from her in the restless wind off the sea, tumbling down the path, hurled and gusted against the rocks, where it would break and smash. Or from the deck of a boat: one twirl, and into the briny, to sink with the weight of its own nastiness. Or she'd throw it in the path of a long low car and watch it splatter under the wheels, all its poison draining out, etiolated, flaccid and dying.

Does everybody have them? Does everyone fight themselves all day and all night inside their own head?

She took off her hat, and spread her arms as she leant on the railing, looking out into the Atlantic, stretching her neck, rolling her shoulders a little. The scent of salt and juniper was clean, aromatic and invigorating; the snow-capped Pyrenees gleamed in the south. The sunshine played on her neck, warm and delicious — but she had to put her hat back on. She could not allow sun on her face. The doctors had agreed. So it is, she thought, that we learn to appreciate things when we lose them.

No! she thought. Get rid of all that. Clean, new. Better. Do something better, be something better. Future! Toughen up!

Across the road, a tall blond American officer was watching her. The town was still full of soldiers waiting to be shipped home, exhausted, hysterical, victorious, in a party mood in this busy town. Teddy Roosevelt had just been, General Pershing turned up; the King was expected. The mayor was a charming chap — Monsieur Petit — with a beard and black eyes, honest, energetic, full of plans for his town. It was terribly clean. The ghosts of pre-war glamour infused the mayor's rebuilding programmes, and all the French were in love with both the English and the Yanks.

The American had been amusing himself with days at the Hippodrome de la Barre and outings to San Sebastien for the bullfight, cocktails back at the Rotonde, and nights at the Pavillon Royal or le Caveau, where Latin-Americans danced with Russian exiles, and undoubtedly there were Secret Service men in disguise. He was a New Yorker, accustomed to fun, and he found Europe droll. His service had been comparatively light, but he had seen enough. He was getting a little bored now.

He knew that she was Mrs Lucke, a war widow, respectable but mysterious, at Biarritz for her health. He had noticed her at the Grande Plage, sea bathing with her personal *baigneur*, her wide hat in place under a veil. The contrast of the revealed limbs and the hidden face had caught his eye. Then he had seen her in the foyer at the hot fountains and mud baths at Dax, and again at the Thermes Salins, where, according to the advertisements, the nervous, the insomniac, the weak, the irritable, the neuralgic or those in need of general healing after injury could take medicinal brine baths, with heliothantic physiotherapy, and massage. He wondered which of those she was — if any. Anyone can benefit from attention — even paid-for attention —

when they have had none for too long. A widow. He had wondered why she never took that hat off. He had wondered what her face looked like. So when she took it off, for that moment on the front, he raised his chin and leaned forward, keen suddenly, excited — but the angle was wrong, and she was too far away. All he got was a glimpse of white-blonde hair, and a gleam of pallor.

When she turned and began to walk again, up towards Maxwell's English Tearoom, he followed her. When she stopped to admire some embroidered slippers on a stall, he paused. The pair she bought were very small, he noticed, and blue: for a child. She passed by Fortunio's English and American bookshop with a glance in the window. He had seen her in there once, having a polite exchange with another English lady about Agatha Christie: Marvellous? Or not? He had caught the other woman's voice but not hers. He wanted to hear it.

And then at Dodin in the rue Gambetta she paused and went in. Her movements were elegant as she slid between tables towards the back of the room, where she took a seat, ordered a *soufflé au Grand Marnier* and a tisane, and took out a book. He took the table next to her, ordered coffee and soft macaroons, looked up, and smiled at her. He saw beauty like a pearl, glamour, and the biggest blue eyes, with sorrow, gayness and determination in them. She saw a man as healthy and handsome as a field of wheat, with good teeth and straight shoulders, frank with admiration.

He said, light and friendly, with a smile, "You're Mrs Lucke, aren't you — what luck. Oh, Lord, I can't believe I said that . . ." whereupon she smiled, and her dignity and pre-war *pudeur* were on the back foot.

"I'm sorry, Ma'am," he said, and she liked that he said ma'am. Then as a courtesy, a patent calling card, he mentioned an acquaintance they shared — but she can't have looked very accepting (Well, of course I don't, she thought, my face hardly moves, how could he read my feelings?), because then he said "Is this OK? Me speaking to you like this in public? You're British, right? So maybe the Empire will explode? And your ancestors start rotating?"

And she was quite disarmed.

"Oh, don't you start that," she said. "That 'America is so modern and Europe is so ancient' business. As if you are all made of plate glass and steel, and we are still wattle and daub. I know for a fact that far more Europeans than Americans are atheists, and what could be more modern than that?"

"So can I take it that you are modern, Mrs Lucke?" he asked, but in a droll way, not a vulgar one, and Julia found herself wishing, really wishing, that her face had expression, because she wanted to give him a look, the kind of look which her features would have formed automatically in the old days, when her emotions and the cells of her muscles and skin were in a direct contact which had nothing to do with her will or her brain . . . but now she had to think about it. How do I make the expression I require appear on my face? She feared any expression she made might be ugly. She didn't know how to deal with that possibility.

She thought of the modern woman she planned to be.

He was watching her, and he said: "It seems as if everything you do, you think about . . ." and at that she laughed out loud, so immediately and so bitterly that her self-consciousness had no time to play its part.

"Far from it," she said. "Oh, far from it."

"Tell me more," he said, and she laughed again, a prettier laugh, and said "absolutely not!" in a most intriguing manner. He pressed a little more, to imprint the matter of his interest, but noted that she did not want to tell her secrets, but to be amused. And so he took it on himself to amuse her. Later, he equipped himself better, with a car for outings, hampers and wine for quiet picnics, and the address of a stables for riding. Today, all he had was a copy of a newspaper his sister sent him regularly for news of home: the *Evening Sun*. He pulled it out, and said to her, "How about this? This guy, the writer, he's called Don Marquis, and he writes about this cockroach, who was a free-verse poet in his previous life, and he comes out at night and writes poems on this guy's typewriter. He jumps up on the keys, one by one. That's why there's no capital letters, you see? He can't bounce on two keys at the same time . . ." And he read the column to her, in his New York accent, about archy the cockroach and his friend the cat mehitabel, who had been Cleopatra in *her* former life, and whose constant chorus on all that life

107

threw their way was: "*toujours gai, archy, toujours gai . . .*"

Julia thought it the funniest thing in the world, and indeed it was. "*Toujours gai . . .*" she murmured, with delight.

His name was Harlan Barker. When he told her he was a lieutenant, she liked the way he said it, lootenant. He was civil and clever and attentive, with a straight nose and hair of a colour that on a woman would have inspired poetry involving sunlight, cornfields and quite possibly angels' wings, but on him was cut short and manly. Before too long Harlan Barker was calling her archy, and in his company she usually found it possible to be *toujours gai*.

On one of the quiet beach and hamper days, in the shade by a rock, on a blanket, sitting a little apart, as they did, for they had not thrown over the habits of respectable society entirely, the shadow of sorrow came over her and he asked her, "What is it?"

She smiled at him, and said, after a moment's thought, "You're so very sensible, I don't think you'd understand."

"Try me," he said, and turned to her, receptive.

She glanced about a bit, nervous, and then thought, Go on! New habits! He's not Peter — talk!

"Goblins," she said.

"What kind?"

"A horrid one that sits on your shoulder pouring poison into your ear, telling you you're no good," she

108

said quickly. She had never mentioned them to anybody in her life. He'll think I'm mad, she thought.

He jumped up.

"You got one of them?" he cried.

"Yes," she said, looking up at him, puzzled.

"Where is it?"

"Now? It's asleep. You've put it to sleep." She gave a kind of smile at the idea, at the fact she'd said it.

"That's not good enough," he said. "Wake it up."

"What?" She was slightly alarmed suddenly. She had offered a tiny opening to her inner world, a first step in something she expected to be tender and delicate, and he was racing in like a cowboy on horseback.

"Wake it up!" he cried. "Where does it talk to you from? Is it inside you? Inside your head?"

"It sits on my shoulder," she said.

"Stand up," he said. He took her hand to pull her. "Stand there. OK." There was a wooden post set into the beach; a fisherman's mooring post, its base drifted with fine sand. He positioned her by it, the sea behind her, and looked her hard in the face. For a moment she thought he was going to kiss her. He hadn't ever, but she knew he wanted to. There was something serious in him which prevented it.

"Let me get this right," he said. "You get that voice, like a teacher or some bully from school —"

"I never went to school," she said.

"Waste," he said. "Clever woman like you," and she was pleased, because nobody had ever thought her clever, and he noticed that she was pleased and smiled at her, and then continued, "OK, the voice — the

109

goblin — is it like your parents when they're angry, or you think they're angry, and it goes over and over all the things that are wrong about your moral character and your behaviour and everything?"

"That's just what it's like," she said.

"That's what it is," he said. "It's not what you really are. Or what you really think. It's some habit you got into when you were little, and you get used to it and it just goes on and on. My sister had an owl in her belly. Did just the same thing. Made her feel nauseous too. So. Is it awake yet?"

She looked at him.

Clever? said the goblin. Clever? You'd fall for that cheap and clearly inaccurate compliment? He's out for what he can get. Probably just thinks you're rich. He'd hardly be after you for your looks, would he? Unless he's desperate . . .

"Yes," she said. "It's right here."

"On your shoulder? Which one?"

"Right," she said, and her mouth tightened, and she thought she might cry, and what was she even doing here? He doesn't like you. How could he like you?

"Put your hands on the post, in front of you," he said. "Just rest them on the top."

He smiled at her. "Don't move," he said.

The next thing was a ferocious loud report, and a hard clean note past her right ear, swift and sudden and gone again with a brush of air and an idea of heat, harder and hotter than she had ever experienced.

She cried out, lurching a little to the left, her foot turning on the soft sand, but she didn't fall. Her eyes

110

were wide as she glanced behind, out to the wide clear sea, and then looked back at him.

He was standing in front of her, a pistol held in both hands, pointing downwards.

"Got it," he said, and he grinned. "Point blank, pretty much."

Back on the rug, she sat shaking. She couldn't take her eyes off him. Lunatic? Hero? What?

But you presented it to him as real, and he dealt with it as real.

He nearly shot you! His bullet went past inches from your head! If you had moved, you'd be dead — but he told you not to move. And you didn't move — he . . .

She'd refused his arm to get back to the rug, to sit. He was squatting now, a little to the side, watching her and holding out his hip flask.

"Whisky," he said. "Sorry to scare you. Had to be like that."

She stared up at him, dark against the bright sky behind him. A flurry of seabirds had been set off by the sound of the shot — gradually they were returning to the rocks and the strand, resettling. She did not feel at all settled. But the voice in her head was not the goblin.

"You OK?" he said. He gestured again with the flask. She shook her head.

"Yes," she said. "I am OK." She sounded a bit puzzled by the fact. But she was OK. He'd shot the goblin.

Later she asked him what had happened to his sister's owl.

"I got rid of it for her," he said. "I squeezed it up out of her tummy, moving it higher and higher till it popped out of her mouth, and then I strangled it and put it in the stove."

"Could you see it?" Julia asked.

"Nope! I had to hold on real tight so it didn't get away and go bothering some other little girl. I just grabbed it right out of her mouth and stuffed it in the stove and slammed down the lid."

She smiled.

Over the next days and weeks she found herself smiling in her sleep, and waking up smiling.

CHAPTER
NINE

Rome and London, June—July 1919
Before leaving London, Riley and Nadine had made
one other visit: to their old art teacher, Riley's mentor,
Sir Alfred, in his white and beautiful house in Orme
Square, behind the magnolias. When they had told him
they were married, he had said, "Good," and "Where
are you living? Want to come and live here?" His
warmth had been joyous. "No, of course not," he said.
"You must go on your great trip." This had been a
dream plan from the years before the war — that they
should visit Amsterdam, Paris, Florence, Borgo San
Sepolcro, Mantua, Rome, Istanbul, Cairo, to see
Rembrandts, Michelangelo, Piero della Francesca,
Masaccio, Delphi, the chapel of Chora, the mosque of
Ibn Tulun. Sir Alfred had sent Nadine up to his studio
to choose a present of one of his travelling painting
cases, and Riley had gone up with her. They had looked
out of the tall windows at the spring sunshine; the
memory of five years before, when he had first touched
her, in this room, had hovered like a ghost, making
Riley's hand ache. The old man's main wedding present
was a truncated section of the Grand Tour — an
extension to their honeymoon — a trip to Italy.

Now, night after night across Europe, following Sir Alfred's itinerary, Nadine and Riley slept under high ceilings in single beds on opposite sides of tile-floored bedrooms, separated by little marble-topped bedside cupboards, glass-shaded lamps, guidebooks, dressing gowns, and deep, terrible misunderstanding. This profound wrongness streaked Nadine's heart. Everything around them was so right, so promising, so surging with possibility and fruitfulness . . . except for what was wrong, and she knew — she *knew* — did not have to be wrong. It wasn't his face. She was getting used to his face. It had become just — the truth. She thought. Or am I still in shock about it? Is he? But we can live with it. Look at us, living with it! We've only another fifty years or so . . . Yes, so far, we're just wandering around, settling nowhere — this is not a real life . . .

Nor was it his speech. She understood him, with only a small amount of extra effort. Other people, unused to him, found it a little harder. When he heard of the Italian mode of speech known as the *bocca aperta*, the open mouth, he noticed how much easier it was to understand, and took to practising it himself — when he wanted to communicate, which she knew was not always. Communication was work for him, physically, emotionally, socially. He did not want attention.

No, the same thing was wrong. The sex thing.

By pure force of will she pushed it away. Distraction! And in this she had a sudden though entirely predictable burst of assistance: Nadine, like so many before and after her, fell deeply, madly, in a most devout, transparent and mysterious way, in love with

Italy. She blinded herself with the glory of the Italian summer. Every time she looked out onto Umbrian hills or Tuscan streets, on to Venice! — every time she breathed pine or fennel or frankincense, or looked into some shaded church in the heat of the day, the fear which had desiccated her in 1918 wilted and shrank. Everything was beautiful, and the beauty began to overpower all her sorrows and regrets. She smelt basil, for the first time in her life, and was intoxicated. The fat and glossy tomatoes made her sigh. This Italian sun was making a nymph of her, mossy-footed, cool-thighed, water-pouring. She loved the world — it's true! I do! I had forgotten! — and she began to wonder what she was going to do about it. She wanted to tell it. To thank it. Is that what art is for? To tell the world you love it?

This educational voyage, arranged by a most knowledgeable guide, was peeling mud and sorrow off her soul. She remembered suddenly, one morning, wounded soldiers arriving from the battlefields after days of travel caked in mud, in a dried-out carapace that had to be chipped off them . . . a clay shell like a gypsy's roasted hedgehog, and God knows what wounds and damage you'd find inside. Every day the cities and the paintings exposed to her long, deep unities of humanity, strong living channels that emerged from the depths of the past like crystal streams bursting from a cavern. She found herself connected not only to the painters, but to their subjects too. All these humans, all these lives, all that time. Look . . .

In Milan she saw a *Supper at Emmaus* by Caravaggio. Jesus sat at the table, looking ill, she felt, with a light sweat on his face, and concern occupied every angle of the three people around him. Just a man, suffering. Such love and fear surrounding him — well, of course I identify with that. Looking at him, some phrases came back to her from the book of Edward Thomas which Peter had given her: "a strong citizen of infinity and eternity . . . I knew that I could not do without the Infinite, nor the Infinite without me". Thomas, she remembered, had died at Arras, at Easter, 1917. She wondered if he had been a religious man. And oh — Peter —

One day at Mantua, she saw another painting, not especially good, in the shadows of a church they had only gone into to get out of the heat. It was typical, showing the Virgin and Child on their throne, with some saints, her in blue, him in a coral necklace. But at the bottom, excluded from the rest of the painting by a marble step and the Virgin's tapestry carpet, scowled at by the Lion of St Jerome (who was offering the Virgin a model of a church), almost trodden on by a baby St John the Baptist, were the heads of four shamefaced people. Two were women, scarved, modest in dark clothing, sad. The others were men: one grey-bearded, aged and wrinkled, the other, younger, guilty-eyed, stubborn, despairing. The women looked down and sideways. The men stared out. Each wore a circle of yellow cord stitched to his coat. At the top of the painting two angels held up a plaque on which was written: *Debellata hebraeorum temeritate*.

"What does that mean?" she asked Riley.

116

"Something of the temerity of the Jews," he said. "I think." It took them a moment or two to get "temerity" across. Some consonants are less clear than others.

The figures seemed to be standing in a pit. Were they a family — parents, a son and a daughter? What had they done? Why were they so banished?

She asked an old lady, who pointed her to a young cleric, who took them to meet a dusty priest who was eating cake in a room behind the church, and he told them in decent English with an amount of gesticulation the story of the Defeat of the Jews' Temerity. In 1493 Daniele di Norsa, a Jew of Mantua, bought a house with a fresco of the Virgin Mary painted on the façade. Having asked the Bishop's permission, he had it painted over. Two years later, under threat of being hung, he had to pay 110 ducats at three days' notice for a new painting by Mantegna, to the glory of the Virgin. A year after that, Daniele was evicted, the house demolished, and the land "donated" for a church to be built. Mantegna's painting was put in it, with great pomp and a procession. A year later Daniele was vindicated of any wrongdoing; but two years after *that* this painting was made, recording his humiliation, and put in the church. This church, on the land where his house had been.

Nadine flexed and wriggled her fingers quietly as the priest told the story. Afterwards, walking between the afternoon sun and the black shadows by the stone walls, she said: "How many times can someone be punished for the same thing?"

"As many times as the culture he lives in allows," said Riley.

It reminded her of scared boys running away from German bullets into the line of the firing squad for deserters. The priest told them that Norsa had been lucky: the punishment for damaging a sacred image was to have your hand chopped off.

They went to see the painting Norsa had paid for: a magnificent thing, showing Francesco Gonzaga, Duke of Mantua, in all his glory and virtue, kneeling in his black armour and his pink and gold brocade. There was no customary image of the donor here, no family symbol or tiny figures of them and their wife on their knees before God. Nadine wondered if Gonzaga was just obliterating Norsa, as a less-than-nothing Jew. Or was he protecting him from further attention and obloquy?

"Christians," she murmured. "Love thy neighbour. And Christ was a Jew, wasn't he?"

"Mmm," said Riley.

"Technically, I think I am too," she said. "Let's not let our children be religious, shall we?" And then realised what she had touched on, and rushed into a tiny shop, where there were new cherries, over which she exclaimed in pleasure.

Children? thought Riley. What does she mean?

She spoke without thinking. That's why she ran off.

For their first hot, starry, delirious nights in Rome, Nadine and Riley stayed at a little place near Santa

118

Maria sopra Minerva, so full of priests that it made them laugh. Even if he wanted to, we couldn't, here, she thought, surrounded by so much chastity . . .

"I'd rather like to try a different sort of hotel," she said, and Riley, who had taken to the ascetic little room with its crucifix and iron beds, was sorry that he had perhaps inflicted lack of comfort on her. They had laughed together at their 1909 Baedeker, where it had said that travels with ladies would cost more, and that ladies should wear blue veils, and on no account go anywhere on their own, and so forth — but he was a man unaccustomed to comfort, and uncertain about the true nature and requirements of women — even a fearless-seeming woman such as Nadine. She liked watching him realise that of course she must have more comforts than this. She liked the pleasure it gave him to attend to her, and began to invent little desires for him to enjoy indulging.

When he proposed an apartment, she almost wept with delight. Their two rooms near the Pantheon, high-ceilinged, tile-floored, high-bedded, green-shuttered, seemed like their first home. The signora sent a girl up with a big jug of water each day. The café on the ground floor was their dining room (the cook immediately understood Riley's condition and they ate whatever she put before them, not knowing half the time what it was: thus for the rest of her life Nadine thought of artichokes as *carciofi* and aubergines as *melanzane*). A heavy linen sheet from the flea market at Porta Portese replaced the slightly smelly velvet bedcover; an empty wine bottle and a handful of tuberoses from the Sicilian on the bridge by the gleaming new synagogue confirmed their occupation. Just before that bridge she found the old ghetto area, a village of its own, with via della Portico d'Ottavia awash with the smell of frying and broth and cinnamon baking. She bought some little buns, and took them home, and sat on their bed. A double.

Now, she thought. But now what? I must be able to do something.

Painting, sex, babies.

She was *shy* of him.

She started drawing again, making watercolours and trying out pastels. She eyed Sir Alfred's old travelling paint box, with fold-up easel, soft, worn brushes, and the smell of ancient turpentine. In the windows of the artists' supplies shops, lead tubes of fresh new colours lay waiting for her, but initially, she just drew: the rippling tiled roofs, overlapping; the bell towers and the domes; the Pantheon from their window, from the café, from the piazza, from the corner. She drew the Trevi Fountain, the nakednesses more harmonious, more playful. She wandered the Vatican museums and caught her breath at corridor after corridor of the beautiful marble bodies of antiquity. The graceful humility of a woman lifting a bowl of water; the magnificence of Caesars and Joves with their great legs and rippling breastplates; Tritons riding turtles, massive arms thrusting massive spears and clubs, the dimpled flesh of nymphs and naiads. She drew an enormous foot. She drew Bernini's Apollo catching the fleeing Daphne, the marble

120

tears cast back on her marble cheeks, the imprint of his marble fingers bruising her marble thigh as she starts to turn to wood in his arms. She drew the Apollo Belvedere and a particular Hermes, a curly-haired, broad-chested, one-armed, flat-nosed marble youth with an air of quiet, intense superiority, an elegant curve to him, wearing nothing but a bit of cloth wrapped round his one arm, and flung across his shoulder.

It's all so sexual! And so utterly, utterly beautiful . . .

And in the Villa Giulia she came across the Etruscan Bride and Groom lying together on their sarcophagus, propped up against their pillow, her leaning back a little against his bare chest, his kind arm round her shoulder, so relaxed, her hands conversational in gesture, her plaits and little hat, his pointy beard, their safety and sweetness. They could be lounging after dinner and talking still — both at the same time, perhaps — with someone across the table — with me! — as if I were their friend — and their conversation continuing — as if at any moment they might turn their heads and look at one another, and laugh, and call each other by some silly name . . . Their physical ease.

The name of the villa made her wonder how Julia was, and Peter, and Tom. No one had written to them — well, they wouldn't — except Rose. Nadine took it that Rose didn't want to bother them on their honeymoon. She would have liked to be bothered, actually. Though perhaps a married lady couldn't write to a single friend about what was on her mind here.

And poor little Tom . . .

*   *   *

In the Forum, under a cloud of jacaranda as purple and glossy as a mallard's wingstreak, she saw a young man kissing a girl, and the girl pulling away, laughing.

She drew the jacaranda, the tumble of it from the column, the lines of the ancient architecture from which it hung, the papery petals, the texture of the stone and crumbling mortar. Then she went home and cried.

It's not the act itself — God, I can hardly remember that, though . . . well . . . but no, it's that laughter, that easy laughter afterwards . . .

Liar. It's lust, is what it is. It's pure filthy lust.

As the summer grew on, the heat became intense. They took to siestas; Riley would put on a clean shirt in the late afternoon before they went out in the long evenings for the *passaggiata*, walking, watching Rome. They lay on their backs on the stone benches of the Campidoglio and waited for the shooting stars.

"It's too early," said Riley, and she shifted position so she could see his face. "They come in August. They're the sparks from the griddle where San Lorenzo was martyred. When they said to him 'Have you had enough?' he said, 'No, turn me over, I'm only done on one side.'"

"How repellent," she said. "How do you know that?"

"Bloke in the café told me," he said.

Riley spent his time reading newspapers in Italian and talking to strangers. It was different here to in England. Here, among foreigners, his difficulties had become a personal challenge to him, an insult he was no longer willing to entertain. Here it didn't matter what people thought, so he was able to launch himself straight on at insurmountable and potentially humiliating situations. He stood firm and patient as people squinted at him, frowned, shook their heads, stopped a moment, considered, began to understand, began to try, smiled, lightened, wanted to help — joined him where he was, because he threw himself forward, so boldly, so shamelessly, so desperately and honestly, so determined. *I don't know how this will be*, he thought, *but I can try it out*. And occasionally a vast sadness overwhelmed him. I cannot just laugh, and chat, and sit around a table eating. I remember it. The ease. I do miss it. So natural and fundamental an activity. So ordinary. So important.

He put to use instead the faculties he retained. He walked the city for hours, exploring and discovering, until his feet swelled. He worked away at the language. He made himself chat. He went to the Sistine Chapel, and lay flat on his back on the floor, the better to observe the ceiling, gazing up, and being thrown out, and going back, lying down, and being thrown out again.

Nothing will stop him, Nadine thought. He will be all right.

When the thunderstorms started, the smell of cold rain on hot stone rose up from the street and intoxicated her. Everything was intoxicating her. The tuberoses; the basil; the wine; the rushing yellow river; the cool and massive churches; the stink of the heat of the day; the splash of cool holy water on your brow; the mighty

123

colours of old oils and bright frescoes as fresh as yesterday; the innumerable colours of the polished marble panels of the floor of St Peter's; the streets; the skulls and bones of the monks in the Barberini chapel arranged like flowers up and across the walls, little scapulae as wings for tiny skull cherubs, set in spandrels formed from vertebrae; the incense, white marble limbs, stone, jacaranda, jasmine, the moon . . .

They were lounging one gold and blue night on the Ponte Sant' Angelo. Above them was Castel Sant'Angelo, on whose roof Cavaradossi had sung of the woman and the garden gate, the stars coming to light, and how he had never loved life more. Over there, St Peter's glowed like a massive pearl in the crepuscule. Beneath them, broad and invisible, the yellow Tiber rushed, loosing its riverish smell and restless sounds. Above, the great stone angels rose, their wings aloft for eternity, each holding one of the symbols of Christ's passion: the sponge of vinegar, the dice with which the soldiers cast lots for his clothes, the lance with which his heart was pierced: *Vulnerasti cor meum*, read its inscription. *Thou hast ravished my heart*, according to the guidebook, but Riley said *vulnerasti* was more to do with wounded, like vulnerable. *Vulnerable, ravished, pierced*, she thought, and the face of Bernini's Santa Teresa, in Santa Maria della Vittoria, came to her, the angel standing above the saint, his lance in his hand, laughing a little at his power over her, and she swooning, half rising, arching from the cloud she lies on . . . Nadine had been reading Santa Teresa's autobiography: "I saw in his hand a long spear of gold . . . he appeared

124

to me to be thrusting it into my heart, and to pierce my very entrails; when he drew it out, he seemed to leave me all on fire with a great love of God. The pain was so great, that it made me moan; and yet so surpassing was the sweetness of this excessive pain . . ."

Lord above, even the saints are at it.

Riley's face, beside her now on the bridge, was the same colour as the stone angels. He had told her once, months ago, about the woman who had cast his face at Sidcup, who had said he looked like a broken statue, like something lying around on the Acropolis. He had given a blokish, embarrassed little laugh.

Vulnerasti cor meum, she thought, in so many ways, over and over, over and over . . .

The moon rode above them, a great calm golden pearl, little sister to St Peter's dome.

I can't go on like this. I love you so much.

She said: "Perhaps . . ."

"What?" he replied after a moment, and she said: "I'm not sure," which made him smile. His smile, so beautifully lopsided and strange. His grey diamond eyes.

He took her hand, lifted it, and put his mouth to it; the half-deadened mouth. It lay there for a moment, like despair. But she felt — did she? yes — in the immobility, a tremor of something — an echo — a nerve — the desire of the mouth to kiss the hand.

He's scared, she thought. She brought his hand back to her own mouth, kissed it with her own undamaged lips. In his skin, the tremor — a strong, thoroughly repressed tremor, seismic, deep deep down. Only just detectable. Strong enough to throw her over.

She felt a flush rising, and went to put her knuckle to her teeth to steady herself but found she was biting her hand, and she was falling, and he was catching her, and his hand was on the side of her breast.

"I should take you home," he murmured, and hailed a horse-drawn cab.

"*E malata, la signora?*" the driver said. "*Vuole che andiamo all'ospedale?*"

"No," said Riley. "She's not ill."

I am going to proposition my own husband, though I know he . . . he . . . .

"Nadine?" he said.

The next day, in the clear summer daylight, she said: "I need to see," so he stood by the window in the sunlight, his shirt collar open, his throat bare, and he swallowed, and he opened his mouth for her, as best he could. She laid her hand against his created jaw, where shifted skin and flesh covered a frame of vulcanite. She traced the main scars, where the skin had been sewn back together; she looked closely at the pores and the shaven hair follicles, where what had been the black curls of his scalp made do now as the beard of his chin. She put her finger on his twisted lip, gently held it down and approached what she might find inside. She said: "Let me look?" She touched the padded flesh, gazed into the unusual cave: flesh white where it should be pink; the tongue lying strangely; the membranes skew-whiff like banners after a storm. This odd attachment, this

126

undercarriage, this jaw. The little uvula dangling innocently at the back, as if surveying the battlefield.

She touched the false teeth, noticed how they fitted with the stitched gum within. She tapped her finger, just once, very gently, on the tip of his tongue, lying there in its unexpected new home. She kissed him.

He stood there, so utterly embarrassed, so certain that he could never be enough for her.

She took his face in both hands, kissed him. Found him, inside it all.

It was as a fully and consummated married couple that they returned to London, a relieved and joyous pair drenched in honeymoon after all; agog at the awfulness of the fate they had each been willing to enter into for the other's sake; each amazed by the other's willingness and ability to make that sacrifice for them, and united in delight and relief that they had not, after all, had to follow through and live forever under the curse of that terrible overgenerous misunderstanding.

They were pursued north, though they didn't know it, by telegrams. Jacqueline was sick.

Jacqueline had the Spanish flu; return immediately.

Jacqueline was dead.

CHAPTER
TEN

Biarritz, towards the end of the summer, 1919
One of the masseuses at the Thermes Salins told Julia
that she thought, *Excusez-moi, Madame,* that *Madame*
should go to the doctor. The doctor, a middle-aged
person with a mouth that managed to be both sloppy
and prissy at the same time, told her she was five
months pregnant.

"A gift, Madame," he said, "from beyond the grave,"
and she felt for a second grateful that her damaged skin
could not show the flush which rose up her neck at the
realisation that by August 1919, a war widow could
hardly be five months pregnant by her husband.

She sat for a moment, before discomfort and shame
stood her up again under his judgemental eyes.

"He died of his wounds, doctor," she said.

"Curious," said the doctor, "what the human body
can do. A mortal wound, and yet, capable . . ." He
waved his hand in a tiny movement of vast disdain. It
was quite clear what he thought.

Julia rested her hand on the edge of the doctor's
polished desk. Moments ago this man had had his
hands on her naked skin. Her gaze fell on her wedding
ring, worn now in the widow's style on the third finger

of her right hand. The ring Peter had put on her finger. Peter, who she was pretending was dead. Peter, her husband who she was lying about and whose child she had inside her. A kind of fury began to moil inside her and flew out, suddenly, at the doctor.

"Isn't it," she said. "To think that his body survived four-and-half-years' fighting. On French soil." She put the tiniest bit of emphasis on the word "French". "And was able to make it home, and be with his wife, and after *all that*, the infection flared up again, and he died. And yet he has left his widow with his child. I agree, doctor. A miracle."

He was looking narrowly at her.

"I wonder where you spent the war, doctor. Saving lives under dangerous conditions, no doubt. A shame you weren't there to save his. Good morning."

Fury surged in her at the doctor's disdain, his disrespect for Peter. If Peter were to die now, he would be dying of the wounds. Whatever he died of, whenever he died, if he were to die in fifty years, it would be of wounds. Nothing bigger, greater, worse, than that war would ever happen to any of them. It never could. Peter was wounded and crippled by the war as much as any one-legged man, any shaking neurological case, as much as Riley, or that man she'd seen in the woods that hot afternoon — the patient from the Queen's, wearing hospital blues and the tin mask which hid his injuries but failed to hide his shamed and lustful look . . . How dare the French fool disrespect Peter when Peter's entire manhood had been dismantled and left in that bloody French mud . . . How dare *anybody* sneer at

129

Peter, mock his body, what he had done, what he had suffered, what he still suffered . . .

As her fury subsided, she felt the irony. And she let the actual matter in: pregnant.

She shivered.

Thank God, thank God, thank God, that Harlan was not that kind of man; that our friendship has been pure. It had a sort of passionate moral reluctance, a shared desire to keep it special, to not be sordid. If he had been a different kind of man, a pusher, a cad, like that one in the pub in Mayfair . . . Well, if Harlan had pushed her, or lured her, she would have capitulated. He knew it, and she knew it. And she would now be in a very difficult and horrid position. But he had not pushed her, in any way. He was a kind man, gentle, and aware of her . . . of my what? My delicacy? My vulnerability?

He'd said, "Everyone gets damaged by war. You don't have to be in it to be damaged."

Well. Harlan and all that he might have been will be over now.

Pregnant.

She put her hand on her belly, and leant with the other against a lamppost. Her stomach still seemed hardly curved. All this time! Her monthlies had been irregular since her breakdown. How had she not noticed? Like an uneducated girl, some poor creature who knew no better . . .

Baby.

Harlan.

Peter.

Tom.

130

* * *

Harlan smiled rather bitterly when she told him, in the privacy of her room, that she was going back to England on family business. "Well," he said. "Summer's lease hath all too short a let. Is this it, then?"

And she had burst into tears.

As good men will, he took her in his arms, he wiped her tears, he held her close. He kissed her, and she couldn't not respond. But then she stopped and pulled away and said — everything.

Husband living, not dead. Husband's state of mind and drinking habits since the war. Existence of Tom. Pregnancy, by husband. It was 5.30 in the afternoon when she burst into tears, and 2.30 the next morning when they stopped talking.

Harlan, sitting across from her on an upright little chair, asked a great many questions. Where had Peter served? What rank was he? Had he come home on leave? How had that been? Had he lost men?

"Yes."

"Where?"

"I'm not sure. The Somme, and at Loos, I think."

"How many?" he asked.

She didn't know. "Quite a few, I think," she said. "He was on leave afterwards and went back to a different company. There were heavy losses and things were reorganised."

He was quiet for a while when she told him. Then he said, "Do you understand what that means to him?"

She thought before answering. "I suppose I don't," she said. "Should I?"

"No," he said. "You can't. But you can know that you can't understand. You can acknowledge that."

She was sitting on her bed. Beyond him the evening was light and golden through the window, and small sounds filtered up from the gardens outside.

"Did you lose men?" she asked.

"Not on and on for four-and-a-half years," he said. "And not alongside them in battle, with their blood on my face."

She opened her eyes wide.

"That's what war is, sweetheart," he said. "I'm sorry to be the one to tell you, but war is your friend's blood on your face and his dead body in your arms. Your husband probably didn't want to mention that. You know why men fight wars?"

"Not really," she said.

"To protect you," he said. "And did he protect you?"

"Yes," she said. "Of course. We won."

He let her sit with that thought for a moment.

"It's an unfortunate fact," he said, "that fighting for civilisation can render a man unfit for civilised society."

She frowned.

His questions started again, and she answered each one carefully but swiftly.

"Does he talk to you about any of this?"

"No."

"To his friends, his service buddies?"

She thought of Riley. "Mm, no."

"Does he *have* friends?"

"Well, no —"

"Does he see *anybody*?"

132

"Hardly."

"Talk to *anybody?*"

"No."

Her face was growing tighter.

"Does he sleep?"

"Yes, a lot — but restlessly."

"Does he dream?"

"I suppose so."

"Do you not know?"

"It's been a while since we shared a bed."

A pause.

"Do you love each other?"

She started crying softly.

"Did you ever love each other?"

"Yes," she said. "Yes. Very much."

He had his hand round the back of his neck, scratching under his collar. He looked up at her sideways.

"What about your boy?" he said, and Julia could only shake her head. "How're they together?" Shook her head.

"How often do you get letters from him?" he went on.

"Ah — I don't."

"Well, how often do you write?"

She said nothing.

"Oh," he said. A silence fell then too. But not a judgemental one.

"Did he like the slippers?" he asked, after a pause.

She looked up. "How do you know about the slippers?"

"I was in the shop when you bought them," he said. "I noticed you."

She liked that phrase. *I noticed you*. It suggested a cleanness of look, no residue and detritus built up about the image one sees: seeing someone just as they are, now. As themself.

"At home," she said, "nobody likes me. I have done an awful lot of silly things. I've gone awfully wrong."

"You can go right again," he said, easily and without thought.

"Can I? How?"

"Just start doing the right things," he said, and as he said it his face broke a little, as if he realised, in the saying, what that meant, here, and now.

With every question he asked, and every answer she gave, a few scales fell from her eyes and clouds divided. Laid out before another person, someone who knew nothing of her family, the story reappeared before her eyes too, fresh and with perspective. She recalled the flood of anger she had had with the doctor — for judging Peter, for not understanding. As if she had ever understood.

Harlan asked: Had she left home before? No. So what had made her do it this time? It was all too much. Had she thought it through? Lord, no! Did *she* have friends? No. Who did *she* talk to?

After a pause, "No one."

Then, "You," she said.

He stood, suddenly, and moved across, and kissed her, her face tilted up uncomfortably, his back too bent

134

over for ease. He stopped, touched her cheek, sat down again.

"What *did* happen to your face?" he said. The light was beginning to fade behind him now.

"I was having a kind of breakdown," she said. "I had the idea that if I could make everything perfect for Peter then he would be happy. Including myself. I wanted to be perfect for him. I had — well, I gave myself — a kind of beauty treatment. Chemical. I thought if I was beautiful enough ... anyway, I was wrong, and it went wrong, and so here it is!" She gave a bold little laugh, and threw her hands up elegantly.

"When?"

"Nine months ago."

"How do you feel about it now?"

She had to think about that for a moment, perched on the satin eiderdown, like some kind of dolly. Through this examination she was going to learn something. How did she feel?

"Foolish," she said.

"You know, though, that beauty isn't your face? It's part of your entire self? You know different people bring it out in each other?"

"Yes," she said, smiling. "That's a nice way to look at it."

"Do you not see that you're bringing it out in me?"

She looked across at him, sitting there. You shot my goblin, she was thinking. For that I will always love you. At least — she thought she was thinking it but she said it out loud, and he looked back at her and smiled, and closed his eyes. Then he stood, and came and sat beside

135

her, and put his arm around her, close. They sat like that for a moment, before he turned and shifted the pillows from under the bedcover, and lay back, and said to her, "Come." He pulled her down to him again, putting her head on his chest, and he stroked her hair as he gazed at the ceiling.

"So," he said. "How much, exactly, is he drinking? Was he getting in to work OK, or had it gone beyond that?"

"Do you know about drinking?" she asked, twisting to look up at him. She could smell his soap and sunshine smell, see the gold glints on his shaven face. A clean man.

He said, "My father fought in the Civil War. He came back a drunk. He'd developed a relationship with spiritus frumenti; used to get it from the medical supplies when there was no whisky to be had, and he acquired a taste for it."

"What is it?"

"Grain spirit — medical alcohol," he said. "It's not good for a man. He died of it. It took a long time and broke our hearts."

He put it so simply.

"But you survived," she said.

He said, "What's important is the spirit in which a person lives. Longing for a particular situation which is 'happy' is not . . . real. But if you're living in a way which leads to the good, then you can die at any point, whether you're happy that particular day or not." Then with some care, he said: "Neither you nor I could be happy if we did wrong by your husband."

136

Is that true?

"He's lost the lives of his men," he said. "He can't lose you too." And when she protested, "But he doesn't want me!" Harlan said, "Oh yes he does. He wants you and he needs you in ways beyond human comprehension. Certainly beyond his comprehension. And yours."

There was longer silence after that.

Then he said: "Is your husband going to die and break your hearts? Yours and your son's?"

At which she wept again, furiously, for a long time, her head on his chest, snot and gulping, ugly crying: for everything she'd done and been unable to do, for Peter, for his men, for Tom, for Riley, Nadine, Rose, the man in the tin mask, the unborn child . . .

And as good men will, he took her in his arms, again, and wiped her face when the time was right, and kissed her. And then, with pauses for tacit permission, he was undressing her, and unwrapping her, and undoing her, and she longed for it and was glad. As he made love to her, from the tentative to the permitted to the suddenly and unexpectedly ferocious, everything that was in her came roaring out: grief and pain and shame and fury and an equally hard and ferocious joy.

Hours later, she lay in the pre-dawn blackness, knowing that this didn't change anything.

He murmured, "Let me at least escort you back to England. I'm doing that at least . . .", and she said no. No. She couldn't bear it.

She did ask him, in the course of it, how he could love her, with her face. He said, "You're tough. You're fun. You're not like a European — you're not obsessed with the past. Even now I don't feel like your past is reaching out to drag you back . . ."

She sighed.

". . . I feel like you're going into your future. Make sure that's what you do, won't you? Though it's not the future I had in mind for us."

He was forty-two, and the way he looked at her, as dawn came up, was very steady. She gave him the address of the small hotel she used to stay in sometimes in London, and said if, if — but he shook his head. "You let me know if he dies," he said. "US military will have my address."

In the morning the hotel manager came to her room, bustling and outraged, but Julia was already packed and on her way. She took a train to the largest town she could identify on the Côte d'Azur. All she needed was a decent doctor and nobody she knew. She couldn't go back. She couldn't stay here. She couldn't be with Harlan. She couldn't live without him.

A strange frozen feeling had come over her. She'd heard nothing from Locke Hill — she'd left no address, nobody knew anything of her or she of them. But the house of cards was about to fall in. She could feel the ghost of the air moving as the cards started to shift, the incipient gust of change.

It's up to me, she thought.

The station at Marseilles smelt of fish. The street outside was full of US sailors on shore leave, and their tough-looking Shore Patrol carrying truncheons. The

138

local people looked evil, poor and miserable. It was neither quiet nor clean. Some small children clustered too close around her, distracting and confusing her, grabbing her coat — begging — or stealing? She moved on to a café, sat, and an African came and spoke to her, kindly, saying: "Madame, you should not sit here alone, trouble will come to you."

She cried for a bit, and several men came and tried to speak to her, none of them kind, and none of them a tall and blue-eyed US lootenant.

She had been a fool, a *fool*, to think she could be free. The only way to be free is to cut out your heart. You cannot live free. You can only live by love. Very well. She would love.

She went to the ticket window.

Part Two

1919

CHAPTER
ELEVEN

London, Wigan, Sidcup, July — September 1919
Riley was on a train again, rattling down to Sidcup. Major Gillies wanted a look at him, see how the old jaw was holding up, that sort of thing. Riley was rather afraid that Gillies might want to talk about his state of mind as well, so he felt obliged, while gazing out at the back gardens and the apple orchards, to go over it, so as to have a quick answer to give.

He was not going to stand for Parliament. Part of him wanted to — to counteract pests like Mosley, who had won Harrow on the sheer force of his own self-belief and ignorance, and to hold strong to the idea of change, that England could be different now, and better. That it could honour its entire population, not just those with the money and the titles. But there was the vicious circle: he had no money and no support. And more to the point, it was not, after all, possible for him to go so directly into the world to challenge and influence it. It was not that his courage had declined — certainly it was not being challenged the way it had been, but it was still there all right. No, the point was that he could not and did not want to squander so much of his courage on being looked at.

He had supposed that he had grown accustomed to his appearance, and to the effect it had on people. Being at the Queen's with the others in similar conditions; being tucked away at Locke Hill; being abroad, where, to be honest, things didn't matter, because he wasn't sticking around, and he wasn't trying to build anything, being wrapped up in Nadine's love and her own courage, he had perhaps underestimated what still remained for him to deal with. Perhaps he had thought that dealing with something was a finite business: deal with it, and then it is over. Or, deal with it, and then you know how to deal with it. But that was not his experience. He dealt with it over and over and over, continually, continuously.

His pride was low, slow burning and constant. He suffered everybody's kindness, he had hugely enjoyed his time in France and Italy, he was beyond joyful that he and Nadine had — oh, God, he was glad — but he found that actually he did not want to have to present himself to strangers. Without an arm or a leg, perhaps he could have campaigned. But without a clear voice and clear human expressions on his face? No. He could not represent the people when he didn't even want to meet them. So Parliament was not going to be the way he would contribute.

Anyway, he was busy. Nadine, usually so sanguine, humorous and reliable, had been distraught about her mother. She was deeply confused about the vagaries of her grief, how its guilt and its paucity could co-exist with sudden streaks of searing loss and misery. Any death brings back every death that went before — she had not known that. She had been flicked back to the state of shock and loss they had all known so well during the war. And half the letters of condolence came on black-rimmed mourning paper, and half the guests at the funeral were weeping for funerals that would never happen.

Riley considered the differences: this kind of death; that kind of death. He dropped his eyes, and thought: The deaths the women witnessed were men who were already lying down. The men I saw die had seconds earlier been standing, running, fighting, smoking, talking. He wondered if that made a difference to how one learnt to live with it.

"Why didn't I like her?" Nadine asked him. "Why didn't I love her? Everybody else loved her. Father loved her! Why couldn't I?"

"Because she was the Queen of Sheba," Riley said. "Anything that happened to her was more important than everything that happened to anybody else." He remembered it from before the war. Often it had been a joyful thing: wardrobes of half-used clothes laid open for the chosen to help themselves, astonishingly generous presents, parties she threw, glamorous people she brought together, admirers, Robert's musicians, young men she had crushes on, young women with crushes on her. "You felt that what she gave you was given for her own glory, not out of love," Riley said, and Nadine smiled at him because he was telling the truth, even though it was harsh.

"It's a shame she never took the trouble with you," she said. "That she never bothered to get past everything. You understood her better than I did." Riley hugged her. He hadn't lost a parent. He couldn't go on wanting all her attention. A whole man doesn't crave attention from his wife in mourning for her mother. But he wanted it.

The loss was compounded by the fact that, on their return from Italy, they moved straight in to Nadine's childhood home on Bayswater Road. Why would they go to Chelsea when the house was empty but for her father, standing there like the last reed in an empty lagoon, desperate? Riley accepted that Nadine and Sir Robert both needed it. A house of grief is a house of grief, and there is nowhere to go, nothing to do. Just wait.

"You take her room," her father said to them. "I don't need it. I'm in my dressing room. You go on . . ." so Nadine and Riley had found themselves in among all the *stuff*, her mother's detritus, the scent bottles, the underwear, the stockings and books and . . .

Riley took one look, and found it unbearable. He had married Nadine, not her mother's ghost.

"Do what you want with your mother's things," Sir Robert was saying. "I know I should help you, but . . ." and with that he had gone out of focus, and Riley very much wanted Nadine to say to him, "Papa, I can't do it on my own," but it seemed she couldn't say that.

Riley telephoned Rose.

It was Rose, of course, who helped; who found the dress shop to take the good clothes, and the charity to take the everyday ones, sorted the papers with Riley, sent the ugly jewellery to the bank and told Nadine, in tears over the jewellery case, that it was absolutely all right, indeed necessary, that she keep and wear the little emerald ring she was holding and staring at.

"I just wish it had been different," Nadine said, meaning so many things — everything, really — Dad's widowing, my mother's wastefulness — what was it I said? We'd have time to get over our tiff? Something — ha! Never assume, never assume. And now she will never have the chance to know what her son-in-law really is . . . and I have lost the chance to make up with her — pigheaded — and now Riley is being strong for me — well, he'll like that — but he's so tender — I must not forget him . . .

And Rose, though she couldn't know what Nadine was thinking, was there to agree.

Riley chafed. He had looked forward to the two little rooms in Chelsea, rent to be paid by him, because he was *going* to be earning, and then things would be right. At the moment, Nadine had an allowance from her father, which was bigger than Riley's pension. Riley hoped that Gillies was not going to suggest he had his pension reviewed, with a view to an increase. He did not want an increase and he did not want to talk about it. He was still glad that the whole pension issue had been dealt with by someone else while he had been out of action, because to be honest he'd rather have no pension at all. But, yes, I am a married man now.

He did not actually know anyone else in his situation: wounded, scarred, a class-traveller, semi-educated, proud — so it was to himself that he talked. Coming up to a year after the end of the war; three years since his wounding. It *was* time to do and to act again. How was he going to be? The trip to Italy had been magnificent. The rediscovery of Nadine's love had been transcendent — Oh, sweet Jesus, if anything could make a man a man again, that could.

But now?

More.

Specifically, work. He had to work. He had to choose, to decide — to commit. All around him were unemployed men.

He had been visiting his father. After the first couple of times, he took to going on Sunday mornings while his mother was at chapel. She was so angry with him, and he could not make it out. She did not treat him as she used to. It was as if he was not himself to her. Since the day when she had burst into the ward and not recognised him . . . does she not recognise me still? In some ironic metaphorical way? Is she angry with herself? Or with me? He suspected that it was her keenness not to make him feel singled out by extra kindness that rendered her harsh, and then regret at her harshness made her suddenly sweet again. It was tiring. But that would be his mother's way. Elen, if she was there, took little notice of him. She made it clear she had better things to worry about: the heels on her dancing shoes; a kitten she found in the street; appointments. Her own life.

He did not feel capable of putting it right. He would, though. It was on his list.

Merry, on these occasions, gazed balefully from behind the teapot and occasionally snapped at them for

148

their harshness, weeping and saying, "How you can be so unkind to him, after all he's been through?" and giving him extra cake, which he couldn't eat, which did nothing to make him feel better. Well, there we go, feeling better is not everything.

His father John was the one who made sense. He would sit in silence while they both looked at the paper, or played a game of cards, saying nothing when there was nothing to say, and from time to time saying something thoughtful.

"Is it time to start working again, Riley?" he asked. "I should think you'd be tired of sympathy and fuss."

"It is," Riley said. "I've got a plan. I'll keep you up to date."

"Good boy." A smile. He didn't need anything more.

That's all there is really, isn't it? Work and love, love and work.

His education had been bothering him — or rather the lack and patchiness of it.

Immediately on his return to London, after doing what he could to help Nadine and her father in their quiet, debilitating business of condoling, reliving and weeping, he had located a working-men's college, and of his own accord re-entered the path of self-improvement he had been on before the war. He took classes in history, political theory, English language, French and Italian. His days, largely, were free, but almost immediately he found a way to fill them. He pretended that he had none of his blessings. He sat in a café with one cup of tea for hours, feeling fake but at the same time feeling more authentic, in some ways, than he felt at home with his lovely wife in her father's house. One morning, leaving a café in Queensway, he saw a card advertising for a waiter. He stepped on outside, looked up and down the road, leant a moment against the yellow brickwork between the shop fronts, swallowed a couple of times. He stretched his mouth wide, tapped his tongue to the roof. He went back in. His hands clean, his clothes good, his face well shaven, his mouth exercised, he enquired of the woman about the job.

Very civil, she said, "You're a fine man and no doubt steady on your feet, but you'd put the diners off their food."

He paused a moment, waiting to see if some burst of anger or shame would make him reel inside.

It didn't.

He nodded. She was right, anyway.

"Thank you," he said, and turned to go.

In the early edition of the *Evening Standard* there was an advertisement from a typesetters, wanting a man. They were just on the Harrow Road, so he walked up there. The girl on the desk gave him the "you've lovely eyes what a shame" look. He glanced across to the men on the floor in their brown coats; they glanced back. He'd spent an hour, once, with the chaps who used to do the *Wipers Times*. It hardly counted as experience, but he'd liked it: the precision, the smell, the skill.

The manager in his shirtsleeves sat Riley down, asked him various questions, nodded at the answers, didn't write his name down. Riley said, "You haven't written my name down." The man smiled, nervous, and said "Pardon?"

Riley stared across the desk at him. "Are you pretending not to understand me, because you have no intention of employing me?"

The man kept the nervous smile and made a face as if to say, I'm sorry I didn't quite catch that.

Riley was ninety-nine per cent certain he was putting it on. He tapped his finger on the desk, thoughtfully. Then swiftly he stood up and walked, under the man's protestations, back to the setting room. He looked around: there were the tiny print blocks with the letters of the alphabet, all the fonts and sizes, upper and lower, spaces, punctuation. There was an empty frame, waiting to be used. Foolish, Riley thought, but he did it — grabbed the letters from the nearest array and wrote out: "If you want a man to think you are taking his application seriously, you need to write down his name." "Name" came out as a widow, so he kerned between the words to bring it back up. The font was spacy on the rack, so he looked for leading, did the little calculation of size, slotted it in. It didn't take long. The expostulations from the manager died down. The men were glad of the interruption. They just stood around watching him till he finished.

Now what? Riley thought. Print it? Hardly. They can read backwards anyway.

And: that was unnecessary, really . . .

He glanced up again at the men, bit inside his cheek, nodded to them. Left. *Yes, that was childish and embarrassing, but perhaps I made a point* . . . He

151

wasn't angry. He liked the accoutrements of printing, though. But no, he didn't want to be a typesetter.

Time to investigate the other end of his social territory. An art gallery in Cork Street needed someone to write their catalogue entries and co-ordinate exhibitions: he'd written to them and the letter, with Sir Alfred's endorsement, had been well received. But in the flesh, one look at Riley's face turned the nice young man pink and flustered, as in the kindest terms he explained that he didn't really — that this was Cork Street — that the kind of people with whom one would — well — and Riley just thought, Poor boy, and said to him, "Never mind."

Later, walking up to Piccadilly Circus, he found his fists clenched. Why now? Did you expect the middle classes to respond better? No, it wasn't that. He shook his head to clear it, and stepped up into Soho, into the first pub he saw. Staring into a pint of half and half, he thought, I might have liked that job. I could've done that job. I wouldn't have been dealing with the public. I had a top-of-the-range recommendation for that job from a bona fide member of the establishment, and even so the lad wouldn't even look at me. Even if — though? — I am only looking in a spirit of enquiry, it's a depressing bloody outlook.

Such assistance as he located, in practical matters of adjusting to civilian life, was attached to churches, temperance societies, and virtuous women of a certain age. Everywhere he looked, he found a shortage of information — or anything else — to assist the semi-educated war veteran — myself. Myself, if I hadn't

152

the advantages of having gone up in the world. Which I have, and I still can't find anything.

And this is London! How's the rest of the country?

He went up to Wigan for a couple of days to visit Sybil Ainsworth and the family. Right across from the station stood the Swan & Railway, where he'd popped one at the barman. Shameful. But understandable. You had a reason, but that's no excuse. He found he was smiling. It sounded like one of Jack's phrases. He let the memory of the man and his kindness wash over him a little, and just stood there, not fighting it, not resisting it or willing it away. Jack Ainsworth. Good man. Glad I knew you. Wish I'd known you longer.

A gang of ragged children had seeped out of the alleys and surrounded him now, crying, "Carry yer bag for a copper!" followed briskly by "Eeeyuugh! Look at 'is face!"

"Thanks, you little maggots," he said, and they squinted at him and ran away. Almost a rank of young men with old eyes were lined up on the cobbles: an arm missing, a peg leg, overcoats shiny, and a tray of matches or pencils hanging across their chests. Next to medals. He didn't look at them direct. A conspiracy of circumstance had robbed one of them of a limb, another of a face, another of his wife, another of his job. They needed something, all of them, but they didn't need to go looking at each other, comparing or pitying.

Riley set his two legs walking, and headed for Poolstock, where his friend's widow and fatherless children lived.

"You're just in time," Sybil said laconically when he arrived. "We've the bakers and the miners out on strike. The demobbed fellas are banned from the union so they're not getting strike pay. You could go over to Liverpool if you were feeling brave, i.e. foolish. They've brought in the troops."

I should go over there, he thought. I should see what's going on.

"You're not going," she said. "I know your type. Too bloody good for this world. You're not going. It's not safe."

It's true, I'm not. He wondered how he would feel in a crowd with the smell of violence and the fear and the anger. He gave a tiny snort of bitter laughter. I don't know what I'd do. Would I cry in public? Want to go home, please? Or would I batter everyone I could get my hands on?

"Ah, well, Mrs Ainsworth," he said. "It's just not safe anyway, is it?"

She gave him a look, and she sighed.

"Call me Sybil," she said. "You daft article." He was pleased to be with them, to help out, take a couple of good long walks on the moor, to listen to Annie's piano practice, to chat, much better than he did on his previous visit. The passage of time, and the family's comments, demonstrated to him how much he was improved. But he remained jumpy. He slept badly on his last night, and was woken first by the knocker-upper, tapping the long pole at bedroom windows along the street, then by the fluttery clatter of clogs along the road as the mill-workers headed in for the day. Later, as he walked to the station, the dank canal

154

on one side of the road and the river on the other, he stopped at the bridge and looked over, expecting the usual, clear water or dirty water — and saw red, bright red. For a moment it was something tremendous: blood, the coats of dead Frenchmen, early on . . . and then Ainsworth's voice came back to him, telling him how the Douglas — the Dougie, he called it — runs a different colour every day of the week, depending what colour they were dying the cotton upstream. You could tell the day of the week by the colour of the river. You could make slides in the ice with your clogs, and skid along, playing the Mucky Daddy. You'd get a black mask if you walked through a pea-souper with a scarf round your mouth. Your dad would take you up to Wallgate or Northwestern to see the trains; he'd call it admiring the locomotives, and you did admire them, because your dad built them. Railway men. Ainsworth, Ainsworth's dad, Riley's own dad.

He walked on, his two good legs, good grateful legs, walking himself into a strange nostalgia, one not even his own.

It was a sunny morning, and he left his scarf hanging loose. The buildings tall and handsome, the shops with their display windows not empty but hardly full. There were too many men on the street for the time of day, and that same look of frustration and confusion as he passed by. Outside the pubs as he reached Wallgate a handful of men in caps were playing pitch and toss in the thin northern sunlight. He stopped in at the Swan just as he heard the dinnertime whistles blow all across the town. He bought a half, and eavesdropped . . . "They're bringing the troops in against the looters and a fella was killed . . . the police are going on strike . . . all hell's let loose over there; robbing and fighting, and even the children running mad in the chewing-gum factory." Riley let it wash over him; the rhythms of Ainsworth's accent, the nervy threat of the words. Himself an outsider, yet again. "There's a battleship in the Mersey, down from Scapa Flow, and tanks on St George's Plateau. English tanks, against English men. After all we've been through. They're saying the coppers'll all be sacked, and the soldiers get their jobs. Which is at least a bit of work. For some."

Would he go along to a pithead to see the strikers, to see what was happening? Something said to him no, go away. He felt troublesome. He wanted no trouble here in Wigan. But the trouble in the air called to him.

Up the road some men were running. The men outside the pubs turned and looked and started to hurry up there. After only the very shortest of hesitations, Riley was with them. Round a corner he heard shouting — he followed it. Summer day that it was, he put his scarf up round his mouth and chin.

When they came to the crowd of men, bustling, jostling, shouting, facing off some enemy invisible down the road, they all just entered it, seamlessly, and became part of it. Riley melted in at the back and became one with the thin overcoats and greasy caps, his boots among their boots, his shoulders among their shoulders: comforting, brotherly. He smelt sweat and tobacco, damp cloth and those industrial smells, engine oil, coal dust, iron filings. An overlapping smell of his father and of war. In the heart of the crowd ill humour

156

had its own smell and its own voice. The jostling was angry, the movement was frustration. Angry scared men were throwing themselves up against an immovable barrier. Bodies crushed him before and aft, and he let them. The shouting was harsh and violent. Riley smiled under his scarf and closed his eyes for a moment. Familiar.

He wormed his way through to the front, as far as he could get. There were more men than he'd thought, and the mood was bad. A barricade blocked the road, backed with other angry scared men, these ones in police uniform, truncheons raised, faces twisted. Some were striking out, flailing at the crowd before them. Beyond them, an important person went up and down on a horse, stamping, nervous. There came the unmistakable crack of weapon on flesh and bone — and then the noise was extreme: shouts, cries of pain and fury. Stones flew — and he felt a warm and familiar rush, beautiful to him in its way, scarlet in his eyes, blood and fury in his heart. The roar of it filled him; he felt entire, hopeless, helpless, familiar . . .

When the metal barrier collapsed, Riley was one of the first over, one of the first to the man on the horse, grabbing his leg, howling, not giving a damn why, revelling . . .

Crack of wood on bone and the bone is his, and he is down. Boots and legs — uh-oh. Then he's being dragged — carried. Someone's got his shoulders and someone has his feet. Just like the old days, he thinks, half conscious, and he half laughs. "Glad you're amused," says a sneery voice, and he's propped up against a wall, cobbles rough beneath him. Someone pulls his scarf down, says, "Jesus, fook," pours some whisky down his mouth, and says, "Who the fook are you?"

Riley just waved his hand.

The men stared at him. One snorted and dashed off again. The other said: "Y'all right? That were a crack an 'alf."

Riley treated him to a twisted smile. "I'm all right," he said, though he wasn't. He could feel his eye and cheek beginning to swell.

"Where you from?" said the man, at the sound of Riley's voice. His left nostril was going up in a look of disbelief. Ainsworth used to do that. Erectile northern nostril. What the fuck am I doing here?

"London," Riley said. "Just on my way back."

"I recommend that," the man said, glancing over his shoulder. "Station's thataway. Here —" He proffered a handkerchief. "Scarf up, cap down, this underneath, and don't pass out till yer on the train."

Riley grinned again, like an idiot.

The man — pale eyes, big nose, face like a piece of granite — looked at Riley, made a decision, swore again, hoicked Riley up, and lugged him down a side street, Riley's arm up over his shoulder. The station wasn't far. The man dumped him on a bench, and said to a guard, "Put 'im on the train to London, Stan." Before he left, he glanced at Riley again, and said, "Where did you get that face?"

Riley pulled his scarf down. He said, "Where d'you think?"

158

The man lifted his right arm: a sort of mittened stump sat there. Taking the fabric elegantly between the fingers of his other hand, and raising his eyebrows in a somehow saucy manner, he pulled the mitten off. A broad, scarred palm. No fingers. He reached across and patted Riley's cheek with it. "Chin up, old pal," he murmured, and turned, and went.

All the way back to Paddington Riley could feel the bruises growing, and alongside them the awareness of what he had risked. He touched the tender bruises. Inches from his remaining bits of original jawbone, and from the wire and flesh holding the artificial one in place. He bit his strange lower lip with his surviving upper teeth, thinking, You utter utter fool. You fool.

His head was throbbing.

He was ashamed to go home and face Nadine. Embarrassed like a fool of a boy. No — like a man. To have risked so much after she had invested so much.

He considered lying to her about how it happened.

At Euston he looked in the window of a barber's shop and saw the black eye emerging, and the dried blood from the cut on his cheekbone. He was rubbing at it with the stranger's handkerchief when a barber came out, saying, "Would you like me to help you with that, sir?" The barber — short, glossy, aproned — led him in and cleaned him up, giving a little commentary as he did on the history of barber-surgeons, and how he'd been an orderly himself, and that was a nice bit of work had been done on his face, if he didn't mind him saying so, and after a while Riley found he was weeping, and the barber had the boy bring him a cup of tea.

Riley looked at it, and sighed, and reached for his brass straw.

She *was* furious. She cried and she wouldn't look at him. She refused to tend the wound, then she tended it roughly, and muttered, "I just don't understand. I do not understand how you would let this happen." She said all kinds of things.

He said, "Well, you wouldn't," because he was thinking of it as a thing about men, that men are obliged to keep from women, for women's own sakes. But it made her angrier.

She said, "You want more pain? You haven't had enough? Do you miss it, is that it?"

For a while he took her righteous anger quietly, as he had done before, and perhaps would have to again. Then he said, "Perhaps I do. I don't know. I got angry. It was stupid."

She said, "That you take it all so lightly that you'd — risk — It makes me want to hit you." Then she was so angry she couldn't speak.

He said, "That's how stupid it is."

Much later she said to him, "I know it wasn't anger that got you into this. You don't have that kind of anger. What could you be so angry about?"

He couldn't tell her about the fighting feeling, about the demon of battle bursting out again in him, so unexpectedly, so unwelcomely. He was just too ashamed. It was like when he wrote to her from the front line that he didn't exist. Even now, he didn't want her to know the worst things about him.

In the days afterward, he found himself thinking about Peter, wondering what precisely it was that Peter was resisting. Does Peter get the heat under the skin? That flush of violence, as strong as sex, as delicious, but hideous? Is he holding that off?

That was not something he felt he could bring up.

I can't change much, he thought. Perhaps I can change one or two small things. I must keep out of big groups of men. It might happen again.

The chap teaching the English language course was a former school teacher, about forty, who couldn't for his own reasons bear to go back to a world of small boys after a war spent with the Navy in the Eastern Mediterranean. Riley and he went to the pub together once or twice; a pint of bitter and a little mild masculine conversation. The teacher — his name was Alan Hinchcliffe — had fallen for an Australian girl in Cairo, and been dumped when she chose to go home. He had no family to speak of, and lived in a room in Brixton where his landlady brought him a pie in the evenings. His moustache was depressing and his tweed jacket smelt slightly, but his mind was sharp and precise and his grammar was perfect.

"Let's do something," Riley said, restless.

"All right," said Hinchcliffe, which made Riley smile. "What?"

"Men like me need to be able to write good letters," Riley said. "Let's prepare a pamphlet."

"Bloody good idea," said Hinchcliffe. "How to write letters and fill in forms, that sort of thing? The college uses a printing firm, you know."

Riley did know. He went down there with Hinchcliffe and they persuaded the owner-manager, a stout man named Owen, to print their pamphlet cheaply as a one-off, with a view to further projects.

"Further projects?" murmured Hinchcliffe, raising his brows.

"Of course," said Riley. "The other pamphlets. Of the series. And the — books."

"Of course," said Hinchcliffe.

Mostly, Hinchcliffe did the talking. Riley just said: "Improved literacy is good for the printing trade," and Owen agreed.

Riley stopped going to cafés and applying for jobs he didn't want. Instead, he and Hinchcliffe sat down together and wrote the first pamphlet — *How to Write Good English* — and delivered it to Owen. They chose a generic layout, cheap paper and a plain soft cover, and watched as Ermleigh, who had the look of a depressed fish and had been gassed, started to slot the little metal bits of type into their wooden niches. He creaked when lifting rolls of paper. They wanted to stay for the printing, but Ermleigh, coughing gently, shooed them off. He couldn't work if he was being looked at, he said. They were back the next day, and nearly smudged the wet ink in their hurry to get the booklets folded and sewn.

Afterwards they all went to the pub, including Ermleigh, who creaked when lifting a pint, as well. He

162

had a wife and children. To him, Riley talked. Not about anything in particular. In fact, the not talking about anything in particular was particularly what they did. The four of them sat in the snug at the Eagle, talking gently, making silly jokes. Hinchcliffe was going to get a motorcycle. Ermleigh painted watercolours. Owen just wanted to keep his father's business going. They found something very calming about each other.

Coming out, Riley was thinking: I'm not going to be the chap with the buggered-up face who gets in fights. I am going to be the chap who does — whatever it is I do. The chap who wrote that book, who published those pamphlets, founded that college, set up that publishing house. Perhaps someone might say, Wasn't he injured? And someone might say, Oh yes, I think he was. But that would not be the first thing they said. I'm not going to spend my life just surviving the war and my injury. I'm going to live my life.

They sold four of the pamphlets in the pub, and afterwards Riley brought some home.

Nadine smiled.

Sir Robert said, "Good man!"

Riley sold them to his fellow students. Hinchcliffe gave a batch to a friend of his, a teacher at another college, who sold them there. Ermleigh took some to the chest clinic. An ex-serviceman's benevolent society heard of them and requested a sample. A little bundle went up to Wigan, and another to Cardiff.

Riley felt mildly sick walking up from the station towards the hospital. The same trees, the same buildings, the same blue benches. Gillies had offered to see him at his clinic for officers at Regent's Park, but Riley had said no, he'd come down to Sidcup. Now he rather wished he hadn't.

There'd be fewer patients. Well, that is good. That is good. No more admissions. Men going home. To what? To family? A job, or chance of one? Somebody to grind up their bloody meals for them?

A few days ago had been Peace Day. The crowds had gathered and the whole of central London had gone bonkers — the park was full of people camping, Allied soldiers from all over. He could not bring himself to look out of the windows at the front of the house. He did not want to see soldiers in camps, and the glorification of military victory. What, was he to put on his medals, with their cheery nicknames — Pip, Squeak, Alfred, and Services Rendered — plus gallantry and wound stripes, and head off for a jolly day out remembering the dead? The King had issued a message to the wounded: "To these, the sick and wounded who cannot take part in the festival of victory, I send out greetings and bid them good cheer, assuring them that the wounds and scars so honourable in themselves, inspire in the hearts of their fellow countrymen the warmest feelings of gratitude and respect."

Well.

It wasn't a sense of being respected that inspired that crowd in Wigan, or the police in Liverpool, or that made the ex-servicemen in Leamington and East Anglia have nothing to do with the celebrations, or the men in Luton burn down the town hall. That wasn't why there were riots from Wolverhampton to Epsom,

164

from Coventry to Salisbury. There were employers in Manchester refusing to take on demobbed soldiers because they'd missed out on four years of experience. Four million returning servicemen, three million munitions workers discharged, one-and-three-quarter million wounded. Women who'd worked men's jobs all through the war being turned out and expected to go home quietly, or back into service. Two-and-a-half-million workers on strike. Revolution in Russia.

Patriotism. Best use of funds. Well. Welcome home, lads. Or am I being churlish? Flags and tea and choirs — isn't that all right?

Well. Jobs and money would be better.

Good cheer — that was Jack Ainsworth's phrase. Be of good cheer, in the prayer he carried around. Good cheer was chin up, basically. Chin up, Riley. Artificial chin.

Same entrance, different chap at reception, same corridor. The garden behind vaguely and unidentifiably changed. The lawn dry and hard after the summer. Fewer patients.

Gillies was in his office, and greeted Riley with joy. "You look almost handsome!" he said, and was interested in how the sunburn on his scalp-clad chin differed from the rest of his face.

"It's weathered," Gillies said. "Settled in. No pain? No tension in the skin?"

"No," said Riley.

"You've had a bash," he said, touching the cheekbone. "Remains of a black eye. I hope you're not taking risks with my handiwork."

Riley flushed, and said nothing. Gillies prodded gently, murmuring, "No pain? No pain?"

"No," said Riley.

"Healed up well. Whatever it was, don't do it again." Then he stopped. "What was it?" he asked. "Temper? Someone have a go at you?"

"No," said Riley.

"I thought you could handle that sort of thing," Gillies said.

"I can," Riley replied. "I do."

And that was true. He behaved terribly terribly well. All the bloody time. Almost.

Gillies was still staring at him. "Looks like a single blow," he said. "From a weapon of some kind."

Riley turned his head away, annoyed. "I'm not ten," he snapped. "My head's my own, whatever you've done to it. And don't patronise me with one of those 'hohoho you're being uppity that's good there's life in the old boy yet' answers."

Gillies said nothing — turned and did something to some papers. In a moment he came back and said: "Smile for me?"

Riley smiled rather bitterly.

"Yawn? Can you?"

Riley could. He did. It was far from the biggest yawn anyone had seen, but it was a yawn. Gillies measured it with a small ruler.

"How's the eating?" he asked. "Liquids, solids? Chewing?"

"Improving," Riley said. "I didn't take on any horse steaks in France."

166

Gillies was continuing to gaze at him, musingly.

"Sorry," Riley said. "Not for getting clouted. But I shouldn't have said that. Of course you have a perpetual interest in my face and its functioning."

"Don't worry about it," Gillies said. "You're absolutely right; you're a grown man. So — your voice sounds a lot better — mind if we run through some of the exercises?" And Riley chanted the tongue-twisters: once again Peter Piper picked his peck of pickled peppers, the ragged rascal ran round and round his rugged rock, and down on the seashore she sold her eternal supply of seashells.

"And how are you?" Gillies asked, finally.

Riley gave him a dark sideways look. "And you were doing so well," he said, at which Gillies laughed.

"Well," he said. "And, so, work and so forth, have you found something?"

"I have," Riley said, and he smiled properly, and took a couple of the pamphlets out of his pocket.

"Here," he said.

Gillies took it to the window for the light, and read it from cover to cover — eight pages of simple, straightforward, cheaply produced practical advice.

"Can you let me have five hundred?" he said, and Riley smiled.

"You don't have that many inmates, sir," he said.

"I've got a great many more ex-inmates," Gillies replied. "Everyone who's left here in the past six months will get one. D'you have them in stock? I'll give you the cheque now, anyway. And what's next?"

Riley took another piece of paper from his pocket: a list on which he and Hinchcliffe had been working.

"How to Write Good English"
"How to Balance your Finances"
"How to Make the Best Impression"
"How to Apply for a Job"
"Everyday Good Health"
"Basics of Science for the Intelligent Working Man and Woman"
"History Up to Now for the Intelligent Working Man and Woman"

He pointed at that last one and said: "I'm going to write that myself. And we plan an annual 'How to Educate Yourself'."

"A Practical Guide for the Autodidact," said Gillies.

"Exactly. Nadine will design the covers." Actually, he had only just thought of it. But what a good idea!

"How will you finance it?"

"No idea."

"Well, let me know if you need investors. I might be able to help."

That easy? Then I must aim higher . . .

"Now —" Gillies looked at his watch. "D'you want some lunch?"

Riley smiled low, and said, "I don't eat with people."

"Am I people? Really? Oh well, let's take a stroll then. We've made some changes. It's quieter now, much quieter. There's more time to get things more right."

CHAPTER
TWELVE

Locke Hill, July — August 1919

Rose's Further Correspondence appeared. They were going to give her £800. She was going to study at London University and then at University College Hospital. She would start in September. If she needed more support in future, she was to be in touch with them. She was a clean hatching thing, with wings to spread and a strength and power that had to be acknowledged.

Her life was not over. She was not some dull unloved creature with no purpose, she was not alone, halfway through a dreary life to a dingy death.

The boldness of it! In so many ways she was surprising herself.

Major Gillies shook her hand, said he was proud of her, and sorry she would be leaving. Should things not go as planned, he said delicately, she would be welcome back.

"Do you doubt my abilities, Major Gillies?" she asked, with the playfulness permitted by their imminent separation and the time they had worked side by side. But she half meant it. She was proud now. Woman Doctor! She bloody well would be the Woman Doctor.

"No!" he said. "No, indeed. On the contrary," and they smiled and it was a little awkward. So then he said, if she ever needed a reference, and so forth, and it was all all right. She would have time for a holiday, even. Scotland, she thought. And so a period of her life was ending, and spinning off.

But to leave Locke Hill! Well, the strangeness should have been in leaving Peter and Julia — but neither of them were there. And that in itself was so strange. The falling apart of things which even if they had not seemed . . . strong, had seemed permanent.

How much we take for granted! she thought, as she folded her vests to pack them. We all said to each other, oh of course, nothing will be the same now — and here I am, surprised because things are not the same. This period of my life will become like my schooldays, calved off from my life like part of an iceberg, drifting away in the distance as I sail on ahead, until I can't see it clearly or remember that much about it. How will I look back on these past years? As something marvellous and character-forming? As something important? And shall I have many more such sections of life to live through and then to lose?

For a moment she wondered whether she was a ship sailing through the universe of her life, or whether she was a rock, around which the river of her life flowed. Then she decided it didn't make that much difference, in practical terms, as she still had clothes to wash and dry, because she was not at all persuaded by the shared laundry at the VAD medical student hostel. And after Scotland she was going to be working very hard.

170

But the main issue was Tom. That is a child, she thought, who has been left enough — but he is not my child. Mrs Joyce and Eliza were his daily companions; they fed him and scolded him and were fond of him, in the manner of decent-hearted women paid to do such things. But it didn't seem to be anybody's job to love him. But it's not my job . . . though . . .

It can be difficult for a capable woman to leave things alone. Rose felt she could — should — do something . . . She, the only responsible adult, couldn't just walk out of this house, leaving Tom with the servants. What a ghost house that would be! Operating around a child, financed at a distance, the absent drunk father, the absent runaway mother, no love, no centre, no . . .

The pang was strong. How could she even *think* of —

Deserter!

But it is not mine! None of this is mine! Well, it is mine — but my life is mine more — isn't it?

Rose went up to London.

Directed by Blakeman, who was quite reluctant to encourage a lady to go to such a place, she went to a pub by the river in Chelsea, and there she found Peter. Blakeman had suggested she go down around noon, and she had understood why.

She walked in boldly, nose in the air, respectability her backbone and good humour her defence. *She* was not scared to walk into a pub. It was hardly likely that anyone would take her for an artist or a lady of easy

171

virtue! (A tiny part of her laughed, and thought, If only! — but just for a moment.) She walked up to the bar. It was like being in a foreign land, and she engaged the same courage. Actually, she thought, never mind Scotland. Why not France, or Spain, or the Alps? The Alps!

That made her think of Julia, the bolter. The thing about bolting is that you must have something to bolt from, and nobody who has not lived your life can understand and judge whether or not your bolting is justified. Rose thought of Julia, in Biarritz or wherever she was now, ordering drinks, buying French toothpaste, sleeping in French sheets, being free. Was she happy? Did she think about her deserted boy, rattling around in that deserted family home?

Try as she might, and angry as she was with her, she still found it hard to blame her. Except for on Tom's behalf. Then she found it very easy.

But Julia is not the only deserting parent here.

Rose raised her head. She was here now on Tom's behalf.

She surveyed the room, with its dark wood panels, dim recesses, etched-glass windows like dirty milk. She saw men. Cigarette smoke. Worn and faded jackets, shapeless caps, hats with brims a little shiny. Braces and shirtsleeves, frayed cuffs. Rolled-up sleeves. Ties, limp with age. Pints of beer. Smell of sweat in cloth. Tired eyes and seamed cheeks. Some crackles of jollity; one or two strapping fellows, red-faced with sunburn, noisy and laughing. A few murmured conversations. Many solitary and silent figures. Newspapers. Coughing.

172

Several sticks, a pinned-up sleeve. Scrawny shoulders, hunched backs. Worn shoes. Cheap suits.

The waiter, after one "are you sure?" glance, took her order for two glasses of sarsaparilla, and then took no notice of her. She realised that perhaps he saw other women like her, respectable women coming in for disreputable men, wanting to take them back to respectability. He probably thought she was someone's wife — and for a moment she felt very keenly Julia's horror — that your husband would be one of these, that he loved the pub more than you and your child, that everybody would know.

Peter was in a corner, reading. As she approached him he jumped up, pushing the wooden chair behind him, and greeted her, politely, keenly. He said, "Oh my goodness, Rose," several times, and tried to steer her out, but she was calm and implacable, and smiled at another fellow who stood and gave her his seat, silenced into obedience by her very presence, by her femininity.

She sat, didn't take off her hat, settled her bag in her lap.

"Peter," she said. "Darling. I have news."

The waiter brought their drinks.

Peter took a sip. "George," he said, "this is the worst brandy I've ever tasted. Bring me the good stuff." His smile was wide and charming. "This is a terrible place you've brought me to, Rose. But how marvellous to see you. Am I in *dreadful* trouble?"

"Peter," she said. "I am leaving Locke Hill."

"Oh, but —" he said, and she continued: "I am coming to London, and I am to study medicine — yes,

173

I shall be an undergraduate! — and I am to become a doctor. Now, listen," — for he was trying to make sense of this baffling and unexpected information, and find a way to respond — "don't worry about anything, I'm very pleased about it, and I wanted to tell you in person, and to thank you for allowing me to stay for so long, and for being so kind. But things move on, don't they, darling?"

The look in his eyes said to her that he had no idea if they did or not. *He looks so utterly lost . . .*

"Still," she said, and his eyes fixed on her. *He wants something . . . what does he want?*

"I will still visit Locke Hill," she said. "A lot, I hope."

He looked down. Like an ashamed small boy.

"And I was thinking, we could go together. What do you think? Weekends? I know Tom would love to —" but at the sound of his son's name Peter's face froze, and she stopped.

"Darling?" she said. "Shall we?"

He said nothing. He glanced quickly around — looking, she realised, for George and the brandy.

"You could come down with me tonight," she said mildly. "Best to bathe and shave," she said. "And not be too drunk."

She read his pale eyes quite clearly. The look, familiar from a thousand patients, said, "It is less trouble to do what you want than to resist you." And alongside that she sensed something else: that he was aware that his child probably needed something from him, and that he might perhaps even be grateful that she could point out things he could do. He may even, she thought, be glad to offer hope that he might oblige.

They walked back to Chester Square together; she took his arm, and chatted, but not much. He had never been anything but tall and thin, with his intellectual aesthetic hunch, like a kind of clever bird; now he was actually bony. His long neck, above his loose and very slightly grubby collar, was like that of a saint in a painting: asking for trouble. His nails were bitten to the raw.

That was on the Thursday. On the Saturday afternoon, Rose was putting a log on the fire in the drawing room when Julia blew back to Locke Hill like a galleon in a storm. A grand kerfuffle of luggage erupted, unannounced, from the cab to the front door and into the hall. The door was banging in the wind; Mrs Joyce was there gasping, and Julia propelled herself into the drawing room, saying, "Oh, hello, Rose. Are you still here?"

"No," said Rose. "I'm visiting Tom and Peter." She turned to rise, to greet — and took in Julia's form, and cried out an exclamation. She could not think of a thing to say.

"How marvellous you are," Julia said. "Looking after my deserted family."

It seemed, absurdly, that somehow now the subject had been changed and Rose had missed her chance to say something about the pregnancy. No words came to her.

"Your mother's here," she said instead. Julia, who had been about to ease the galleon into berth on the sofa, snapped upright again.

"Oh?" she said.

Rose gave a bemused little smile and a small gesture of the hands. Just like that, she thought, just like that, not a word to anyone, and chaos resumes. She went to the hall to call Mrs Joyce to make tea. Dear God, she thought. Does Peter know? Does anyone know? And even — Is it Peter's? As far as she understood, they weren't even — *really* that was none of her business. But she couldn't help racing through the dates in her mind — and felt vulgar. She wasn't going to join in. She wasn't even going to call Peter — but he and Tom were already there, coming in from the garden, where they had been looking at a dead bullfinch, in which Rose had hoped they might be interested.

Peter was heading for the library when he saw the luggage, and stopped. For a moment, all was frozen: nobody wanting to approach anybody, none of them wanting to face whatever it was that would happen next. Then Peter sighed, flinched almost, and Julia came to the door of the drawing room, and stood there. Tom stiffened at the sight of her. Hellos passed between the three of them, and fell to the floor like clumps of dust. Tom did not kiss his mother; she didn't invite him to. After a moment he asked if he might go upstairs. Peter said yes, Julia said no, please stay. He went.

"I gather my mother is here," Julia said, with a bit of a smile. Of course she had been practising what to say, Rose thought. And of course now it will all be irrelevant. Script changed by the presence of an unexpected character.

"I gather you're having a child," Peter replied.

"Yours," she said, and at that he said, "Oh for Christ's sake," and went finally into the sitting room, pushing past her, and sat down. His head fell forward into his hands. "If you'll have us," she said.

He flung his head up at that, his hair flopping back, his bony face suddenly young. Rose watched warily. There was after all a sweetness in the way Julia spoke. A real sweetness. Oh, Julia . . .

"It *is* yours," Julia said. "That time —"

Rose, in the doorway, ducked out of sight, embarrassed but unable and unwilling to remove herself from earshot.

"I made a terrible mistake," Julia was saying. "Leaving. I should never have — but when you left — I thought I wanted a new life — and that you did, too — I'm sorry . . ."

"Oh, Julia," he said, and Rose could hear the gentleman and the drunk struggling within him.

Then he said, "You can stay here. I'm living in town anyway. Do what you want. Perhaps your mother will stay and look after you."

"Don't be foul, Peter," Julia said, and then a harsh sound of Peter laughing.

"When I saw your bags," he said, "I assumed you'd come back for a divorce. Not for our marriage."

"Peter," she said again. "My dear — I do want our marriage. And I want it to be here for you whether you want it now or not. So that if you change your mind or whatever happens, your wife and children will be here."

There was a pause. Then: "For you," Julia said, quite gently.

And then there was a very particular silence. Peter — like Rose, in the hallway — was taken aback. Each the same thing: When did Julia last say or do anything for someone else?

And then they were all interrupted, first by the appearance of Millie with tea — Rose took the tray — and then by the vast implacable ocean liner of a woman that was Mrs Orris, a sweeping, brown fur-trimmed vessel which made Julia look suddenly vulnerable, an overripe fruit on a delicate stalk. Even the heads on Mrs Orris' fox tippet looked depressed and borne-down.

At her entrance, Peter and Julia turned to her as one, and smiled, and snapped into propriety. They had long experience of her. Rose, in the doorway, unable to get through with the tea, saw them through a gap in Mrs Orris' hangings.

"Hello, Mother," said Julia, glittering slightly. The tenderness of the moment before had disappeared from the surface. It did not stretch as far as Mrs Orris, but it had not fled.

Mrs Orris held her dramatic pause, scanned her daughter up and down, and said: "Well. Here you are. We were worried. Where on earth have you been?"

"She's been taking the waters at Biarritz," said Peter. "Delicate condition, and all that. Do join us. I think

178

we're about to have tea, if you could perhaps allow Rose through."

"You didn't tell me," Mrs Orris said, to both of them.

"Well, I'm an adult now, Mother, and I don't tell you everything," said Julia and, before her mother could retort, added for herself: "as you can see", and followed it up with, "What are you doing here, Mother? I wasn't expecting you."

"I came to see my grandchild."

"Oh, well, I hope you've seen him," Julia said, "and found him well. Do have some tea, won't you, before you get your train."

"I'm here for the weekend," Mrs Orris said with an ironclad smile.

"Only if you really want to," Peter said.

Julia smiled sweetly, and started to lurch up to help Rose pour and pass, but Peter stopped her with a gesture. Rose was transfixed by the sudden alliance in the face of a greater enemy. With Peter backing Julia up, Mrs Orris could do nothing but sit and drink her tea and fire off useless little shots: Julia was looking thin, she was surprised at her going to France, the sea air could hardly have been good for her complexion, they really might have told her, and surely it was time they considered boarding school for Tommy — at this last Peter reared up again and repeated that Tom was fine, absolutely fine. Rose, smiling low, uttered the same lie.

Dinner displayed everybody as they were. Julia, dragging her chaos with her. Mrs Orris, freezing

179

everyone up like some great Medusa. Peter, flinching and exploding, flinching and exploding as if he were still at the Front. Everything was uncomfortable until Mrs Orris had retired. Then everybody seemed to breathe out, and shared relief at her absence left them for a moment united.

Rose went up to bed shaking her head at the immutability of people.

And me? What do I do?

They are not my responsibility. They are not my responsibility.

Then stop thinking about them.

She picked up her reading list and started to put ticks by the titles she would start with. Even with her scholarship money, she could not afford to buy all of these. And some would be vast — volumes and volumes. But she would buy some. I wonder how soon I will be allowed into the college library. Or the British Library! Oh my . . .

She fell asleep to visions of domes and books.

CHAPTER
THIRTEEN

Locke Hill, August 1919

Julia had walked into her old home as though through a clingy fog of past habits and old behaviour, which draped itself over her and required of her the brittleness, spikiness and defensive perfectionism she had paraded over the past years. She was wrapped in it almost before she noticed, as if she had learnt nothing. This knocked her.

To start by being rude to Rose! *No.*

Of course her mother being there had surprised her — but never mind. It wasn't anything to do with her mother. It was a long-term matter, and it was about Peter and Tom and this new child.

Peter was sober, clean, properly dressed. The sight of him, so thin and pale and delicate, like a heron, huddled against things, made her feel, what, tender? She still wanted what she had always wanted. And here it all was: him, the house, children. It was her business to make it work.

After the ridiculous stilted dinner, Rose left, tactful as always. Peter was staring down the gleaming dining table.

He looked up at her at last. "Well," he said. "Julia. You and the baby must of course live here. Hire a nurse and so forth. I'm sure Tom will be glad you're back." He stopped, as if realising that there was no reason whatsoever to think that. "I won't be here much, won't get in your way. But this is your home. Please, um, cherish it. I would appreciate your not . . . offering any further threat to its security." He drifted into a small silence.

Julia broke into it. She just said, "Thank you."

Peter said: "Probably neither you nor I deserve the . . ." — the word evaded him — ". . . but Tom does, and this . . ." He gestured towards Julia, suggesting the unborn child. "It's all been very unpleasant," he said, and then pushed his chair back rather suddenly. "Happy to finance everything and so forth, but you *will* need to pay attention to the children," he said. And retreated to his study.

Tomorrow, Julia thought. There will be many tomorrows.

The following morning, Julia sat down with a second pot of tea in the sitting room, and wrote to Nadine.

Dear Nadine,
    It seems so long since I sat on the edge of the guest bed upstairs, the first time we met, when you were upset about Riley, and

She stopped in the middle of that first sentence. Riley.

182

When she thought about her own face, about how its damage had changed her and was changing her, had she ever — ever — for one moment — thought about Riley? Not just about Nadine and Riley, but about him, as a man and a human being? How it must be for him?

Why have I never talked to him, never even tried to, about a problem we — about, well, this common ground?

Why don't I know how to talk to men? Do I think they're not quite human? Do I think they can go off and get shot at and wounded and so horribly scarred, and somehow they're just meant to bear it all? I couldn't bear one iota of it.

Riley can't eat easily, he can't talk properly, everybody stares at him and pities him. She remembered again, suddenly and clearly, the man in the woods, in the tin mask. I couldn't bear it for one second, and yet I haven't even tried to understand them and help them.

Her pen hovered over the paper, sort of useless. She found she wanted to write something else entirely. What? A letter to herself? Her former self? Or to Riley? To Tom? To Harlan?

To Peter?

No, I will put no pressure on Peter for anything, until he's ready. Dear God, I have been a fool, and I have missed out because I was a fool. I have so much to live for . . . I will get over my own shame and my own idiocy. I will be good to Riley. I will admit all my failings to everybody, very lightly, and apart from that I will let them talk about themselves.

Yes.

She turned back to the letter.

. . . It seems so long since I sat on the edge of the guest bed upstairs, the first time we met, when you were upset about Riley, and Rose brought you here. When I think now about all that has passed, I am surprised, and bewildered. My own folly, in particular, surprises and bewilders me — my idiotic beauty treatment, of course, but also my terrible inability to know what to do for Peter. But I am writing to you now about Peter. I hope you don't mind. It just seems to me that you and Riley seem to have found ways of dealing with what fate has dealt you, and they seem to work well. I need advice!

I am — perhaps Rose has told you — to have another child. Tom is silent and sad. Peter — well, you know as well as I do that he drinks. I say to myself, be kind, be strong, be this, be that — but I don't seem to know really how to put these intentions into action. I would like to talk to you about this, if you could bear it. I

(She crossed that out. Enough.)

Please come and visit, as soon as you're back. It must be soon now; you've been gone for ages. Bring Riley.

Yours affectionately,
Julia

For a second, writing "you've been gone for ages", her eyes filled suddenly with tears. She felt, actually, as if tears were always there, just under the level of spillage.

It's love. I can apply it to one man, or to another. I will be grateful to Harlan for ever.

She decided to walk into town herself, to the postbox, and went to find Tom to invite him along. He was in Max's basket, which he had dragged behind the sofa.

"That looks cosy," she said, and smiled down at him. "Do you want to come for a walk? Max could come too."

Tom looked at her proffered hand, and up at her face. He took it joylessly.

Later, Tom told Rose that he and his mother and Max had posted a letter. Rose raised her eyebrows.

For the rest of the weekend Peter was quietly, completely, drunk. Julia did not pursue him, nor try to talk. Before lunch on the Sunday he saw her upstairs and retreated, suddenly, holding his hands up flat towards her, almost as if to ward her off. Later, as she was coming out of the bathroom, he turned violently and howled at her as if she had come at him out of the night: she ran off in shock, and sat in the kitchen, trembling. Mrs Joyce found her, and said that he was all shaken up, not to mind. Julia asked was he often like that and Mrs Joyce said, well, she hadn't seen that much of him as he was up in London mostly, but when she did see him, things weren't getting any better. She looked pleased to be asked, and as Julia looked at her she thought, for the first time, Mrs Joyce is a human being too.

"Tell me about Mr Joyce," she said. "If you don't mind." She was supposing that Mrs Joyce was a widow, and that the emotion of the moment and the confidence exchanged would allow such a question.

Mrs Joyce smiled. "There's no Mr Joyce," she said. "Never was. It's a courtesy title, Ma'am."

After tea Julia told Rose she would like to talk to her if she had a moment. She said, almost before they had even taken seats in the drawing room, "I want to thank you and I want to apologise."

Rose nearly fell back into the sofa, she was so surprised.

"You know what for," said Julia. The brittle urgency was still in her voice. She could hear it. Slow down. Be kind. "You know so much and you're good at things, and I've never responded very well to that. I'm sorry I've been awful to you. And thank you for everything you've done for Tom. I know Peter is more sort of your area as well anyway, because of you being his special cousin — but thank you, anyway, for looking out for him, if that's all right . . ."

She took a breath and started off again before Rose could say anything and put her off track.

She said, "It seems to me things were better for him when Riley and Nadine were around. Do you agree?"

Rose agreed.

"So I thought if we could get them down to visit, regularly, that would be a help. And Riley might know of other friends — from the war — I don't think it's much good having only us to talk to . . ." Here she fell silent, because of course she hadn't even been here for him to talk to anyway. "I think he needs other men, with the same sort of . . . Oh look, Rose, I don't know how to do anything for him, but it's not too late. It's not. We can help him. A baby is a miraculous thing and my dear mama will not be whisking this one away — let's try? Will you carry on helping? And advise me? Because you know about soldiers, and I just don't . . . but I'm going to stop wanting things from him. That'll help, I think. I'm going to be lovely to Tom, and to the new baby, and I'm sure that'll wash off on Peter."

"If he's here," said Rose.

"Of course," said Julia and then she smiled and said: "I was thinking, Riley's brought him back from danger twice already. You know, in the war, and then when he got him down here for Christmas last year. Perhaps he can do it again. Third time lucky sort of thing."

"In the war?" said Rose.

"Yes. On the Somme. When Peter was wounded, and Riley carried him back. Didn't you know?"

No, Rose had not known.

"I don't know the details," said Julia.

"Did Peter tell you?" asked Rose.

"No!" cried Julia, half laughing.

"But Riley didn't," said Rose doubtfully.

"Peter talks in his sleep," Julia said. "It's often as if he isn't asleep at all, so much is going on. Lots of carrying. Peter carrying things, and being carried. When he was first back there was an awful lot of Thank You Purefoy. I asked him about it. About the Thank You Purefoys."

"And did he tell you?"

"No. I worked it out," Julia said.

They both pondered that.

"And . . . did you work out anything else?"

"No. I don't understand any of it, Rose. I've nothing to back it up with. It's another world, and another language."

Rose made a little face of understanding: raised eyebrows, *moue* of acceptance. Then she said, "Two things are bothering me, Julia."

Julia looked willing.

"Where have you been, and is that my cousin's child?"

Julia smiled and blinked.

"I've been in Biarritz," she said. "Taking the waters and realising what a complete fool I have been. And yes. It is."

There was a pause.

"I have never been unfaithful to Peter," Julia said.

She didn't have to say that. Nobody was asking her to. But as she said it, she knew it to be not just necessary, but true. This was no lie, no adulteress' self-justification. Without Harlan, she could not even have come back to Peter. Without the confidence he had shown in her, she would not have had the courage to come home and face her own folly; and even if she had, she would have continued to fail as a wife. She would not have found it in her to love Peter, really love him, with patience and compassion and quietness, as he needed. She would never have realised her mistakes. And if Harlan had been a different man, she would have gone off with him, and lived in a lie with him, or been deserted by him, the child adopted, Julia's heart and reputation shattered, and whatever developed from that — tragedy and pathetic shame, probably — would have developed. But Harlan had shot her goblin and given her insight, and her night with him had sealed her fidelity to Peter. It had been an act of faith. How strange. But true.

Rose and Julia made a list together before Rose went back up to London: Dr Tayle, maternity nurse, speak to Eliza, new shoes and jacket for Tom. And Rose promised she would ring the next day.

Remarkably little was said. Julia had been on a rest cure. Apart from Rose and Peter, everybody assumed that somebody else had known about it. This version took its place as a kind of truth, and it was not mentioned again.

CHAPTER
FOURTEEN

London, September 1919

Nadine made linocuts for Riley's covers. She didn't know what he wanted, so she did what she wanted. They were beautiful, simple and modern, with swooping calligraphy and an elegant cartouche. She took great trouble with them because she wanted him to understand that she had forgiven him for scaring her so badly with his escapade in the north.

She had watched him go off to work: to his classes, to meet Hinchcliffe and Ermleigh, in his jacket, doing his man things. She had thought: What's he going to do? What's he going to do today?

She had a terrible fear that she didn't trust him. Not his intentions — she trusted those completely. But his ability to control himself. She wanted to race out after him. She didn't.

She was afraid too that he didn't like living with her father; that he was bored with the grief of their household; that he needed more light and beauty to continue his recovery. She didn't like that he didn't seem to be seeing his family. Though perhaps he did see his family. She didn't know. Was she allowed to know? Is that the sort of thing a wife asks a husband?

She let it wind her up tight, until one day, walking along Westbourne Grove on her way to Whiteley's for a reel of thread, she saw his mother, and ran up to her, heedless.

"Mrs Purefoy!" she said, and had no idea what she wanted to say to her.

"Mrs Purefoy," said Bethan, unsmiling.

"That's quite funny, I suppose," Nadine said, but Bethan was having none of it, and just looked at her.

"How lovely to run into you," Nadine said. "I do wish you'd come to call." She was lying. She didn't wish it. And Bethan would see that. Damn.

"I suppose I'm to enquire of *you*," Bethan said, after a pause, and with a very slightly disdainful look, "about the wellbeing of my own son." And at that Nadine's own wickedness came bursting up.

"Not unless you have any interest in it," she said, and stared at her right back. "Though if you don't, then I have to say that's entirely between you and him. Personally, I always thought it might be nice when married to have a mother-in-law one could talk to about things. But there — silly me. Good day, Mrs Purefoy." She turned round, started walking back the wrong way. Damn damn damn. No cotton reel. Ruined relations with mother-in-law. Damn. Fool.

Bethan was calling her name. Nadine turned around again and walked back, trotting like clockwork, her head down, so fast she practically walked into her. "I'm so terribly sorry," she said. "Totally uncalled for and awfully rude. I'm so sorry."

Bethan, standing there with her basket over her arm, said: "Your mam died, I heard."

"Yes," said Nadine. "Yes she did. She did."

"My condolences," said Bethan, and something of kindness in her voice made Nadine look up, and burst into tears, and find herself on Bethan's shoulder, about a foot below her own, crying like a loon, and trying to tell her that he went to Wigan, he got in a fight, he could have been hurt, he's moody still, it's been better since he's had this project, but why would he take risks like that, why would he do that, take such a risk when everything is still so fragile . . .

They went back to the little house, walking together. Perhaps she's just shy, Nadine was thinking. Perhaps she thinks I'm snooty. If it's up to me, then I'll do it. I'll be happy to do it.

They drank tea, and Nadine made a point of smiling a lot but not saying thank you too often. She didn't want to tell Bethan anything Riley might feel private about, so she told her things about herself instead: how she hadn't always got on with her mother, but she missed her so much. She asked after the girls. Merry was training for office work. Elen had a gentleman friend — then Elen came in, and Nadine could see from her face she was going to say something snide, as was her way, as was her mother's, and so she jumped in first. Just be human to them, burst these bubbles — so she said: "I'll stop you right there, Elen. He'd love to come home more, and see you all properly. But let's be nice. I'm your sister, whatever you think . . ."

"I see Lady Muck's got it all sorted, then?" Elen said, looking to her mother for approbation — but Bethan raised her eyes wearily and said: "Elen. Her mam has passed away. Grief makes people immediate, you might have noticed. And what's more, she's right."

When Nadine left, Bethan said to her, "Don't be a stranger."

Riley saw that her prints were beautiful. He grinned at how clever she was. And a tiny thought floated by: One more gift from her world to mine . . .

Stop that. You invited her to do them.

But he couldn't stop it. He was aware of resentment, and he didn't like it. He resented it! And he resented that, too. And he was aware that this cycle was almost funny. Almost.

There was another thing.

Sir Robert one evening said: "Riley, old man, might I have a word?" For a moment it was like when Riley had been looking for a library to take Sir Robert into to tell him he had married Nadine.

"Of course," Riley said, glancing around.

"Won't beat about the bush," Sir Robert said. He had his most urbane look on, which meant he was probably feeling a little embarrassed. "I asked you earlier this year about prospects and so forth, and possibly gave the impression of being less than confident in your capacities. Want to take that back. Very impressed, actually, by your gumption — shouldn't be surprised really — and so, got a bit of capital — probate and so forth — from reorganising —

Jacqueline — you can imagine — and I'd like you to allow me to invest in your press."

Oh!

This Riley had not expected. He didn't want it, that he knew. Could he refuse? His mind raced. No. Or yes? Was he allowed to say he'd think about it?

He sat silent.

"I hope you'll allow it," Sir Robert said. "I think it's a very likely investment."

He means he doesn't think it is at all. He doesn't believe in me. He's putting out a safety net to protect Nadine, and to allow me a little time before I cock it all up.

"Robert," he said. "I'm touched and honoured." He hated lying. This was unpleasant.

A light knock, and the door pushed open: Nadine. She was smiling and looked questioningly at them.

She knows about this. They've planned it.

Solicitous and loving, she said: "Isn't it a wonderful idea, darling?"

Which it is . . .

You'd think a fellow had a right to decide about his own investors . . . but no.

Riley could see perfectly well that a shot of financial back-up at this early stage would be extremely useful: the initial pamphlet had gone down very well, so he and Hinchcliffe had quickly put out another two, and had new ones in the pipeline. But damn it, he hadn't even been going to take money from Major Gillies. He would accept no money, no investment, that smelt of sympathy, war shame, or guilt. Not a penny. He was a man like any other and would make a living and build a business like

194

anyone else. Enough of being given everything on a bloody plate and being denied the opportunity to prove himself.

So, everybody thinks it's a splendid idea, except for your pride. Ha!

Of course a business needed investment. He would be happy to accept investment from men who had served. Or widows. Or nurses and VADs. Ambulance drivers, orderlies, chaplains, drivers of ambulance trains, etc. because 1) it would make him work all the harder to make them a decent dividend and 2) they didn't need to pity him, because they had their own sorrows.

So is Jacqueline's death not a sorrow?

Yes, of course it is.

Riley, you're tying yourself in circles! Your logic is self-punishing! Your logic, face it, is not logic.

He accepted the money — as a loan, not an investment. (Sir Robert, who hardly knew the difference between the two, was happy with that.) What he intended to achieve was more important than his pride. Bite the bullet, lad. Riley put Hinchcliffe on a salary and came to an agreement with Owen the printer. He came to an agreement with himself, too: he would pay his father-in-law back within three years. By which time he also planned to be paying the household bills, and with luck buying out the lease on the house on Bayswater Road.

"You're practically a publishing empire," Hinchcliffe said, the lunchtime Riley offered him a salary, in the Leinster Arms.

195

That was good to hear. Yes, he could build an empire.

"We," he said, and Hinchcliffe looked pleased, but Riley was a little tired. "I'm not going to go out talking to everyone," he said. "You can do that. What do you think?"

"I think yes," said Hinchcliffe.

"And we'd better get someone to answer the phone. A wounded man."

Hinchcliffe agreed. (Riley took on a perky and remarkably agile Cockney boy with a wooden Anglesey leg, the younger brother of one of Gillies' patients. "He can run errands," Riley said. Hinchcliffe didn't dare say a word.)

"Let's think up some new ideas then . . ." — but they were hardly short. Everywhere he looked, Riley saw mental, emotional and intellectual hunger. No one knew what would emerge from the chaos, and people wanted to be both prepared and reassured. The end of civilisation, the collapse of all that we once knew, whither this, and what about that . . . the Peace, the Armenians, religion, Communism, Ireland, jazz, unemployment, girls putting on lipstick in public. Civilians, in particular, seemed bothered with these issues. Riley, having looked death in the mouth many many times, was a secure man — secure in the knowledge that he was going to die, and so was everyone else, that human life was a vale of tears, and that consciously or willingly adding to the world's harvest of fear and misery was a waste, a waste, of the nebulous glorious moments one might be able to snatch along the road. Not that he

196

judged. He knew how it felt to come out of danger into relative safety, and to burst into tears and piss yourself with relief. He saw the world around him doing this. It's what Peter was doing. Even Julia perhaps, with her bolt to Biarritz.

He had spent a long afternoon in a café in Amiens with Peter telling him about the Spartan Army and their techniques. Esoteric harmony: how to release fear from your muscles, from your face, from your soul. Exoteric harmony: how to be united with your brother warriors like limbs on a beast, fingers on a hand. The Shedding: part of the training in phobologia — the knowledge of fear. After a battle, the Spartan warriors would go somewhere — Riley had imagined them standing around in fields, knee-deep in the dead and blood-stained asphodels, greaves and breastplates glinting in evening sun — and they would shake and weep, releasing the tension, the adrenalin, the fury, the ice-cold control that kept them invincible in the fight. And when that was done — a respected part of the process of battle, something necessary — they would come back and proceed with their lives. It was not only the soldiers, now, but the whole country, the whole world perhaps, that was shaking, after what it had been through. Phobos was a creature of many forms. And Riley knew all about that. So he addressed it.

The approach was practical. From the initial pamphlets for autodidacts and the lost and confused, the Orme Press planned to move on to pamphlets of policy and ideals, written by intellectuals and those with experience of their field. Robert Waveney was writing them a treatise on the power of music, practical and emotional, to raise the spirits and motivate the low. This had already attracted the attention of the Horrabins, who Riley hoped would agree to write something. They might even get the Coles, even H. G. Wells . . .

"How about improving memoirs, for men and women?" said Hinchcliffe.

"Yes. Let's find some. And — crime stories." Riley said. "The modern ones. Of the rather lurid, tersely written and very profitable type. Bitter old soldier turns detective kind of thing."

Hinchcliffe expressed his surprise.

"They will fit in perfectly," Riley said. "All our publications will tend to peace and social justice, and crime stories are also about righting wrongs and understanding human nature. There's too many soldiers going to the bad." He wondered for a second where Johnno-the-Thief Burgess was. Probably gone back to going to the bad. Perhaps he'd look him out. Perhaps not.

"But who will write them?" Hinchcliffe was saying.

"You," said Riley, and Hinchcliffe snorted. But Riley knew he'd like the idea.

No conversation with Riley could be very long. He had come to recognise the little tensions in his cheek muscles and a certain strain on the tongue that told him he was talking too much. When he stopped talking, he just stopped. He didn't notice that that was how he did it, and that it might be seen as rude. It didn't matter. He only talked to who he wanted to anyway, and his grey-diamond eyes still spoke clearly to anybody who cared to listen.

Hinchcliffe, tapping his fingers on the dimples of his pint mug, said, "By the way, you know Owen has sacked Ermleigh?"

"No. Why?"

"I gather because he wants someone who can work harder."

Riley closed his eyes and bit the insides of his peculiar cheeks. "Come on then," he said, and stood up.

At Owen's, Riley stood slightly too close to the man and said to him with great clarity, "Mr Owen. Now, we've been to the pub together, haven't we? We're on the same side? So — how's your German?"

"Sorry, Purefoy, I don't . . ."

"Without men like Ermleigh, you'd be printing umlauts, Mr Owen. Do you have umlauts in your printstock?"

"I, er . . ."

"You should get some in. I'm planning a series — 'My Life as a Hun', by some ordinary German boys — their side of the story. How being thrown into the pit of hell by a German government differs from being thrown into the pit of hell by a British one. Only war isn't hell, is it? It's worse. Because hell is just for sinners, but war gets everybody, no matter how innocent. And then some of us come out of it worse off than others. Probably even harder to feed your family in Hamburg or Berlin at the moment than it is here, I should imagine. Not asking you to sympathise with the Hun, Mr Owen. But you might consider the position of the Tommy."

"Well, Captain —"

"Put Ermleigh back, Mr Owen, or our business goes elsewhere."

God, this is so easy to do. No skin off my nose. (And he caught himself for a moment. He'd used that phrase to Jarvis once, during the phase when the bridge — or what was to be the bridge — of Jarvis' new nose had been carrying a delicate little horsehair stitch, crimping it in place so at least the great sausage was narrower at the top than at the bottom . . . wonder where Jarvis is now. Find him.)

"But Captain Purefoy —"

"Mr Owen. With the Empire collapsing, we're just a clever little country. That's all. But we are meant to have standards. In theory — in principle, we have principles."

"But —"

Riley said, "I am never going to do the wrong thing again, Mr Owen. Do you understand?"

He said it quite gently. The red mist of fighting was not far away at all. Just below the surface. But this anger was sleek. He could feel it in his eyes.

Owen understood.

Walking back, Hinchcliffe beside him, Riley shed it. Rolled his shoulders and threw off ripples of anger to let his calm return. Hinchcliffe was silent all the way.

Riley was thinking: It seems to me that once you've been damaged, if you don't become a healer you just get . . . more damaged. You need to be able to envisage a future. To acknowledge how scared you are, and yet carry on, and help.

After a while, Hinchcliffe said: "So, um, Purefoy. Are you going to sack me for not being wounded?"

"Oh, you're wounded all right," Riley said. One-and-three-quarter million wounded, and that's just the wounds you can see. "You got your heart broken."

Coming back to his father-in-law's house that night, Riley fancied a cup of tea. The coat rack in the hall was, as usual, full: Sir Robert's smart velvet-collared cashmere, his raincoat and his walking coat, Nadine's new blue cape, her light coat and her tweed, plus several things of Jacqueline's that had escaped the clear-out to the dress agency. Riley didn't like to move anything, but when his own coat slipped off the mound of cloth for lack of any kind of purchase, he felt a low fury.

He didn't know how to live here. At home, as a child, he had his own hook and there was only one coat each anyway, and he'd make his own tea, or his mum would. In the trenches you didn't take your coat off, and if you did you were asleep under it, and the tea came round in its billy when it wanted. In the hospital you didn't have a coat, or tea, unless someone thought you should, in which case they'd bring it. But here? No room for your coat, and tea involved ringing a bell, waiting for someone to come and ask what you want, then go away and make it and bring it to you. And no one expected you to want tea when you came in in the evening. You were meant to want sherry. (And then you didn't have your actual tea till eight, and they called it dinner, and your actual dinner they called lunch. Well, he was used to all that.) Several times he'd found himself going round to Sir Alfred's instead. Being a straightforward guest and being straightforwardly offered a cup of tea by Mrs Briggs who had loved him since he was a boy was easier than this half-guest half-family position in his father-in-law's home. Or his wife's dead mother's-in-law's home. Or the home of the girl his wife used to be.

"Remember when we were going to live in Chelsea?" he said to Nadine, later that evening. "Our two little rooms, and you were going to study art?"

"Remember when I was going to get a motorbike and ride around the world with you on the back?" she replied, with a smile.

Is living in Chelsea that ambitious? he thought. Oh.

"I'd like to live in Chelsea," he said.

"But we live here," she said carefully. "Don't we?"

"We *could* move," he said.

"Why?" she asked. He looked around the pretty room; glanced out the windows towards Kensington Gardens, wide, leafy and dim across the road. Because of my pride, and my lack of ease here, because I want our home to be our own home. Is that selfish? Probably.

He thought of another tack.

"Shall we get a little place in the country?"

She said, "I can't think we could afford it."

"In a few years?" he said.

"Thinking ahead!" she said, and she smiled.

It's just teething troubles, he thought. Settling.

"I ran into your mother," Nadine said, with a little smile. "Almost literally." She waited to see what he'd make of that. *What do I make of that?*

"Oh," he said. "How is she?"

"She's well. I went back for tea. Elen was there. Don't look so surprised! We're family."

He hadn't thought of it quite that way. But — he glanced at her suspiciously. She looked happy enough about it. *Hm.*

"I told them to pop in any time," she went on, "but I'm not sure they will. Perhaps a more formal invitation, just to make things easier . . . in a month or two. Perhaps around Christmas. Boxing Day lunch or something. They know about my mother . . ."

Hmm.

She was looking at him.

Family.

He went round a few days later, braving the possibility that Elen would be no less withering now than she had been on his first visit. Being withered by Elen he could do without. But as it happened, he was just in time to learn that Elen was getting married. Her man friend was called Gavin, a ticket inspector on the Great Western. He was Welsh (Mum was over the moon about that). No war — asthma. He seemed all right. Jokes were made.

Walking home (home! Which was home?), he thought about it all. There was, of course, another way to make her family house *their* home — children. At some stage no doubt he would find he had got her with child. That sounds very biblical. Get her pregnant just sounds vulgar. What is the polite term? It didn't matter that he didn't know. He wasn't exactly going to be talking about it to anyone. But yes, fathering a child seemed pretty manly, something to be proud of. Something, more to the point, that nobody else could do for him. But he did not bring up the matter of a baby. He knew nothing about babies. How long it was meant to take, or — anything. And there's another pamphlet! "All About Fatherhood, for the Newly Married Man".

All this was the kind of thing he would have been able to talk to Ainsworth about. He had a letter from Sybil: "We had some grand Walking Days in the summer. Little Annie says she is going to join the Band and the character of the lass is such I believe she will, whether they will have her or not. The Sadness is never far away but there's too much to be done to think about that. We raise a prayer to him each Sunday, and to you, and Annie says to be remembered to you. And by the way — there was talk of a lad from London being involved in the trouble here when you were visiting last. He answered your description, though I've no doubt you've too much sense to get involved in anything ridiculous, so it must have been some other facially injured lad up from London heading to the station that dinner-time. Let's hope he's the sense to keep his damaged head out of hot water the next time."

Sybil's voice seemed like one of comfort, from long ago. There was no reason why it should, but it did. I'll go and see them again, he thought, one of these days.

A few days later, as they were going to bed, Nadine said to him: "About the future. I've been thinking. I think I will go to art school. You've inspired me by commissioning me."

He was very pleased. This was to do with them, their future, not the past.

"You don't mind?" she asked.

A tricky question, as it tends to lead to "why would I mind?" which immediately sounds defensive. But then, why would I mind?

"Why would I mind?" he said.

"You might want me to stay at home and have babies," she said.

"Well, I do want you to stay at home and have babies," he said.

"When?" she said, smiling.

"When they come," he said, with a little frown.

"You do know where they come from, don't you?"

"Yes, thank you," he said, with very mild *faux* outrage.

She put her hand over her mouth for a second, laughing or covering embarrassment, he didn't know. What's she doing?

"What is it?" he said.

"Darling," she said. "I've been being very modern and I hope you don't mind."

"What?" he said.

"I've been reading both Marie Stopes and Annie Besant."

This meant nothing to him.

With the expression of one making a leap, and blushing scarlet, she said: "I've acquired a diaphragm."

"We all have diaphragms," he said. "You've had one all your life."

"Oh, Riley!" she exclaimed, and she went into the bathroom, and came out with a little bag. Inside it was a little box. Inside that was a rubber thing, circular, mysterious, important. He gazed at it, perplexed.

"It's a contraceptive," she said, almost giggling. "You don't have to worry about it. I do it. But I want you to know about it."

"Blimey," he said.

"I haven't used it yet," she said. "But it means we can have our babies whenever we want, and I think perhaps not yet. What do you think?"

"Blimey," he said. Then, "But you do want some in the end?"

"Certainly," she said. "Lovely little curly babies. But I want more of just us first. Not Papa all the time, not sadness, not work. Papa's been invited to tour America. I've told him he must go. And I'm going to redecorate a bit. What colour shall we have the bedroom?"

"I couldn't care less," he said, with a smile.

"Marvellous," she said. "And can we go dancing? I won't mind if you want to wear your scarf — I could get you a lovely silk one — but I'd love to go dancing. Hear the music and hold you in my arms. All that."

"Blimey," he said. How many times can you fall in love with the same person?

CHAPTER
FIFTEEN

Locke Hill, October 1919

As it couldn't matter less to Peter where he was, he stayed at Locke Hill. The comforts of home did comfort him. His study was there for him; his clothes, clean. He wasn't sure what everyone was going to say to him, how much of a fuss they were going to kick up, or when, but for the moment they seemed pleased that he was there, and mostly engaged with Julia and the imminent baby. And Julia herself, vast now and oddly passive, smiled at him, was kind to him, left him alone. It was pleasant to have Nadine about when she came, and when Riley came down they took some walks together, quieter than ever. He was aware of these things, but they were not his world.

It took Odysseus ten years. I have not even had one.

His world was in his head, and in Homer. He read the *Iliad*, again, and then the *Odyssey*, again. He read the Greek alongside the dictionary alongside the Chapman, against the Dryden, and the Pope alongside the Cowper alongside the Greek, and the more recent translations. He read, all the time comparing what Achilles and Odysseus did, and what happened to them, with what he had been through in France, what he had seen and done, and what had been done to him.

He found himself translating bits, here and there. Words which did not seem quite right to him — well, of course they were right, but they were right for something else, somewhen else, for some other translator. For what he was thinking, now, they were not right. So much liberty a poet could take with the original! The chronological series of translations was like a pile of poems built on each other; like sedimentary geology.

Was Chapman a soldier? Had he any idea? Homer — or at least some of the many who contributed, who were parts of Homer — at least one of them was. How else could they know to use the same word for the giving way of a man's legs with fear, in battle, and with lust, at the sight of Penelope in all her finery? And for Patroclus falling dead in battle and Achilles falling in grief by his body? How else could they understand?

He noticed that the word for truth meant, precisely, not forgotten. A *lethea*. Not in the Lethe, the river of forgetting. Is that what the truth is? What you don't forget? What does that mean? Well, for a start it means that everybody has a different truth ... He thought about Calypso, the sex maniac who kept Odysseus prisoner in her cave for seven years; he thought about how Odysseus, in disguise, testing his wife, felt so strongly for her grief as she wept over the husband she thought was dead, yet he kept his eyes dry as pieces of horn beneath his lids. He thought about trust, and how when the ships of Odysseus' fleet moored in the safe-seeming inlet to sleep, every man aboard those ships was killed, and only Odysseus' own ship survived, because Odysseus had moored outside: he had not trusted. He thought of the firestep, sentries, all night, awake. Of the modern ways he had used to keep awake: nightclubs, cocaine, prostitutes, jazz. And of the Sirens, who sang of the truth of the battlefield.

Truth itself a drug, he thought, an addiction. A man could lose his life after war to wanting and needing to know the truth of what happened. Harking on the past. Am I doing that? Or am I drowning the truth? It's not that I don't know what happened — I don't understand. I don't understand.

He would go to sleep and wake in a panic: he should not be sleeping. Bad things happen when officers fall asleep.

On the study sofa one afternoon, sleeping in the comparative safety of daylight, he was woken, just as the silvery autumn sky was turning to lead, by the cold point of a blade in the softest hollow of his throat. It was quite real. Lying, eyes closed, he knew that if he sat up suddenly and swiftly enough, his throat would be pierced, and death would be his. He moved his head gently, very gently, to and fro, to feel the sharpness against his skin. He thought it would be right, and a good way to end it.

In one movement he swung his arm across the blade, and he opened his eyes. It's nothing. There is nothing there. Here's the truth: it's all in your head.

Some neighbours, the Baxes, back from Yorkshire now the war was over, invited them to dinner. Of course he didn't want to go, and actually neither did Julia, but because each felt that the other might like to, and because both knew that on some level it was a good idea, they ended up going.

Mr Bax was too old to have fought; his children too young. The other guests, a vicar and his wife, and an accountant and his sister, were of an age. Peter was next to Mrs Bax, who seemed to know a great deal about the peace terms, and where everybody was going wrong. She knew almost as much, indeed, as the vicar. The accountant was full of good information on stocks and bonds. Peter ate his chop and felt like a savage, and felt that surely he was not meant to be still feeling like a savage.

The vicar's wife, courteous and intelligent, was keen to talk about the decline of civilisation. What future, she wondered, for religion and art?

"Madam," Peter said, "you should know — you of all people are civilised, a civilian . . ." He meant it kindly — he thought — but it came out oddly.

After dinner the vicar took to the piano, and there was singing. Very civilised! Mrs Bax, with her white throat and her generous embonpoint, took her place by the upright piano and, aware of Peter's service record, made sure to keep the songs cheerful.

Peter was all right for "I'm Forever Blowing Bubbles", and "A Pretty Girl is like a Melody", and "By The Light of the Silvery Moon". But when Mrs Bax started singing "How Ya Gonna Keep 'Em Down on the Farm (After They've Seen Paree)?", feeling herself no doubt rather modern and bold with the lines about how "wine and women play the mischief/With a boy who's loose with change", he started laughing not with merriment but with a note of desperation, and the memory of Mabel at the Turquoisine, singing it so differently, so beautifully, with such profound understanding of why a boy needed that mischief and was helpless in the face of wine and women — and oh, God, she sang it on Julia's birthday last year, which I forgot, one more tiny offence among so many — only last year. Jesus, must time go so slowly?

Perhaps Mrs Bax thought her choices too frivolous — anyway, she and the vicar changed their tune, and decided on "Roses of Picardy", sweet yet respectful. And yet, when she sang, really quite beautifully, the lines about how the roses will die with the summertime, and our roads may be far apart, Peter started laughing again, laughing hard.

Mrs Bax stopped singing. The vicar lifted his hands from the keyboard.

It's the same to them. It's all the same. The silvery moon from before the war, the silvery dew from 1916, the wine playing mischief — it's all just entertainment and civilisation. They know nothing. Phaeacians. They're bloody Phaeacians.

"Darling?" Julia murmured.

Peter rolled his eyes sideways towards her in a kind of desperation.

"Let Demodokos touch his harp no more," he said in a tone of resignation and finality. "His theme has not been pleasing to all here."

So then they stared, like bullocks over a fence. Not unfriendly. Just uncomprehending. Rich tourists in the land of pain.

"Well!" said Mr Bax with hostly responsibility in mind. "The old songs still have their potency, I see!"

"Old?" said Peter. "Old? Are they so old? Is it all past, now? You want war songs? I have some!"

He stood up, and caught eyes with his wife, and her eyes were open, kind and loving. He was weeping, he realised, with a sense of idiocy and of letting everybody down, but they were not his world, so who cares?

Idiotes: *he who cares only for his own interests.*

He raised his eyes to gaze around at them, and said: "The famous harpist sang, but the great Odysseus melted into tears . . . as a woman weeps, her arms flung round her darling husband, a man who fell in battle . . . she clings for dear life . . ."

He said it furiously and clearly, but he said it in Greek, and nobody, not even the vicar who might have been expected to, recognised it. Only Julia picked up the word "Odysseus".

It seemed that the duty of pacifying him fell to the vicar, who stood up from the piano stool and said something calming and appropriate: "Now now, old man, no need to be angry," that sort of thing, in ecclesiastical tones . . . but Peter turned on him, and said, starkly: "You liked my fury well enough, didn't you, when you thought the Hun was coming for you. You were happy to have my fury protect you then. Weren't you? But now? Now, oh no. Now I'm to shut up and behave. Now you're not afraid of the Hun any more, you're afraid of *me* —"

The vicar's wife flinched and blinked; Mr Bax bumbled to his feet, exchanging glances with the vicar, thinking about ringing for a manservant.

Julia, breathing lightly, went and stood beside Peter, very close.

"I'm so *sorry*, Father," he was saying bitterly. "That I don't just *slot back in*. Terribly inconvenient. I do understand."

She put the size, the pure volume, of her body alongside him, touching. She put her hand on his shoulder and leant in, leaning a little of her weight and her breast on his back. It was a movement of trust. He turned his head sharply over his shoulder to look at her, profile to profile.

Everyone was staring at him.

Her eyes were clear and steady.

She leaned up, and kissed him, very softly, on his cheek. It felt to him — actually, physically felt to him — that every nerve ending was peeled raw. Her kiss was on skinned flesh. He thought: I love you. His mouth formed the words: "*s'agapo*" — in Greek. And she smiled, because that was something he had taught her, in Venice, naked on a bed under a golden glass chandelier, with canal water reflections rippling on the vaulted ceiling.

"*S'agapo*," she said back to him now.

When she came out, he was standing by the car, smoking in the night air, his expression alert, puzzled, miles away, as if listening to something only he could hear. They were silent in the car on the way back, and she held his hand.

At home, he looked for whisky and she did not stop him. Instead she found his books, his spectacles and his glass of water and brought them up to her bedroom, to the bedside table on what used to be his side of the bed. She went carefully downstairs again, pausing to breathe, leaning back a little to counteract the weight she was carrying, taking care on the dark wooden treads. He was standing in the hall, looking lost: again she went and stood by him, her vastness alongside him. With a touch of her hand on his arm she brought him up to her bedroom.

Propped up on four pillows beside him in bed, she listened as he told her, carefully and with much apology, the names of the men who had died at Loos and on the Somme, and something about the dreams he had been having.

He didn't say, "Your body beside me in bed turns into a German boy, a dying boy when I stumbled into the shell hole beside him, a dead boy by the time I left. The sounds you make are the cries and gasps of death. His voice was light and young. His hair was fair. His body was warm and heavy." He didn't tell her that he didn't know whether or not he had killed the boy, and if he had, if it had been to put him out of his misery or to shut him up. That he didn't know whether, if he had, that was any worse than killing him in battle. He didn't tell her that his haunting memories meant nothing because surely, to be valid, one should be haunted by only one terrible memory — there being so many

214

surely, by definition, meant they could not be so outstandingly terrible? He didn't tell her that he still wrote lists of terrible memories, and changed the order, and wondered if something you are still in, every day, even counts as a memory, and that he screwed them up and threw them in the fire, because even the phrase "terrible memories" became ridiculous, prissy somehow, through repetition.

1) Stealing the boy's knife to cut his throat to shut him up, and cutting his throat. Or,
2) not having the courage to do it, and letting him — how old was he? Sixteen? — take all day and all night to die.
3) Not knowing.
4) Leading the men over the top, on the Somme.
5) Carrying.

But he told her some names.

She said nothing. Sometimes she closed her eyes; sometimes she looked at him; once or twice she stroked his arm.

"I keep carrying them in," he said.

She thought about it for a while, and then she said: "You are carrying death. I am carrying life."

And he said, "Arcadia is a sin, you know. That's why they had to tie him to the mast," which she didn't entirely follow, but she put it away to think about later. Instead she said, "So are you dead? Or will you live?"

"I'm tied to the mast," he said. "But I think the ship is moving." He didn't really think it was. But he thought, for the first time, that if it were, that would be a good thing.

When he fell asleep, she manoeuvred her great self to reach over to his bedside table, her full belly hanging from her frame like a packed hammock, to pick up his book. And she eased herself back to her own side, and sat back, propped again, with Volume I of Chapman's Homer resting against the slope. She patted the child through her nightdress and her tight tight skin, and started to read, from the beginning.

CHAPTER
SIXTEEN

London, August — October 1919
Two letters reached Nadine. The one from Julia, and
a smooth cream envelope with an Italian stamp and a
Rome postmark, addressed to Nadine's dead mother,
care of the Albert Hall, crossed out and sent on. She
still didn't feel quite that she deserved to perform this
most personal of duties to the dead, so she held it for a
moment before opening it with one swift movement of
her mother's bone paperknife.

Piazza San Bartolomeo 22
Isola Tiberina
Rome

Dear Signora,
   I hope and believe you are in my family. My mother
who was name Chantal Elia Fiore before Mendoza
tells me you are her sister in her family from Paris. I
am living Rome. I was soldier but intend architect.
I am curious if you are my aunt. What do you think?

Thank you dear Signora,
Aldo Elia Fiore

Nadine read it again. How charming! You open an envelope and out pops a man in Rome who thinks he is your mother's nephew. And an aunt! But Jacqueline had never mentioned a sister. Parents, yes — Rafael and Berthe. They were there in the wedding photos, beaming, shiny little creatures from the old century, well dressed, beetle-like. They had visited, Nadine thought, when she was very small. The seventy-three small ivory elephants that she would see if she raised her head, lined up, promenading still in their glass case, had belonged to Berthe. When had they died, the grandparents? Did they even make it into the new century? She remembered how during the dark days in 1918, during that strange interlude in Paris, she had stared at the street they used to live on, wondering if there were unknown cousins on the pavement around her, her own blood passing unrecognised, close by. She had been too weak and shocked to do anything about it then, in the full flood of . . . then. But the thought had crossed her mind. And again, on honeymoon.

Jacqueline had *never* mentioned a sister.

Nadine found herself sketching a little family tree on the envelope.

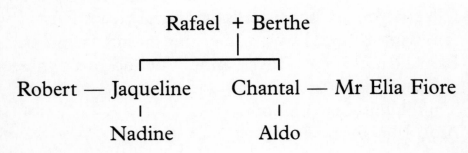

It was so small and neat.

But perhaps it wasn't! She'd always thought that apart from poor cousin Noel on her father's side, there was only her. But if there can be an aunt, there could be other cousins.

When Riley came in that night after a day soothing printers in Cheapside, he was still standing by the coat rack when Nadine, fizzing with excitement, showed him the letter.

He hung his coat and took the letter she held out to him.

"How extraordinary," he said, as he read it.

"I'm writing back," she said.

He trailed his hand along her shoulder as he went into the drawing room, his cheeks widening with his idiosyncratic smile. "Rather exciting," he said, and she touched his hand as it trailed off past her.

She said: "Why do you suppose Jacqueline never talked about her sister?"

"She wasn't interested in the past."

"True. But a sister isn't the past."

"Jacqueline had her way of wanting things to be," he said. "Of course she should have told you. But she did what she liked."

"Or perhaps I was just a terribly difficult person to talk to. Or a difficult child. Was I?"

"You were sweet," he said, and she thought again what a miracle it was that they had found each other and kept each other.

"Perhaps I was a hard birth, or she wanted a boy! Oh who knows." Nadine was irritated at her own sorrow.

The previous year, while still in the extremes of the peculiar emotional landscape where the war had dumped her, she had decided that she would never again be upset by anything that wasn't concretely and immediately offensive to her. Her peace of mind was precious; she would value it. She would not let it be upended by a late bus or an uninterested mother. If there was something to be done about a problem, then it must be done. If there was nothing to be done, then you might as well shut up about it. That's all. It had worked well, so far. But it hadn't helped with confused grief for a mother she . . . couldn't say it. So ashamed. Didn't like.

But an aunt might be able to explain to her . . .

This Roman's letter just toppled into the small abyss in Nadine's heart where her troubles with Jacqueline still creaked and lurched. His existence soothed it: food to an empty stomach; water to a dried-out pond. Later that evening she sent a telegram to her father in Chicago:

APPARENT COUSIN TURNED UP ROME APPARENTLY MOTHERS SISTER ANY IDEA LOVE NADINE

The reply came at breakfast:

NO NEVER MENTIONED STOP NEITHER RAFAEL NOR BERTHE STOP WISH COULD TALK PROPERLY STOP HOW ODD HOW RILEY LOVE PA

She wired back:

AM TAKEN WITH MYSTERIOUS POSSIBIL-
ITY RILEY WELL LOVE

The reply:

HUMPH

Nadine wrote back to the Roman, a kind, cautious letter, explaining and enquiring. The reply came in the same ambitious and inaccurate English: Aldo Elia Fiore was so very sorry to hear of the passing of the signora, his aunt. He sent his sympathies, and he hoped his letter written of ignorance had not been a grand intrusion at a time of grief. He was extremely happy to have the knowledge of his cousin Nadina. His information was from his mother, now also, sadly, no longer with us.

Oh. Chantal was dead.

So that was a curious grief: to lose the brand-new aunt she had never known she had, and the link to Jacqueline. It made her decide very quickly that she would not lose the cousin. Meanwhile she saved the Italian envelope for Tom. The stamp had a picture of an aeroplane on it, and little as he was, he loved aeroplanes.

The second letter, from Julia, was, frankly, welcome. It would be — dear Lord! — refreshing to have something other than her darling bereft father to think about; to have some female company — and perhaps

Rose would be there; to see Tom, and get some country air, and be out from under of the wing of mourning. She had intended to go to Locke Hill anyway, but the fusses of returning from travel and being flung into the emotions and duties of bereavement had prevented it. Knowing little of Julia's excursion, Nadine took her condition, and Peter's being "in London", as signs that normality was gaining a little territory in the everyday life of Locke Hill. She was glad of it. She did hope, though, that Rose would be there. Rose did make everything easier.

To Nadine, coming in from the station, up the curved drive to the handsome porch with roses bouncing above it and sunlight pouring down, the house seemed empty. The front door was unlocked and she walked in as if she still lived there. Memories of last winter strung the door like autumn cobwebs: of arriving from France, of Riley turning up that mad night, of how they had sat outside on the lawn smoking under the freezing stars . . .

It is a simple fact that wounds don't heal the moment the cause of them stops. Rose said something, early on, about deep bruises taking for ever to come to the surface. Broken bones are forever weaker. Scar tissue has no feeling, which is a wound in itself. It's no good not to feel or think at all — or is that self-protection because what you would feel or think is unbearable? Is that why so many people are being harsh and brittle, and going out dancing all night? But it's all so recent still. And probably when you think you are recovered is when you are most vulnerable . . .

I have lost my mother. I have Riley. I have Riley. For a moment she recalled them dancing under the Chinese lanterns at the Hammersmith Palais: ridiculous kicky jazz dancing, breathless, laughing, falling against each other, all that romantic stuff. Walking home wrapped round each other. One arm round him inside his jacket, thumb hitched on to his belt; the other hand resting on his heart, stroking his face, holding his hand flopped over her shoulder. All the closeness. They fall asleep holding hands. If I never have anything in my life again, having him back is enough for me.

"Julia?" she called.

Mrs Joyce poked her head out of the kitchen door. Nadine was so pleased to see her. Floury hands were clasped, and a flurry of "oh goodness" and "oh never mind that" passed between them. Nadine found herself wanting to ask Mrs Joyce how the household was, how was Peter, how was Tom. Indeed she was about to, when Mrs Joyce said that Mrs Locke was in the glasshouse, and to go on through.

Nadine wandered through the house — quiet, well kept as ever — and out through the French windows down to the walled garden and its greenhouse. There were signs of digging and replanting in the old vegetable garden — Harker must have been busy. The lawn that Julia had had dug up for extra food production was weedily overgrown now, lumpy and full of ground elder. Nadine laughed at herself for looking for symbolism, for signs of how they all were in how their gardens grew. Julia's garden was bedraggled with seed heads and late roses and the huge flaming marguerites, which seemed to have thrived on the neglect of the war years. As if that proved anything. The poppies were apparently marvellous in Flanders this year. She'd read it in the paper. People were going on battlefield tours. There were guidebooks.

Julia was there in a pinafore, poking seeds into ridges of compost in planting trays on the wrought-iron shelves rusty beneath their flaking white paint. Tom sat on the shelf beside her, swinging his legs, asking questions, and trying on her trug as a hat.

"Julia?" Nadine said, curiously.

"It's practical things I need help with," Julia said, leaning against the glasshouse shelf. Tom had been sent to find long straight twigs for seedlings to climb when they sprouted. Nadine had been put to sit on a slightly cobwebby painted stool. They had had a polite squabble about who should take the seat, with Julia insisting that she found it more comfortable to stand. "I don't really bend very well in the middle," she said. "I hardly showed at all till a few weeks ago and then I just expanded . . ."

Nadine wilted a little inside. More about Julia's needs. Well, I owe it to her. They were supremely hospitable, even though neither of them was entirely conscious. And her letter was — different.

"Well," Julia said. "You've probably heard that I've been away. I wanted to think about life and the future.

224

I went a bit mad. All the past and regret and sorrow and grief — everybody's — what we've lost . . ."

Nadine inclined her head. She didn't want to talk about what was lost. She had, after all, managed to regain. She was all future, now. Art school. Riley working so hard with Hinchcliffe and the pamphlets.

"I've done the most awful things," Julia said. "I just make awful decisions and everybody suffers, and then I feel — no, I *am* — the most awful fool. I want to be a better person but I can't seem to see how . . . I seem to have muddied everything so much I couldn't see my way — and when I tried I just made it worse — and part of me knows that Peter is trapped in exactly the same thing. Exactly the same. And we didn't talk. We — well . . ."

She glanced at Nadine, who looked steadily back at her. A waterfall seemed to have opened up. Well, let it come. This waterfall of me me me.

"Sorry, I'm going on —" Julia said. "I don't want to be stuck in my own stupid feelings. I don't. I want — and then I feel, I feel, oh damn it all, I shall drink all the whisky in the house. Why not? If he can, why can't I? He's killed people, all right then! I have given birth! Blood! Violence! It's human, isn't it? Isn't it? And ruining my stupid face — and Nadine, don't think I don't think about Riley's face. I do — and I am so ashamed, and ashamed of my shame, and how it paralyses me — anyway, no more! Nadine, this is what I want to know. How can I love Peter?"

Nadine was extremely surprised. Julia looked at her anxiously, as if to check, and went on: "It seems so much easier for you and Riley. When Riley had his awful wound, and yet you manage to deal with it and yet I can't. What must I do?"

Nadine moved her head an inch. Julia stared at her, her wide blue eyes holding what — concern?

"While I was away," Julia said, "I realised that I can have no future anywhere except here. Look! I have my new child coming. I have Tom. But I don't want to talk about me, really I don't! I want to talk about Peter — Nadine — you and Riley —"

"What about us?" asked Nadine, quite kindly. Resigned.

"How is Riley?"

Nadine gave a smile, a quiet smile of such glowing intensity that Julia actually blinked. "He is — marvellous," said Nadine. Then she felt embarrassed.

"Gosh," said Julia, and Nadine dropped her head a moment, and they both quickly moved on, because *that*, for sure, was not what they were going to talk about. It was Julia who picked up the thread. "So when he came back," she said. "When he was still, you know, full of the battlefield — when he was at the Queen's, and he sent you away, and it was all so difficult —"

"When you invited me to stay here," said Nadine, remembering suddenly Julia's awkward sweetness to her at that time.

"Yes," said Julia. She turned her head to look out of the cloudy glasshouse window, and Nadine followed her gaze.

"I suppose," Julia said, and then started again: "Please don't mind my asking. How did you manage not to just get stuck there? Because Peter and I are stuck there. And on the face of it you and Riley had — Oh, Nadine, I am sorry — what a thing to say!"

But Nadine just looked up at her and grinned and said, "Julia, don't worry a bit — I've used the same expression myself and kicked myself for it. On the face of it we what?"

"You seem to be capable," Julia said. "Happy. Getting on with it." She glanced up as she spoke, to check the effect of her words.

"Yes, I suppose we are," Nadine said.

"How do you actually *do* it? Each day? When you wake in the morning, what do you say? How do you not annoy him? How do you not hate him?"

Ah.

How do we not hate each other? The sex thing, of course . . . but before that. Loyalty? Faith? What . . . right at the beginning . . . And something came back to her.

"The night he turned up here, when I was just back from France," she said, "we sat outside in the garden. It was terribly cold. And one of us said — I'm pretty sure it was him, but he thinks it was me — well, one of us said, 'Tell me one thing.' So we did."

"What did you tell each other?"

"That doesn't matter. What matters is . . . that they find it very difficult to talk about things — we all do, but the men who've been at the Front specially do — and they sort of need to. So you just need to give it a form. Tell each other something each day. Something factual and true about yourself and your life and what you've done, or learnt. We did that. And then gradually you come to understand each other."

"That doesn't sound too difficult," Julia said.

"It needs patience," Nadine said. "And — Riley doesn't drink much. So Peter will always be harder to get to."

"Nadine," Julia said, "the other night, he got awfully upset when we went out to dinner, and I really didn't know what to do, he was talking Greek and shouting at the vicar, and everyone was hideously embarrassed — and I thought, well, I'm either on their side or on his side, and I didn't know what to say, so instead I just sort of *did* it. I went and stood beside him. Just that! Do you think that was right?"

"Yes," said Nadine. "I'm sure it was."

"And — later — he told me the names of men of his who had died. Burdock and Atkins and . . . Lovell . . . and . . ."

Nadine's eyes filled suddenly, full, overflowing. Dead men, dead boys, dying men you couldn't help, who would never come back . . . The terrible ache of the deepest bruises . . . There was nothing she could do about it. Tears rolling down her face, a flood, and she felt suddenly, rackingly sick.

"My dear!" Julia cried, but Nadine was sobbing, at how these men of theirs had been chained to death, how death had held them in its cloud for years on end, throwing itself at them from every side, and at their companions, drenching them, beating them up, threatening them, battering them, torturing them, taking their friends, taking them — but only so far, then throwing them back, or just taking part of them — their sanity, or their capacity to breathe, their leg, their arm, their face, their speech — laughing at them . . .

"Oh my dear," Julia said. "Oh my dear."

"We are so lucky," Nadine said with a kind of gasp, and went on, in a sobbing gulping rush, "Julia, we are so lucky to have them. We must love them and hold them and feed them and be with them and — Julia, we must do anything and everything for them. We must use all our kindness, our intelligence, our strength, our patience — everything God gave us. It will be a life's work, I swear it, to make things possible for them, I daren't say easier for them, but possible — Julia do you ever think how — they spent those years believing — knowing — that at *any moment* they might very well be killed, and be *dead*. All day, all night . . . and they kept on fighting, and they kept on joking, and they kept on doing their best . . . Julia, we are so lucky to have them . . . and death hasn't left them yet — I don't know how long it takes to leave — but it's still here — isn't it?"

"Jones," said Julia, frowning. "And Bloom, and Bruce, and . . . Merritt . . . There were more." She went to Nadine, sitting sobbing on the stool, and put her arm round her shoulder. After a while she gave her a handkerchief. "It's clean," she said, and sighed, hugely. "We can't any of us do this on our own, can we?"

At this, Nadine felt a new rush of tears. At the miracle of Julia realising.

Later, faces washed and tea served under the same tree where Tom had thrown stones at himself, Julia said, shyly, "So, I do want to ask you two favours."

Nadine, her eyes red, smiled a little sideways.

"It seems to me that Riley is good for Peter. Bring him down? He's saved Peter's life twice. Perhaps he can do it again. Third time lucky!" She laughed the small laugh of nervousness and relief.

"What do you mean he saved Peter's life?" Nadine said.

"He did," Julia said. "When he brought him back here before Christmas. He was just drowning, I think, in London. I mean, I don't know, of course, but — he hadn't come home! And Riley brought him home."

"And?"

"And the other —" Julia paused. "Has Riley not said anything about it?"

"About what?" Nadine asked. "I don't know what you're referring to."

"Well," said Julia, "I don't even know if it's true, but I think it is . . ." And she told Nadine what she had told Rose, that when Peter was wounded on the Somme, Riley had carried him in. That Peter talked in his sleep. Her speech, previously a river of her own feelings, became a rivulet as she spoke of Peter, constrained and rocky. "And — he sort of relives things. Carrying men in. And being carried."

Nadine looked at Julia carefully. She saw something in her that she knew from herself: wanting to confide, but not wanting to betray his privacy. The time has come, I think, to betray all the privacy there is. We can't battle on in this silence, this sort of continuing silent war with what happened . . .

230

"But *Riley* was wounded on the Somme," Nadine said. "His arm. How could he have carried Peter in? He was in the Casino hospital at Le Touquet."

"So was Peter," Julia said.

"That's when Riley was promoted to captain," Nadine said.

Julia said, "I don't know."

"Nor do I," said Nadine.

"Do we have to go back over everything?" Julia said. "To be all right now?"

"Half left," said Nadine.

"What?"

"Joke of Riley's," Nadine said. "When people say is he All Right, he says Half Left."

"Oh goodness," said Julia. Then, "But he never mentioned carrying Peter back?"

"No," said Nadine.

They were both thinking, That was three years ago and we still don't know.

Julia said, "Do you know, I'd never seen Peter's scar. Three years. I was pregnant when he was wounded. I saw it for the first time the other day."

In a rush Nadine said: "Riley and I didn't kiss until last month."

Julia's eyes opened wide. She said, with a blink, putting her hand to the base of her throat, "Peter and I — only twice. Since 1915. Tom, and . . ." and here she made an open-handed gesture down towards her pregnant self.

They stared at each other for a moment, and then retreated, alarmed by the sudden scale and pace of intimacy.

"So what's the other favour?" Nadine asked.

Julia sat up, a little formal and polite, in preparation.

"Would you," she said, "could you, be here when the baby comes? I hope you don't mind my asking you — but I would like it — if you could?"

"But don't you want Rose?" Nadine asked. "Or your mother?"

Julia gave her a very straight look. "My mother is a monster," she said. "And Rose — Rose was in love with Peter. I don't think she is any more, but it's good that she is building a life away from here. Isn't it? Are you pleased for her? I really am."

"Good Lord, Julia," Nadine said. "You're rather taking to this telling people things business, aren't you?"

Julia stared at her quite steadily.

"I don't like who I was," Julia said. "I don't want to be how I was. I want to be different. Do you know about Arcadia and Utopia?"

"Ah — no," said Nadine. "Not in particular."

"Arcadia is the lost heaven of the past," Julia said. "Utopia is the possible heaven of the future. Peter talks about it. Anyway, I'm more for Utopia than for Arcadia. That's all. And I know I can't just stamp my foot and demand it. I have to work towards it step by step. So I'm going to. Anyway," she said, "come round the garden with me and talk to me about your mother. If you want — I mean — I know we're not really friends — we couldn't be really, could we? Before? Things can't grow, sometimes . . . but if you like. I mean, talking, and being friends. If you like. But I didn't even say

232

anything to you about your mother. I'm so sorry, Nadine. I know you haven't always been marvellous friends with her, but that makes it even harder to lose her, I should think. I'm sure I'll be completely miserable when my monster mother dies. But I'm not saying your mother was a monster! Oh dear — I mean we could talk about loving our mothers. Because I do understand about not liking a mother very much, so if you wanted, I am somebody you can admit that to . . . and if you don't want to talk about your mother, might we talk about Tom's birthday? We should have a party for him with cake and so forth . . ."

They stood, and walked down towards the walled garden.

Nadine was quietly amazed.

CHAPTER
SEVENTEEN

Locke Hill, December 1919

As the nights grew longer and the baby grew due, Peter stopped sleeping at all. Julia might need him.

He took to walking: round the garden in the icy night air, so dark, skies heavy and clouded, or bright and star-spattered; or the upstairs corridor at night, slowly and repetitively, to and fro. He checked and double-checked the locking of the doors: front, back, garden and French windows. He moved from one bed to another and lay down, briefly. The sofa in the study where he had been sleeping, he ignored. From time to time he lay down beside his wife and stared at her, in wonder. Then he would spend the main part of the night sitting on the velvet chair in her bedroom, watching her. If anything bad happened to his wife now, then the whole war, everyone's death, would have been in vain. She is to be protected.

He hardly drank; he didn't snarl, he didn't go off anywhere.

Sometimes he brought Tom in to sit with him during the days. He whispered to him, "This is Ithaca. This."

Tom, with a child's faithfulness, curled gratefully on his father's lap, very still so as not to disrupt the miraculous moment.

Riley and Nadine came for a weekend. Under instruction from Nadine, though without much hope himself, Riley was looking for Peter to see if he would come for a walk. He tracked him down and found him sitting with Tom. "He looks so innocent," Riley said, and Peter replied: "Oh, Riley, children know nothing of innocence. They don't even know it exists!"

And Riley said, laughing, "Lord, you're right. The moment they realise it exists is the moment they lose it."

"That's the point," Peter said.

He saw that this tiny scrap of conversation, for all its inherent sadness, gave Riley pleasure. "Can I show you something?" he said.

"Of course." Peter shuffled and Tom climbed down from his lap. "You're getting big," Riley said. "Can you drive a car yet?"

Tom looked up at him and said, "No!" in a tone of considerable delight.

Peter was fishing in the inside pocket of his jacket. He produced a small flat box, and proffered it: a string of pale golden pearls, on blue velvet.

"Will she like them?" he said. "Her birthday."

"I have no idea," said Riley. "Yes?"

They did go for a walk, hoping perhaps for the comfort of effort, the feeling of strength you get from striding through nature when she is being slightly uncomfortable. Riley felt it, and determined to find a way to walk more in London. Peter was just uncomfortable himself. He wanted to talk. He couldn't. Riley, so capable, seemed to be drifting away from him.

Peter was there in the chair, wide awake in the dark, when Julia's contractions started, long before dawn, two weeks early. She was turning under her blankets, giving the odd low moan in her restless sleep. He watched her fretful waking, and when she suddenly sat up with a cry, her satin eiderdown falling to the floor, he lit the lamp, took her hand, and gave her water from the nightstand. She was warm. He took the eiderdown and folded it on her chaise longue.

Soon after the late midwinter sunrise, in cool grey light, a dark figure in a dressing gown looked in, hair muddled. Nadine.

"It's started," Peter said to her, briefly.

She gasped softly, and whispered, "Have you rung for Dr Tayle?"

Peter looked at her impatiently and said, "Of course not. No need for a medic. No one's hurt."

Julia's face glowed in the dim light.

"How are you?" Nadine said to Julia.

"All right," said Julia. The women's voices were quiet like ghosts, as if pretending they were still asleep, that it had not, actually, after all, started. "Probably do need the doctor though." She was a little out of breath.

"Peter," said Nadine. "Would you call him? I can make Julia comfortable . . ."

Peter stared at her. For a moment he saw in her eyes the look — what was it? The woman who — ah — yes — when he'd been shot in the leg, and Riley had brought him in, shot: there'd been Riley, then the stretcher bearer with the eyebrows, then the nurse at the hospital at Étaples.

"Peter," Nadine said. "Go on."

He went. He rang the doctor at home and summoned him as if giving orders. He could see the light, such as it was, was coming up outside the drawing-room windows, and through the glass panel above the front door. Night patrol; dawn patrol. When he'd hung up the telephone he opened the front door and went outside into the cold cold air. There was a little frost; it crunched under his feet. He lit a cigarette and watched the smoke coil for a moment. Then he set off: down the drive, through the shrubs down to the spinney, across and round the back of the walled garden, into the paddock, up round the lawn and the outhouses, and back the other side of the house. All quiet. Only a rook or two yelled at him in their moaning way.

He re-entered the house and went to take off his hat — but he wasn't wearing a hat. In the distance, over the low hill to the east, he could see an orange glow, the odd flare. There was no sound — odd. But he could see it. It was all going on.

He wasn't sure where he was. Behind the lines, anyway — somewhere safe, for now. Nice billet. He'd better go and take a look around inside.

Just about then a medic turned up — out of uniform, sloppy — been off duty, presumably, but someone was yelling blue murder upstairs. The MO was taking his coat off and so forth, so Locke ran up ahead of him. If they'd set up some kind of hospital here someone should have given that poor blighter his morphine or something by now.

He burst in where the cries of pain were coming from — a room, a nice one, familiar. There were women in there — nurses — but the wounded soldier seemed to be a woman too, and yelling like he was still at the Casualty Clearing Station . . .

"All under control here?" he said, and one of the nurses — they weren't in uniform either, what is this place? — said yes it was, but could he bring some hot water, as if they thought he was an orderly — "Not entirely my role, old girl," he said, but he went and got it anyway because needs must, though it did seem odd, and then he went back in and sat down, suddenly, on a small velvet chair, and lit another cigarette.

When the MO came up, he tried to steer Peter from the room — took his arm in a chummy manner, and tried to sort of lift him and move him towards the door. It was very embarrassing. They all seemed to think he should be somewhere else, whereas he knew for a fact that he needed to be right here. Though he wasn't sure why. So he stood up, a head taller than the doc, and stepped up close to him and stared down at him, eye to eye, as if the doctor had committed treason. He said, "You do your bit, and I'll do mine. How about that? Everything's under control here." And he sat down again.

They didn't bother him again after that. He just sat there, and smoked. He wasn't going to leave the poor fellow alone. Is it Purefoy? Ainsworth? Who is it?

They were doing some kind of emergency surgery. Evidently it went well, though it seemed to take some time. After a while — a long time — *hours?* — the soldier's crying out and gasping and weeping stopped. The women stepped away from the bed. The angle of the doctor's shoulders changed — there was a kind of rolling back, an assumed uprightness. He turned, carrying something: It'll be whatever they just amputated. It was wrapped in cloth, and looked like some kind of small limb — half an arm, perhaps. Lower leg. Poor bastard.

Within one moment he realised that it was crying, and that the doctor was trying to give it to him. Its voice was new and limp and high.

"Don't be ridiculous," Peter said, standing and pushing past to where the soldier lay, grey-faced and silent on tangled sheets. She seemed to be asleep, or drugged. Just as well.

One of the nurses had taken the amputated limb, and was crooning to it.

What a bloody extraordinary —

"Get this place cleaned up," he ordered. "And what is that thing?"

"It's your daughter, Peter," said a calm voice, a woman — and for a moment he was on a lawn in Paris with a beautiful black-haired girl, drinking, outside the Tuileries — and then he snapped back.

He let his head fall back, way way back. Raised it again, and found Nadine staring him in the eye.

"Is everything all right?" he said. The word seemed hollow.

"Yes," she said. "You have a daughter."

"Splendid," he said. "I'm just going to . . ." and he smiled politely, and left the room.

He went into the garden again, for the cold clear air to clear his head. He walked round again, a fearsome concentration on him. What the hell was that? What was it?

Every now and again, over the past year or so, he heard things which logic told him could not be there: snaky streams of cool saxophone jazz, late at night, in the Kent countryside; distant explosions in the office. His dreams had seeped a little into reality. He had accepted that. It didn't seem too much. You wouldn't tell anyone about those things anyway. They'd have you at Craiglockhart within the week, signed and certified as a lunatic.

But this?

He knew perfectly well that nothing as bad, as strong, as interesting, as terrible as the war would ever happen to him again. In effect, nothing would ever happen to him again. His entire life from now on would constitute nothing but getting over the fucking war.

He went back into the house — all the doors were double-locked, and he had to go round again to the front — and drank coffee, and smoked. Then the memory leapt out at him like something quite new, or something totally unreliable.

Baby!

Julia. Baby. Daughter!

He washed his face, washed his hands, and went back upstairs. There they all were. The baby was clean now, washed and pink, making damp little scrawling noises. Its face was rather purple. Julia lay back, exhausted, wrung out, smiling and gentle. Supported by cushions, she was able to hold the little girl, and she was trying to feed it, holding it to her beautiful white breast, blue-veined, marbled. "Don't laugh," she was saying. "It's the best way — honestly! I've been reading about it. It's the best for the baby . . ."

Dr Tayle was saying that it would be better for her not to.

At that she sat bolt upright in bed, holding the baby close, and cried out to him that she would not be dictated to as to how to look after her child.

Peter stood in the doorway, a little crooked, smiling at her. She glanced up and smiled back. "Darling!" she cried out. "Look!"

"Well, well, all right," Dr Tayle was saying. "Good that you feel up to it. Jolly good. And as for you, young man," he said to Peter, "you need a proper night's sleep, and you're to come and see me. You look exhausted."

Peter murmured something pacifying, along the lines that he would, of course, he'd take the dressing-room divan . . .

But he didn't. He sat all day with Julia and the baby, talking, smiling, while Nadine and Mrs Joyce popped in and out, hurriedly seeing to the things they had thought they would have more time to see to. Harrington squares, towelling nappies, the crib. Burying the placenta. Someone had to call to see if the nursemaid could come sooner. Chicken broth and arrowroot biscuits for Julia. Cabbage leaves for when her milk came in properly. Lunch! They'd forgotten all about it. Mrs Joyce produced a lovely soup, and came up afterwards to congratulate Julia, standing in the doorway grinning like a fool, nodding and, "Well then. Well then. That's good. Lovely little thing."

Peter sat quietly and watched it all, accepting congratulations, being shaken by the hand and patted on the shoulder. Nadine telephoned Riley and Rose to tell them the news, and reminded Peter to ring Mrs Orris, which he did, aware of his healthy and normal disinclination to speak to her. But shouldn't a moment like this be an opportunity to be flooded with love and forgiveness? He was not flooded with love and forgiveness. He was very aware of everything, as if drapes had been lifted, and windows washed. It hurt his eyes.

After lunch, Tom came up to the bedroom, and patted the tiny bundle.

"Her name is Katherine," Julia said. "We'll call her Kitty." And Tom said, "But she's not a kitten, is she?" and everybody laughed.

That night Peter climbed into the marital bed alongside Julia, gentle alongside her body.

"Is this all right?" he said, and she smiled, and said, "You can be nursemaid — wake up when she wakes!" and he kissed her, very tenderly, wrapped in miracle.

242

In his dream, he was holding his wife, and they were
very happy.

He was woken by blood, blood everywhere, flowing,
warm blood.

The weight of her body was against him — German
boy, oh, poor German boy . . .

Burdett Lovall Jones Atkins Wester Green . . . STOP IT!

He pushed back the blankets and scrambled from
the bed. He didn't want his bloody dreams to disturb
her, to pollute this bed, even. He stood on the mat for
a second in the dark, thinking, it's so real. He could
make out the glass jug of water on the nightstand,
glinting a reflection of some scrap of light: he poured it
over his hands. Sticky.

He tore off his pyjama top.

It is real. I've believed such things to be real before, in
dreams, in confusion — but this is real.

Real blood is all over me.

He went back to her: he took her in his arms. She
was all blood, and blood swept through his mind.

That was not where the others found her. Twelve hours
after the last patrol he had made around his garden,
seeking out any dangers that might threaten his people,
he carried the corpse of his beloved out from his tent
and laid her like Patroclus before the walls of Troy, at
the foot of the lawn.

CHAPTER
EIGHTEEN

Locke Hill, December 1919

They were out there, both of them. Julia was lying down; Peter sitting by her on the grass, in the dim wintry dawn. It looked for all the world as if she were reposing, having a picnic among the icy bones of the garden, the stiff twigs and frozen seed heads. It looked romantic.

What on earth are they doing?

Nadine saw them from her bedroom window, 6.30 or so in the morning. What she saw didn't make sense. She went down the stairs, cold feet in slippers across the hall, through the drawing room where the French windows hung open, across the grey and green of the winter lawn. She saw the white nightdress clinging, streaked and drenched from waist to hem with scarlet. She saw Peter smoking. He was wearing his greatcoat, and Nadine thought, He could have taken that back and got the pound for it. Too late now, probably. His pale chest was bare inside the coat, and his face was smeared.

Nadine walked across, shivering, bent down, sat by him. She reached over and took Julia's hand. It was not stiff, not yet quite cold. Nadine held on to it, and put two fingers across its pale wrist. Nothing was happening. No movement, no small throb, no warm blood.

"Are you dead?" Nadine whispered. "Julia?" She couldn't take her eyes from her face: the white skin, the closed eyes, their deep sockets, the fine skin of the lids. No movement. The veins seemed empty. Nothing but bone within the white skin.

"Julia," she whispered, and with great and tender care she reached across and put the pad of her forefinger to Julia's white eyelid. The gentlest movement slid it up, as delicate as skin on the surface of warm milk. The eye beneath was the emptiest thing Nadine had seen since . . . well, Nadine had seen empty eyes before. Nothing there but the very slightest cloudiness.

"Julia," she called, softly.

Julia gazed at the grey sky, unmoved.

Nadine lifted her finger, and the eyelid drifted very slowly down over the clouded blue. It was so slow in its settling, drowsy almost — but inanimate. Passive. The skin, as thin as a mouse's ear, seemed already to be drying out. Closed, it lay settled like a snowdrift at the end of a storm.

Nadine held Julia's hand, and turned her head to look at Peter. He met her gaze, but dear God, his eyes are almost as empty as hers . . . She held her look steady, trying to hold him. He was grey-skinned and gaunt, and looked twenty years older.

"What happened?" she whispered.

He shook his head.

She reached over to him and took his hand: warm, alive, beautiful. "Peter," she said. "Oh, Peter. Oh my —

Peter," she said, and she moved over and sat very close beside him; he was terribly thin. She huddled next to his coat, bringing his arm to put it round her narrow shoulder. "Dear Peter," she said. "Poor Julia. Oh dear. Oh, God. Oh dear."

It was very quiet out there. Peaceful. The world seemed far away.

The baby! she thought suddenly. Tom —

She expected this thought to bring a flood of duty, fuss and horror down on her, but it didn't, not yet. There was instead a calm estrangement. Is it because we are outside? Is it like the war? Are we reverting to war reactions? No children in the war. Not little ones. No newborns in the trenches. The observation floated off again.

"Peter?" she whispered. "Will you come in now?" He shook his head again, a quick sudden jerk of fear and horror — so she kissed his forehead, bending over to him, and squeezed his hand, and whispered, "I'll be back in a moment . . ."

Mrs Joyce, at the French windows, had been staring for a good five minutes. As Nadine came running in from the frost in her nightclothes, Mrs Joyce stood mute. There was blood on the carpet all across the sitting room. They saw it now, a trail across the carpet, extra red petals on the Aubusson.

Nadine said: "No, wait." She didn't want even to close the French windows behind her. "No," she said. "I need to think . . ."

Mrs Joyce stood, muffled up in a pink quilted dressing gown. Her hands were up over her face.

"She's dead," said Nadine. "It's all blood."

Mrs Joyce gasped.

"Major Locke doesn't want to come in yet, so perhaps we should take him a cup of tea. It's awfully cold," Nadine said. "You should have one too. And yes, me too."

"I'll make tea, then," said Mrs Joyce.

"Let's just — yes," said Nadine. She thought, carefully, counting and remembering to breathe. "Tea." She looked up helplessly.

"The children . . .?" Mrs Joyce asked.

"Mrs Joyce, don't telephone the doctor yet. I'll look at the children. You put the kettle on," said Nadine.

"I'll be in the kitchen," said Mrs Joyce. "Millie is still asleep."

"I'm going upstairs," Nadine said.

Everything needed placing.

It all seemed to be a terrible inversion of the day before.

Max was barking in the back hall. "I'll feed him," said Mrs Joyce.

"Thank you." said Nadine. She took the stairs very slowly. Her heart was too big in her chest to allow room for breath. Her legs weren't working well.

Tom was asleep in the nursery; angelic.

In Julia's room the velvet chair was on its side, the water carafe spilt, the sheets dark with blood, and tangled.

What had happened?

The baby, in her crib at the bottom of Julia's bed, uttered the tiniest noise, like a creak, or a mouse, peaceful, scarcely human. Nadine went to her and picked her up, very gently. The baby didn't wake, just made her tiny noises as Nadine wrapped the shawl around her, and tucked her into the crook of her arm. Tiny eyelids fluttered. Unfocused blue eyes beneath.

Unfocused blue eyes.

Nadine carried the baby down to the kitchen.

"Could you ask Eliza to dress Tom," she said, "and then if you could take them all into town, please, Mrs Joyce. When he wakes." Her thoughts were in the wrong order. "Not now."

"I don't want to leave you alone here, Mrs Purefoy," Mrs Joyce said.

Nadine said, "I won't be alone. Peter's here."

Mrs Joyce put her head a little to one side, as if to say, "And?"

"I'm going to telephone my husband now," Nadine said. She could barely speak.

"Shall I take Kitty?" Mrs Joyce said, but Nadine shook her head. She let Mrs Joyce come and look at her, though, gazing and clucking. Mrs Joyce said, after a long moment, "I'll bring you your tea to the telephone."

Nadine said, "Thank you," and in this infinitesimally careful way the two women proceeded. No surprises. Nothing fast or unexpected.

Riley didn't usually pick up the phone. But it was so early. He'd know it was her. Answer — answer.

What came out was: "Julia's dead."

"Did he kill her?" Riley asked, straight off.

Her relief at his straightforwardness gave her voice: "No," she said, and her breath roared through her, followed so swiftly by the thought: How can I say that? I don't know. That's loyalty and affection talking, not an open mind. "I mean — no — her nightdress — the blood is all — um . . . There's no reason to think that . . ."

"Who have you rung? Who is there?"

"Mrs Joyce and I," she said. Breathe. "I rang you first. She's making tea." Breathe. "She'll take Tom out. I am just here. I have the baby."

"And has he said anything?"

"No. But Riley, darling — they're in the garden! He's smeared his face. With mud, I think. He's been crying." Her voice was rising with imminent tears. "I don't know why they're in the garden!"

"I'll take your father's car," Riley said. "Hold fast. Do nothing. Lock yourself in the house if you feel you should."

It was still so early. Grey milk sky. Them, out there. Us, in here. What has happened?

She went upstairs again, carrying Kitty. Tom was sleeping sound. She stilled the urge to wake him and hug him, came down again and sat on the sofa. Kitty was tiny in her arms. She found she was rocking gently: something automatic in her was responding to the scrap of life in her arms.

When Julia wanted to feed the baby. When she smiled at Peter across the bed, so tired and a little sheepish, so sweet — and he smiled back. That moment.

The fireplace was cold and ashy. She wanted to make a fire but she found she physically could not put the baby down. But without a fire the whole house is dead. Julia is dead.

Where's Millie? She'd need to tell Millie. She should go and do that. The girls shouldn't see this.

She dozed off. Woke again, totally confused, thinking, He didn't kill her. She was certain of that. But she had not been surprised when Riley asked, and Riley had not been surprised that she had not been surprised, and that said something, didn't it?

I had thought people had stopped dying. Even when Mama died. And now . . .

After a while Mrs Joyce put her head around the drawing-room door.

"Tom is up and dressed," she said. "He's had some bread and milk, and we're going into town now. Would you like me to take the baby?"

How are they meant to live through this? Peter? These children?

"Too cold," said Nadine. "Too soon. Too new." She was not yet a day old. She had not even fed yet.

"You've no fire!" Mrs Joyce said. She made it up, swiftly and effectively. "I told Millie to stay in the kitchen. I'll bring some goat's milk," she said. "It's best. Mrs Paine has a nanny goat. I won't tell anyone what for."

Nadine mouthed "thank you" to her.

"Tom likes the goat," Mrs Joyce said. And, "If I were you, I'd call Dr Tayle now."

"My husband is on his way," Nadine said. Mrs Joyce nodded, and went. Nadine did not want the doctor. If the doctor came it would be true.

Nadine couldn't even put the baby down for long enough to make a proper sling to carry her in. She just sort of pulled at the cloth, wedging it in order to be able to tie it. In the end the baby was slung across her chest like a peasant child, or a foreign one. She did not want her to be unheld even for a moment. She did not want her to be alone in any way.

The fire was burning now, stuttering and breathing. Nadine stood, pushing herself up, though the child weighed practically nothing. She went to the French windows. The tableau was unchanged: lawn, the slope, the two figures at the end. She could see the tiny orange dot of Peter's cigarette. It was impossible.

For a moment she wanted to rush out and check. Perhaps they *were* just having some astonishing picnic.

The hall clock had struck nine when the doorbell went. Not Mrs Joyce; she had only gone fifteen minutes before; she had a key and would come in round the back. Not Riley — too soon. Nadine felt a flash of panic. Who? What could she say? What if they called the police or tried to take Julia away? She thought about hiding until they left.

Shuffling outside, and a cough. Dr Tayle.

Of course he'd make a routine visit.

Well.

Nadine let him in. He said obvious things. "Ah, giving Mother a rest, are we? Good, good. And how is our new arrival?"

What am I to say to him? Her nursing experience was giving her nothing. Of all the things she had dealt with, that she had not been equipped to deal with . . . *but that was meant to be over there. Not here. And not now. It's meant to be over.*

The doctor was making for the stairs.

"Please wait in the study, doctor," she said, and her voice sounded all wrong to her. He went in, a little puzzled, but not very. Nadine went and sat at the kitchen table, and thought: *When is this going to be over?* Her tea stood cold on the hall table by the telephone.

Then she went back to the doctor, wishing he were a thousand miles away, and that he would leave them alone. But she couldn't ask him to go. She understood that. It would be wrong. Reality, of its nature, was going to intrude.

"Mrs Locke is in the garden," Nadine said. "Perhaps you'd follow me."

He followed her, huffing surprise and disapproval. "She should be in bed! She needs to rest! Far too cold to be up and about outside, really . . ."

But then he caught sight of the mad tableau at the end of the lawn, and the sight propelled him forward, urgency catching at him like a flurry of wind at a dead leaf.

Peter glanced up as the doctor blew towards him. Said nothing. Nadine, following, stood back.

Dr Tayle was saying, "What — what — we must get her indoors. We must get her indoors." He let out a little grunt as he collapsed to kneel at her side. "Come on, man. Help me. Take her feet."

Peter drew on his cigarette, and closed his eyes, and said, sadly, "Oh come, come, Doctor. This is a perfectly

252

good place to be dead . . ." And then the doctor leaned back, and turned grey, and seemed suddenly as much at a loss as everybody else.

Nadine thought: If she were in her bed, it would be completely different. It would be a tragedy but now it is a farce as well. Or . . . She went to where Peter sat, and knelt down with him, his bloodied coat, his cold white hands. She laid her fingers on his arm.

"What happened here?" Dr Tayle was saying. "Major Locke . . ."

Peter let him look at Julia. He stared at the doctor like a dog all the while he took her non-existent pulse, felt her dead belly, looked at the spread and amount of blood. He would not let him move her. Dr Tayle tried to persuade him, mentioned decency and things like that. There was a horrible moment when the doctor's sense of propriety seemed to overcome him, and he took hold of Julia's shoulders, and seemed to be about to try to pull her up and carry her himself, and Peter roared. Nadine feared some horrid foolish physical squabble was about to break out over the body, pulling and grabbing — but the doctor backed down. He took a vast handkerchief from his pocket and wiped his brow.

"Major Locke," he said, "you know it's a criminal offence to prevent burial of a body?"

And Peter smiled and replied mildly, "Well, she's only been a body for a few hours. Is there not a transition period, during which she can still be my wife, while I get used to the idea that she is my dead wife and once again the corpses rule?"

The doctor said, "You need to come inside too, Major Locke. It's too cold out here." But that was nothing new to Peter. He stared until the doctor finally turned away.

Inside, Dr Tayle wanted to see the bedroom. He followed the trail up, and down again. Nadine put a log on the fire in the drawing room, cuddled Kitty close, and left him to it. It occurred to her, as she tended the fire, that the wild smearings on Peter's face were not tears and mud, but ash.

Dr Tayle came back down. He seemed lost — to be looking around for a man to speak to, some other head-of-the-household figure. There being none, he spoke to Nadine. "I believe it was a haemorrhage. Alas. It's not unusual, God preserve us — women die like that all too often, God preserve us. There needs to be a proper examination and under the circumstances another doctor should — see her — but nothing could have been done. Nothing could be done. There's no sign of anything other than haemorrhage."

Relief?

"But it's not my decision."

Ah.

"And the police must be informed."

Silence. Her heart pounded strong and her thought was simple: No.

Why? Because you think he could have?

"But there's no wound?" she said quietly, after a moment.

"Would you have expected it?" he said, frowning, looking at her. He said it very carefully. Each of them

254

knew that the other was thinking: Peter was strange last night.

"Not at all," she said.

"I saw no sign of any wound," he said. "I was not able to give a full examination. But I do not expect to find any wound. If that is of any comfort. But procedures must be followed. And it is unusual that she should be in the garden."

She said thank you, not knowing what else to say.

"And you, Mrs Purefoy?"

"I'm all right," she lied. Half left. "Shocked." She let go a huge sigh. "Shocked." Do babies feel the shock of the person in whose arms they are? She's so near my heart . . .

"You were a nursing member of the VAD, weren't you?" Dr Tayle was saying. "Do you feel capable of dealing with the situation, for the moment?"

She did, and said so, but the doctor did not want to leave her. He seemed indecisive. Flustered, almost.

"Have a cup of tea, doctor," she said. "Or a glass of sherry. It's a terrible shock for everybody."

He nodded.

"It must be best to leave them for now," she said. "My husband is on his way, and will speak to Peter. Mrs Joyce has taken Tom into town." Was she repeating herself? "No upset is required," she said. "Please allow my husband to speak to the police later if he thinks it necessary. There is not the slightest danger." She fixed her eyes on the doctor's quite firmly. No lunatic specialists, no policemen, were going to barge in here to upset Tom and shred Peter even further, just because he needed to sit with his dead wife in the garden.

It had all been perfectly usual. Nothing. The only oddness was that they were outside. Had she gone there? Run there in panic? Had Peter taken her?

It's very odd. All of it. Oddest of all that a person could just die, of nothing. And that another person could take her poor body out into the garden and lie it there. And just sit. That too is so odd. Is that what happened?

"He was upset and he carried her body outside. That's all," she said. "Give him a little peace." And in that moment she knew that if he did not, she herself would explode in some way; would hit him or shriek or make some wild accusation that would see him removed — He has to leave now.

"Are we agreed?" she said.

The doctor left. He said he would be back in a few hours.

Peter sat out there, and time suspended. He accepted nothing, not even a cup of tea.

After standing at the French windows for half an hour, staring at him, Nadine had a realisation. Julia's words came back to her: none of us can do this on our own.

She went over to the sideboard and poured two large whiskies. She put on several coats, Kitty tucked inside the layers, then picked up the glasses, and just went and stood on the lawn beside them. She was not going to just look at them through glass in their odd tableau: Julia like Ophelia, her little white foot poking out on the icy grass, the lace on the clean nightgown they had given her after the birth spread at the cuff and throat like frozen sea surf on the lawn, and at the hem like rotting, frothing weed; Peter, sitting, in his heavy coat, smoking, one knee up, one leg out — with all the lazy elegance of a soldier on a war memorial, ruined, beautiful, his long hands fluttering in the dull winter light as he lit cigarette after cigarette. She belonged with them.

He was whispering.

She squatted down beside him to hear.

He looked up at her, his eyes so pale and so cold.

"I suppose I killed her?" he said, very very quietly.

"No!" she said. "No, you didn't!"

His eyes were disbelieving.

"Go away," he said.

"No," she said, gently.

She took up her previous post.

She was still standing there when she felt Riley's hand on her shoulder, his arm around her. "Go inside," he said. "You're cold. Make me a cup of tea, would you?"

"Have you told Rose?" Nadine whispered, as he unfroze her with his touch.

"She's on her way," he said. "Go on. Go in."

I love you.

Tom and Eliza were making up the fire in Peter's study (view to the north, other side of the house from the lawn). He handed her logs, with due awareness of his own importance.

"I put the dog in the shed," Mrs Joyce said, and indeed now she mentioned it, Nadine recalled hearing some low howling.

"Riley is here," said Nadine. "So I am going to make some tea. Tom, will you come and help me?"

The baby was still tucked into her shawl. Nadine wanted to know where everybody was. That they were all right. Though they weren't.

Mrs Joyce looked questioning.

"Riley is here," Nadine said again, as if that answered all questions. Then, "Where is Millie?"

"Upstairs," said Mrs Joyce. "I told her Mrs Locke has — had an accident. She's upset. Best thing. Out of the way."

"And the maternity nurse? Was she not asked for for today?"

"Yes, Mrs Purefoy, we expected her this morning."

"Can you speak to her? I will, if you wish."

"Between us we'll do, Mrs Purefoy."

"We will. Thank you, Mrs Joyce. Oh! Harker?"

"He wanted to chop some more firewood," Mrs Joyce said. Their eyes met and for the first time Nadine felt that she would cry.

She went and put the kettle on the hob. There were the arrowroot biscuits. She took one from the tin with the picture of the rocking horse on the lid, and gave it to Tom, and her eyes settled on him.

Do I wait for Peter to tell this boy his mother is dead? Will Peter be able to?

Do I have to tell him?

Do I tell him now?

258

Riley had told her a phrase of Peter's, about children knowing nothing of innocence; of how you only recognise it when it leaves you. Eliza had put Tom in his sailor suit, and he looked absurdly sweet.

Is he going to hate his sister now? Will he see her as his mother's murderer? Or his father? If . . . is there any way out of this?

She was suddenly lividly angry. It had been going to be all right! They had been smiling at each other! Things had been better! There's this beautiful baby, oh, Christ . . .

She said to Tom, "Hop up on the table, sweetheart," and he did.

Rose could tell him!

She sat next to him.

"We're not normally allowed to sit on the table," he said.

"Today's not a normal day," she said.

"Why?" he asked.

"It's a very sad day."

"Why?"

She put her arm round him and realised she was holding him too tight.

"Why?"

Damn it, Rose can do it. Rose is practically his aunt.

"Is it Mummy and Daddy in the garden?" he said, and for a moment it seemed her stomach slipped out of her body . . . This is where I slaughter innocence, she thought. This is where I watch it die.

All right, then . . .

She said, "Did you see them?"

"I'm going to see them again," he said, and slipped off the table and started towards the drawing room.

"No!" she shouted, but then — but then.

Do we still do what is expected? What has always been done? Or what it might be better to do?

Do we look back, or forwards?

"I'll come with you," she said, and she took his hand.

They walked out together across the lawn, damp now and dull. Riley was sitting with Peter, both smoking. Riley was talking softly. When Tom dropped Nadine's hand and trotted straight over to his mother, the men looked up, paralysed as it were, with surprise.

"Tom!" Riley exclaimed, and looked round, and Nadine was there, and Peter looked up and round, with one of his beautiful beatific smiles, his blue eyes light.

"Poor Mummy," Tom said. "She's got blood."

"Tom," Nadine said gently. "Darling," and she put herself close to him, and touched his arm.

"Nadine!" Riley said, and she made an arm-lifting what-could-I-do gesture, a gesture of I'm not in charge, I can't prevent, I can't control . . .

She knelt by Tom.

"Is she asleep?" he said, and Nadine took her breath, and looking at Peter, and then back to Tom, she said gently, "Darling, your mummy is dead." Peter blinked softly at her, his eyes kind.

"Like the bullfinch?" Tom said.

"Yes."

"No more flying?"

260

"No more nothing, darling. Her soul has gone to heaven."

"Where's heaven?"

"Somewhere we can't go, until we die."

"But I want her."

"Sit with her now," said Nadine. "With your father. Sit with her and say goodbye. Then in a few days we will have a special sad party for her body, to say goodbye to it, and then her soul will go to heaven."

"I don't want it to," Tom said, dry-eyed.

"We have no choice, darling."

Silence.

"We have no choice," she said again.

Before anyone could say anything more, Tom burst through the vanguard of his father and Riley, jostling their coats and their knees and their adulthood, and flung himself to the ground. He patted his mother's hair, kissed her cheek. "She's too cold!" he said, angrily — and at just that moment, a noise behind them — it was Rose, a Gladstone bag dropped on the terrace, rushing down the lawn.

Tom jumped up. "Rose!" he shouted. "They're going to put Mummy in a hole in the ground like the bullfinch and I don't want them to!" — and Rose was weeping and weeping, floods of tears.

Tom stared at the ground. All around him were the dead matches of the men's cigarettes.

"For God's sake, get him out of here!" Peter shouted. "Everybody just go away!"

CHAPTER
NINETEEN

Locke Hill and London, December 1919
There followed a period of confusion which afterwards
none of them could recall clearly. Rose's furious
determination to get Peter inside. Riley's quiet
conviction that he should be left alone. Nadine's desire
to take Tom and Kitty away. Tom's equally profound
desire to lie down by his mother and make her wake up.
Kitty waking, finally, and mewling like a bird inside
Nadine's shawl. Peter sitting, smoking, ignoring it all,
looking at Julia. Julia lying there.

Rose finally said everyone should go away and leave
her with her cousin. Riley picked Tom up, kicking and
yelling, and held him very close and tight and safe as he
carried him up the lawn. Very soon Tom subsided, and
Riley put his hand over the back of the boy's head as he
sobbed against his shoulder. Nadine walked beside
them, her hand gently on her husband's back.

So then Rose could go and sit across from Peter, and
call his name gently.

He looked up, his eyelids drooping, exhausted.

She had been going to speak softly to him, to be kind
and strong and sensible, but she didn't. She just wept.
How utterly she had failed them both. How utterly. After

262

all. The moment I leave. As soon as I made the break — and look at us now.

After a while he held his hand out to her, and she took it.

"I killed her," he said.

"I don't think you did," she said.

"I thought I did," he said.

"I don't think so."

They were too far apart to hold hands for long, arms stretched out. They let them drop.

"Go on in," he said, and she looked at him, and she went.

She spent the next fifteen minutes in her room, howling: for him, for Julia, for everything. Among the things she howled for was the fact that now she could never leave him. She would now stay here for ever, looking after him and the children. The future she had imagined was exploding in her face. She didn't berate herself for having dared to imagine a different life, a free life — her *own* life. She just recognised the truth. The woman is needed by the man — the sick man — and the children. Goodbye, medicine. Goodbye, independence.

Then she went back out to sit with him some more.

The maternity nurse, Harding, had arrived, young, cheerful, appalled, calm. Eliza had said she was very sorry but . . . and run away. Millie was in the kitchen, crying. Harker had retreated to his room, and came out only to speak occasionally in a low voice with Mrs Joyce. Peter was still in the garden. Riley was talking to someone on the telephone. Rose had come in again and kept swallowing and walking round in circles, her chest heaving quick and shallow. Nadine wished she would sit down, or go and rest. For herself, Nadine just wanted to lie down with Riley and the baby and weep.

He came and sat with her on the sofa, and for a moment it wasn't clear which of them was going to subside against the other. In the end they both did, and sat in silence together, hands entwined, shoulder to shoulder, heads together in the beautiful closeness.

"What did you say to him?" she asked. "Outside?"

"Nothing," Riley said. "I can't say anything to him. He was talking about Odysseus and Penelope and — Tiresias? I couldn't follow him."

"Tiresias was the prophet, I think, who Odysseus went to find in the Underworld. When he met all the dead heroes from the battle of Troy."

"Oh, Christ."

Mrs Joyce called him. He was wanted on the telephone again.

Nadine was feeding Kitty, staring into her great eyes. Poor Julia, she thought, not to have the joy of this. Poor poor Julia.

And were my mother and I ever like this? Did I gaze at her with great big eyes?

She sat, baby in the crook of her arm, the bottle in her hand, being stared at across the room by Tom. His eyes were narrow under his little cap, his small tie like a noose around his neck.

264

"Come here to me," she said, but Tom did not slip to her side with the same ease as he used to the winter before.

"Come on," she said. "It's only me." He came, and sat stiff and thin beside her. Nadine could see his eyes closing over, as if layers of ice had solidified between him and the world.

Riley was out with Peter again. They didn't seem to be talking.

At dusk, Peter was alone out there. He stood up and stretched his long arms and let out a firm deep breath. He raised his head and shouted: "Come on, then!"

Riley had been waiting for it. He went out — and found Harker coming from the shed, dragging behind him a stretcher knocked up from a tarpaulin and two poles. Riley looked down at it.

"The Boers, sir," Harker said sadly. "Spion Kop." Riley glanced at him, and nodded.

They lifted her on to the stretcher as best they could. Cold and rigor mortis prevented much movement, but Peter had laid her out beautifully earlier. They spread her nightdress clumsily and covered her with a blanket, and carried her upstairs to the bedroom.

The bloody mattress was already out in the yard. ("Don't burn it till everyone's gone away somewhere," Riley had said, so it stood propped against dock leaves and nettles behind the wall.) Millie and Mrs Joyce had brought the guest-room mattress in and made the bed up: just two white sheets. Mrs Joyce had gone to Rose's room with her mouth very pale and small, and asked, Was she to put on the good sheets, or which?

"The good ones," Rose had said.

Riley and Harker lifted Julia onto the bed. The blanket had slipped from her face. They looked down and were embarrassed to see her in so intimate a state.

The women took over.

Riley went out, thinking of corpses tipped into ditches, lost in mud, bursting from the sides of trenches, never seen again. How were they, out there, the dead boys? Would any of their poor bodies ever come home and be honoured? That bloody poem — *some corner of a foreign field that is for ever England* . . .

Poor Julia. Poor everyone.

Oh God, where's Peter?

He was in the kitchen, drinking tea with Mrs Joyce. At about six, two policemen came. Dr Tayle had spoken to them. They came into the drawing room, didn't sit down, and told Peter, Rose, Riley and Nadine that they had come to say, in person, that there would need to be an autopsy. They were embarrassed.

"Is there an idea," Riley said, "that a crime has been committed?"

They said no, no. They said they could say nothing till after the autopsy. They left.

"Well," said Peter.

"It doesn't matter," Nadine said again.

"What doesn't matter?" said Peter. "It was the police, wasn't it?"

"It just means they have to look at her," Nadine said.

"I know what it means," said Peter. "To look at yourself."

"As long as it doesn't show any —" Riley began, and Nadine broke in.

"It won't," she said. "Hush. It won't."

Peter was looking at them, one by one.

"There's no need to fear," Nadine said. "We're all just scared . . ." But Peter said, "Will they chop her up?" and that silenced everyone.

Then, "You didn't kill her!" Rose burst out. "There's no wound."

The men stared at her.

"We looked —" Rose said. "I mean — we didn't *look*. But we would have seen."

Peter's face was impassive. "Are you sure?" he said.

"There is no wound," Nadine said. "We would have seen. The autopsy will show that she haemorrhaged."

"You didn't kill her," Rose said. "Nobody will think you killed her. She wasn't killed."

Peter said nothing. The three others stood, hoping, each of them, that they had not betrayed their fear to him.

"Do you need to see?" Rose said quietly. "For proof? So you really know?"

Peter raised his eyes to hers. "No," he said, courteously. "Thank you."

They all went to bed early and lay sleepless — or so they all assumed. In fact, Peter sat in his study all night, and got through a bottle and a half of whisky; Tom slept soundly, Rose read, Mrs Joyce prayed, Kitty mewed quietly in Nadine's arms while Nadine dozed, and Riley sat outside Peter's door on the floor till about four, when he went upstairs, removed Kitty to her cot, and made love to Nadine with the full force of a man who is consciously and thoroughly glad that he is not dead.

Riley had to go back to London. The proofs of three new pamphlets had to be passed today or held up till New Year. He'd come back to Locke Hill the following day. First he went with Peter and Rose to the undertakers; then they dropped him off at the station. All was to-ing and fro-ing. What he really wanted was to stand beside Peter, to be there beside him, all the time, forever. However things were between a man and his wife, to lose the woman — to lose the woman — and now Peter was so losable, again . . .

Suddenly on the train he had a vision: himself coming home to Nadine, with the black eye and the bashed-in cheek. How cavalier he had been, racing off into the world of his own demons as if nobody else existed. Reaching back in time to that perverted familarity, that rush of thrill and violence. That stupid little show of masculinity which was actually as weak and foolish and cruel as anything he had ever done. How that recklessness had hurt her.

That little word, "hurt", which catches in your throat.

If she lost me . . .

I am important to her.

She loves me.

Peter, coming back into the house, thinking, What is it now? This house? This home? found Nadine standing in the hall, with Tom holding her skirt and Kitty a white woollen bundle in her arms. He stopped dead and stared.

"Bit of a pickle," he said.

"Yes," said Nadine.

"I don't know what to do."

"Of course not," said Nadine. "No one does. It's too cruel."

Peter blinked, and said, "Yes, it is rather, isn't it? I suppose we could have a cup of tea." Mrs Joyce was crying in her room, so Peter put the kettle on the range and made the tea himself. He brought it in to where Nadine and the children had settled back on the sofa.

"That sofa!" he exclaimed. "What it's seen . . ." He walked over to the fire, back to the sofa, then remembered the tea, and poured it. "Thank you for taking care of everything."

"I'm glad I was here to," she said.

Peter looked at the baby, and frowned.

"Can I see her?" he said.

He could tell Nadine was pleased that he wanted to. She made to give her to him, but that was too much — he almost stumbled back, his fear and bewilderment visible, no doubt. Does she know I can't abide human contact? Does she wonder how this creature even got conceived?

He looked down at the baby in Nadine's arms.

"Sweet," he said, rather hopelessly. How extraordinarily soft she is. She's like a petal. The light would shine through

269

her, like through ripe gooseberries, or a mouse's ears. Somewhere in his battered heart a spark of love blinked. "Is she all right?" he asked.

"She is," said Nadine. "She was underweight, but she's feeding well."

Peter startled, and Nadine stopped.

"What am I meant to do now?" he asked, like a small boy. He was thinking, Surely this is where women sweep in and take care of everything . . .

Nadine said, "They need to be loved and looked after."

And Peter said, tentatively, "Yes — but how? I don't — can Tom go to school?"

"He's three," said Nadine.

"Is that too young?"

"Yes," Nadine said. "And he doesn't need school. He needs a mother."

"And the baby too," said Peter.

"Kitty," said Nadine.

"Kitty," he agreed, humbly.

She had one hand laid still on Tom's head, and looked like some Victorian painting, *The Soldier's Departure*, or *The Widow's Fate*, or something. But she looked happy, and competent. Peter glanced at the floor.

"I don't suppose," he started. What don't you suppose? Whatever it was, Nadine understood.

"I mean — Rose —"

"Rose is busy," Nadine said quickly.

"Yes."

"I'll stay here for a bit," she said. "But my father — and Riley . . ."

"No, of course."

"But they could come up to London with me," she said. "Till we can sort things out. Papa won't mind. It will help to take our minds off things."

"Thank you," he said. "That's very good. Just for now."

Peter chose to appear relieved, but in truth they had both known it was going to happen that way, since the moment Julia died. How else could it be?

"Mrs Joyce could come . . .?"

"Oh no, you'll need her — but Harding . . .?"

"Of course. And — will Riley . . . um . . .?" he asked. "Just till we sort things out?"

As he echoed her phrase, he noticed how empty it was. When or how on earth would anybody sort things out? Let alone me.

"He'll be happy to have them," she said. "And he'd do anything for you, Peter."

"I should speak to him," he said, as the vast possibilities of debt and friendship and obligation spread out for a moment in front of him, before the clouds of shame and necessity blocked off that view again.

As he left he turned and said, "Dread grief is upon me. It is, you know."

Rose, coming in from the kitchen, saw that something had been settled. She raised her eyebrows to Nadine, who nodded.

"What?" Rose said.

"The children are going to come and stay with us."

Rose frowned. "But," she said.

"Don't you dare," Nadine said.

"What?"

"Don't you even dare," Nadine said again. "Don't you even *dare* think about coming back here and looking after him. You are going to live your life, Rose. You just are."

"You'd take the children on?" Rose said. "Have you thought it through?"

"It needs no thought," Nadine said. "There's no 'would'. It's how it is."

"Does Riley know?" Rose asked.

Nadine just looked her. Her face read clearly: As if Riley would not instantly recognise the situation and do the right thing!

"And what about Peter?" Rose said, tightly.

"If it comes to it, Peter can come and live with us," Nadine said. "Or — or something — but you are *not* giving up medicine."

"Oh." Rose drew herself up a little. Is it that simple?

"You're not," Nadine repeated. "Stop taking on responsibilities which aren't yours. It's your life."

Rose paused, looking at Nadine. She considered saying "but" again. But she didn't want to say but.

As she went over to the fire, she punched Nadine very lightly on the shoulder.

CHAPTER
TWENTY

Locke Hill, December 1919
A few days later, Julia's body taken, the funeral fixed for the following week, time hanging like a noose, Rose and Nadine dragged an old cot down from the attic, to paint trills of flowers on it for Kitty. It seemed wrong, but then why? "There's a birth here as well as a death," Rose said. And they had both laughed a little hysterically.

Nadine said, "It does all still seem out of our hands. I feel so — buffeted. I can't remember when I last made a decision, an active decision, rather than just responding to what jumps out at me demanding a response."

"That's normal, though, isn't it?" said Rose.

"I don't know. I was trying to think about it. First you're a child and you're meant to do what you're told, then there was the war, and you did what was required, and then Riley's wound, then peace and then — my mother, and coming back home and now Julia, and Tom and Kitty . . . Of course, it's not really like during the war. But something is — I'm sort of helpless before fate. There's no calm moment to say, all right, I would like to go this way, and do this. Like you've done."

"What I'm doing wasn't entirely done as a result of calm reflection," said Rose drily.

"But you made a decision," Nadine said. "You are doing what you've chosen."

"So are you. You chose Tom and Kitty."

"That was emotional," Nadine said. "Nothing rational in it at all."

"And you're going to art school."

"Well, that now does seem irrational . . ." Nadine said, to which Rose replied: "Ha! Now, don't *you* dare. If I may quote."

There was a short silence.

"Oh, we'll work it out," Nadine said. "And aren't we lucky? That what we want to do and what we should do match up. And that we *can* do them." Another pause. "So far," she added. "But it's as I said: out of our hands. Future buffeting is bound to occur. I used to just accept it. But now I know that I want to do something. Something proper and real in the outside world. There are women doing things all around us. Lady Astor, in Parliament! Virginia Woolf and Rebecca West and all the ladies on committees. You! It should all be possible now. I seem to have stopped being so terribly passive."

"We all have," said Rose. "Even Julia. She seemed the most accepting person of all — but then she just upped and chucked it all in and ran off."

Nadine glanced up.

"What do you mean?"

"When Julia did a bunk," said Rose. "Over the summer. She went off in May, and wasn't seen till August."

Nadine's mind flickered. "Oh! She mentioned she'd gone away somewhere, but — oh I wish I'd paid more attention! You just remember the daftest things, and nothing that really matters. Because you just don't think someone's going to suddenly die! Even though, really, we ought to know by now that they do. War or no war."

"Yes," said Rose.

Nadine painted four more little leaves.

"Rose!" she cried. "Is Kitty Peter's?"

"He believes so. And she looks awfully like him."

Their eyes were wide.

"She went to Biarritz," Rose said.

"*How* long for?"

"Nearly four months."

"Gosh," said Nadine. "I thought it was two weeks or something — she never said. Biarritz! Rose — would you like to travel?"

"Sometimes."

"I have cousins in Rome," she said. "We're corresponding and I'm going to go and see them. One of these days."

"You liked Italy, didn't you."

"I loved it," she said. "I felt like a person in a novel. Wildly adventurous — I suppose that's what Julia wanted, as well. Were you *very* angry with her?"

"Furious," said Rose. "For dumping Peter like that, for deserting Tom. I said she was decisive — certainly she was very good at making bad decisions. But I don't know if she was quite sane. And I'm not sure people can be expected to be what they're not."

"But if what we are is not good, aren't we expected to *try*, at least?"

"I think Julia tried very hard," Rose said. "And everything was swept out from under her. Peter has been very difficult, you know. Much worse after you and Riley left. He stopped bothering to maintain appearances. Because of Riley, I think. While Riley was here he didn't want to disintegrate in front of him."

Nadine gave a little shiver. Yes, Riley obliges you to keep things together. He's a sort of — not a *memento mori*, but a *memento vitae*. Memento fortunae. "Do *you* think Peter has some kind of shell shock?" she asked.

"I think it's grief and shame, and the deluded notion that drink can help you through."

"But," and here Nadine rocked back on her heels, her paintbrush pointing skyward like a *flambeau*. "Is there *anything* we can do for him? Now, I mean?"

Rose laughed. "Look after his children," she said. "For goodness sake, look at what you're doing!"

"That's for them. I mean for him. Medically, or psychologically, or — you know. Him thinking he had killed her. The way ... he didn't know. It seemed almost as if he wanted to have done it."

"That's a black thought, Nadine."

"And one that you've had too?"

"No," Rose said after a moment. "Though I have wondered why he is so intent on punishing himself, when he has been punished so much already. I assume it's just the usual thing. Like so many of them, he was put in some impossible position, and blames himself for not having been able to put it right."

"Is it really that simple?"

"Oh no!" said Rose. "It's far more complicated!" — and they almost laughed.

276

Nadine covered the moment by looking down at her palette. The lovely dark crimson, for tiny roses. Dear Rose. Loyal friend, clever, ambitious, funny, flawed.

"Rose!" she cried suddenly, as an idea struck her.

"What?"

"Is that why you're studying medicine? To heal Peter?"

"Peter will be ancient by the time I qualify. Specially if I were to be an alienist. No — it's — no. I'll just be a GP. I think."

"You might get terribly interested in something and want to delve into it and discover cures. I could see you doing that."

"But curing the human mind? How would we do that? When over and over again it starts more wars? How can we cure it of that?"

Nadine dipped her brush into the jar of turps. Carefully, she cleaned it.

"Oh, Lord, Rose," she said. "You're right, of course — but thinking like that just makes us all mad." (Neither woman used the term lightly. They knew what it was.) "I was just thinking of individual minds, like Peter's. It seems so unfair." Her own mind was racing around. She wanted to paint a picture for her friend: maybe those dark roses at the corner of the glasshouse, against the red brick wall — come the summer, she'd go down and paint them, thorns and all. Maybe Peter would be — she stopped her thoughts. No good looking ahead. It's almost as pointless as looking back — with which thought, of course, she found herself looking back, helpless not to.

"What was he like before the war, Rose?" she asked.

277

And at that Rose blinked, before being able to say, "Oh, Nadine — Nadine, what was anything like before the war? You tell me. Was everything better? *Was* it a heaven of long sunlit afternoons and dappled meadows and honey still for tea? Or was it just that we were young? *You* were — you and Riley, you're young *now*, look at you — and at what you've done . . . What was Peter like? He was clever, thoughtful, gentle. He was everything he still is, but he was not bitter, and he didn't lash out. He's brought the war home with him, I think. Sometimes, the look on his face, you'd think *you* were the Hun. I don't know how long it will take him to realise that it's over, it's done, he *needn't* be haunted by it any more. His mind has fallen into a pattern. He reacts as if he were still at war . . ."

"Have you told him that?"

"I think he knows," Rose said. "And can't do anything about it. But now — I don't know. We must stick together." Then she said: "I'm rather proud of you, Nadine. I suppose it's rather ridiculous how we all sort of thought that after the war was over people would stop dying, and we could — tidy ourselves up again. And now look."

"Yes," said Nadine. Another little red rose appeared under her paintbrush, followed by a crimson tip on a bud. Then she said, "Poor, poor Julia! Things will get better, the children will grow and be all right, more or less, and she will never know the joys they will bring —" And Nadine burst into tears, her head falling forward suddenly like a heavy flower, the paintbrush laid down on the newspaper.

278

"Oh, Nadine," Rose said, and so for a few minutes they sat there.

"But Peter seems to be holding together, doesn't he?" Nadine said, hopefully. "For the moment?"

"In a rather bleak way," said Rose. "He's still just reading all the time. He's not talking to anyone. Has he talked to Riley? Or you? And he's not eating again. I can be there for the holidays but in January I must go back to London — and — Nadine — we do need to talk about Christmas . . ."

"Can we do it in London?" Nadine said. "You and Peter come, of course — oh you know. We could have it small and quiet. I know Mrs Joyce would like to go to her sister."

"Yes," said Rose. "I don't know if Peter will want to come, but I'll do my best."

"Rose," said Nadine, in a changed tone of voice that made Rose wary.

"What?"

"You wouldn't — after a decent interval — but — oh dear . . ." She's not even buried yet . . .

"I'm not going to marry Peter," Rose said.

"But you were attached to him, before, weren't you? You don't mind my saying? Julia thought you were —"

"Did she! Well, perhaps I was, back in the days of innocence, before any of us knew the first thing about anything. Before-the-war! But I'm not now."

"Well, I don't blame you. You see those marriages of — a kind of combination of pity and affection and convenience — they may be practical and so forth, but I don't think it would do, really."

Rose smiled at her. "It wouldn't for me," she said. "For one thing, I'd have to give up medicine, and that I will not ever do. Certainly not for a man. And you and Riley," she said. "Are you happy? I mean in general . . ."

"We are," Nadine said, feeling again the amazement that such a thing could be true. "But — I know it looks as if Peter is the suffering one and Riley is fine — but it's not like that."

"His face is all right?" Rose asked.

Nadine wondered whether to tell her, and in the wondering found herself already saying it.

"It's not his face. It's inside his head. Like Peter. The darkness is still there. This summer he — well, I suppose you'd say he got himself attacked. He wouldn't tell me what it was for weeks. I was very frightened."

"You!" said Rose, but Nadine gave her a look, and they both silently acknowledged the idiocy of the view that because somebody gets on with stuff it means they aren't troubled by it.

"He'd gone up north to see Mrs Ainsworth, and he got caught up in a demonstration — a strike. He said he did it on purpose — one of those other senses of purpose one gets, you know — not the sensible, reasonable sense of purpose, but the compulsion. He said it was all the men. Being a man in a mob of men, and it being like battle. All the emotions. Whatever it is that gets into their blood."

"Was he all right?"

"Black eye, big cut on his cheek. But when you think about the surgery, Rose, and the delicacy, and the risk — but I can't tell him not to be a man, not to do man

280

things, and not to suffer what he suffers, just because I'm afraid for him. Of course I was furious. I am furious! I don't in the least understand — but I know those things exist . . ."

"Will he do it again?"

"I don't think of it in terms of him doing it. It's more that it happened. He was overwhelmed. It's not as if he has no self-control — but you know, I rely on him so much. It's so frightening and infuriating when the strong one shows a weakness."

"We all just have to take it in turns," said Rose drily. "Is he happy to have the children?"

"Oh yes. Though we'll want a couple of our own as well, in due course. He's —"

"He's a man!" cried Rose. "Of course you will."

Nadine smiled, and for a moment she had to bite her own lip because she loved him so so much.

"I hope everything goes tremendously well for you now," Rose said.

Nadine blinked, touched. "You too," she said. "It's about time." And each felt the friendship ratchet one little cog higher.

After Rose left, Nadine reconsidered the question of happiness. How wonderful it had been to be around birth instead of death. How lucky that they were there to help with the children.

She shook her head, slightly aware that nobody had thought it through at all.

Be grateful. Be grateful, every day, that love is strong, and nothing worse is happening.

CHAPTER
TWENTY-ONE

London, December 1919
Riley sat alone in the Leinster Arms. He was angry, and he was ashamed of his anger. How can you possibly be angry about this? What is wrong with you? And at such a time?

He had got his wife, for this miserable, poisoned Christmas, a book of photographs of the sculptures of the Vatican museums. A good present; thoughtful, very much appreciated. Then Sir Alfred took him aside, and confided that he was intending to give her the money to pay for art school, and all the resentment loomed up again. How could he mind? Only a pig would mind. And it was so delicate of Sir Alfred to think to ask . . .

But he minded. *Of course* building a life and a business takes time; *of course* he had not, so far, been able to provide his wife with much. That he accepted. But here, everything was already provided — and by those who had everything. It's easy to take when you're a boy, you don't think of it. A dry shirt, an opportunity, a little job, an education, a new life as a different kind of boy . . . And then as a soldier, everything is provided. And then as a wounded man, they do their best to heal you and mend you. And then, after the war, what do you need? A release! A change — here, have the honeymoon, the marvellous trip.

A house? Sir Robert not only has one, but he actively needs you to come and live in it. Money? Well, there's nothing so urgent about that, we have enough, and a man in your condition, Riley, well, you take your time . . .

And of course I can't afford to pay her fees . . .

Oh, it's not about Christmas and the bloody art-school fees. It's about the children.

Of course, *of course*, there was no question but that Tom and Kitty would come and live with them, for as long as it takes, whatever "it" was. For as long as poor bloody Julia remains dead? For as long as Peter remains in his own world? For as long as Nadine has a heart in her body and arms to hold these poor infants?

But I want to give her children. And we'd agreed, not yet . . .

His father-in-law provided the home and investment in his company. His mentor was to pay his wife's fees. And now, in a final indignity, his former CO had provided the children.

What kind of a man lives like that?

But what kind of a man could refuse any of these things, individually? No one.

Ha. Look at me! Angry Englishman sitting alone in a pub, staring at his beer.

He had in front of him some Christmas cards, bought by Nadine, signed by both of them. He stood, stuffed them in his pocket, wrapped his scarf round his face and headed up towards the station.

His dad opened the door, and stood aside to let him in, a warm smile. "They're still at church," he said, and Riley knew that John knew that that was why Riley had chosen this time to visit.

"I'll just leave the cards, then," Riley said, but his father shot him a look and held out his hand for Riley's coat. Then he sat him down, a hand on each shoulder, and put the kettle on.

Riley put the envelopes on the table and shrugged. "Christmas cards," he said. "And, Nadine invites everyone to tea. New Year's Day."

"Good," said John. "We'll all come. Mum told me they'd run into each other. You staying for lunch?"

Riley shook his head. The meat smelt delicious. Roast beef, roast potatoes. *Well.*

John handed him three biscuits with his tea. "So?" he said.

"What?"

"You must be able to think of something to say to me," John said.

Riley glanced at him, and got his straw out. "My CO's wife died in childbirth," he said. "The funeral is on the twenty-ninth. His children are living with us."

John stirred his tea.

"And how's that?"

"It's wonderful," said Riley. "Tom, the boy, is — he's very pale and quiet. We knew him before when we were living there. He's had a tough time, and we're going to warm him up. The baby is just a baby. Very sweet. *Very sweet*, actually."

"Nadine's dad like 'em?"

"I think he does. He chucks Kitty under the chin and calls her 'little chap'."

"And will you have your own?" John said.

284

"I think we will, yes," Riley said. "Nadine's modern —" he blurted. "She has a little rubber thing and you have your children when you want them."

"Very sensible," said John, and smiled. "And how's business?"

"We're proud producers of eleven little pamphlets so far."

John said, "So you've a wife, and a father-in-law to look after, and children, and a business. And plans."

"Yes," said Riley.

"Good lad," said John. "Not bad for twenty-three years old."

Riley dipped his head, and grinned. You don't grow out of wanting to please your parents.

"I've had a lot of help," he said. As he said it he could feel his face harden.

John said, mildly, "And you think you don't like that."

Riley looked up and burst out: "No, I bloody don't! It's pity!"

"Is it," said John.

"Yes."

"Or is it wanting to make up to you for what you did? Thanking you? Not wanting to stand around like a bunch of lemons leaving you to it when you lost four years, half your face, and you can't talk proper?"

Riley said nothing.

"Don't be a berk, Riley. Only a right bastard wouldn't want to help you. And your Nadine and her family ain't right bastards. Surprise surprise."

Riley said nothing.

"You're doing well," John said. "Don't cock it up. Don't you read the papers? You won the war, now you got to win the peace!"

As he walked back up Praed Street, Riley found himself remembering Ainsworth's prayer: Courage for the big troubles in life, patience for the small. And when you have laboriously finished your day's efforts, go to sleep in peace. (Be of good cheer. God is awake.)

Good God, Riley, after all you've lived through, you can certainly survive a couple of children landing on you. Winning the peace, for all of us. Go on. This — taking on Tom and Kitty — is what is needed, just as much as education, and reconstructive surgery, and Hinchcliffe to have a purpose, and every lost soldier a gravestone, and Ermleigh not to lose his job. In the Spartan Phalanx, each man used his shield to protect not himself, but the next man along — and the work continues. The work continues.

And there's Christmas, and there's a funeral to go to.

Christmas was all right, but the funeral, of course, was terrible.

Mrs Orris had tried to take charge from the off. First she wanted Julia buried at Froxfield. Then she wanted her buried in her wedding dress. She was angry with them all for having Christmas in London and not inviting her. Then she said she washed her hands of the whole affair. Then she came to stay at Locke Hill, and then she left without telling anyone. Then she came back.

Nadine said, "We must be patient with her. She's lost her daughter."

"Yes, now there's nobody for her to be so absolutely foul to," said Rose, and Nadine snorted with laughter which turned into tears.

Mrs Orris challenged Peter's choice of hymns; she wanted "Onward, Christian Soldiers".

Peter had laughed in her face, and said: "Madam? Over my dead body. He chose "Come Down, O Love Divine", and two utterly obscure, deeply sad seventeenth-century ones which nobody knew. Rose persuaded him to drop one of them for "Jerusalem". Then Mrs Orris wanted to read a poem. Peter agreed she should. But the one she wanted to read was a sentimental horror which everybody else thought half-witted. She insisted. She telephoned the printer on Christmas Eve — Riley's printer, Mr Owen — and put it on the order of service, and changed the typeface without asking anyone, so the lines no longer fitted properly, and she was so rude and bossy about this that a situation developed, with Mr Owen blaming Riley, and the new pamphlets being late after all. And then she announced that there would be full mourning, for everybody, without consulting Peter, and nobody had full mourning, and there was no cloth to be had to make any up, and anyway no time, it was Christmas, it was mad, everything was closed . . .

Peter rescinded the order, and Mrs Orris declared that nobody had loved Julia except for her.

Then she wanted to read the letters of condolence people had written to Peter. He hadn't read them himself. He pushed the bundle towards her. "Have them!" he said. "Read them, eat them, make a hat of them. As you wish."

Rose, of all people, had been the one to lose her temper with her. There had been a huge silent fight about whether or not the children should attend. Nadine was still not letting Kitty out of her sight, or her arms: Kitty had to go. So how could Tom not?

Mrs Orris said she would have them all arrested if they tried to force this young innocent to attend his mother's funeral; it was disgusting, she said, just the sort of indecent suggestion she would expect from her reprobate son-in-law, a man without any kind of morals at all, just the type one would expect to lose his self-control at the first sign of trouble, even the Army had sent him home . . .

Peter said, in his polite manner, "Well, next time, Jane, perhaps you'd like to join up? You could scare a Hun to death just by appearing —" and left the room, rolling his eyes.

This was when Rose took her firmly, physically, by the overpadded shoulders, and shouted into her face that this was a decorated and wounded war hero, the backbone of the British Army, the man to whom they all owed the fact they still had heads on their shoulders and furthermore the father of the grandchildren she presumably expected to see again in her lifetime — and *furthermore* a man who had lost his wife and was left alone with two children to bring up.

And then she felt absolutely terrible for abusing this woman, this older woman, who had lost her daughter.

288

Nadine said, "Nobody's forcing anybody. Harding could perhaps take Tom for a walk."

And when the day came, it was the wettest and most miserable kind of English winter day: light for only a few hours, and you could hardly call it light anyway. Kitty had colic. The train was delayed so people were late, among them Peter's mother, who appeared like the ghost of the old century, frail and worried in a crinoline and bonnet, Scottish mists settled into the folds of her shawl. In a church full of prurient neighbours, shocked and buttoned-up friends from long ago, sniffing relatives, and individuals weeping repressedly for some other bereavement of their own, only the doctor cried all the way through.

"Afraid we're going to sue him for incompetence, no doubt," Peter said loudly, afterwards, sitting on his father's grave with Kitty in his arms, smoking, smiling his bitter smile, and declining to come home for the wake.

But he's holding Kitty! Nadine thought. That's good.

And that was the end of 1919. Cold dingy weather, hypocrisy and misunderstanding lurking, all a year older, a year further away from it all. One woman down, one new girl entered, otherwise the same group in the same house. They were all, some despite themselves, aware of the symbolic power of the passing year, and the passing decade. And each was thinking, in their various ways, as they cuddled their teddy, caught each other's eyes, raised the glasses of sherry which seemed a decent substitute for champagne in this time of mourning, but early, because Lord knows nobody wanted to stay up till midnight, thank God that's over.

289

Part Three

1927

CHAPTER
TWENTY-TWO

Locke Hill, August 1927
Time passed. It had no choice. As various people felt it
worth saying, during the war, after the war, at Julia's
funeral, in the weeks and months afterwards, Life Goes
On. Riley Purefoy, thirty-one years old, sitting in the
Leinster Arms after work one high summer evening,
sipping a pint of half and half through his brass straw,
heard someone say it at the next table.

It does, it does. Its doing so had been on his mind. It
was ten years since his war had finished. Do I feel safe
yet? Am I still afraid? What do I fear?

He feared that Tom and Kitty might be taken from
them — that Mrs Orris might decide to cause more
trouble, or Peter recover, and want the children. What if
Peter were to die? He had wondered if he and Nadine
should try formally to adopt them, but when he had
brought it up, she had said no. "They have their father,
flawed as he is. We can love them and keep them, but
blood is blood. It's not so much about him having
them, as them having him."

It was, he felt, unsettled. But then things are unsettled.
It's their nature. Whatever we may think is going on.

He feared that nothing would ever happen to them again. More often, that fear was a hope. Occasionally he would say to her, "What about the motorbike, Nadine? Weren't you going to have a motorbike and tour the world?" and she would laugh and say, "Oh yes, I'm going to, you on the pillion, Tom and Kitty strapped to the handlebars." Or, "I have my world here, sweetheart." Or, "Plenty of time."

Did he fear that he and Nadine would never have their own children? He thought not. They had ceremonially and rather gleefully thrown the rubber thing on the bedroom fire in 1926, but nothing had happened yet. They were going to give it another six months before thinking about seeing a doctor. Nadine had relaxed into the combination of art and children with great grace and a good nanny, involving the children and retreating as she wished, unburdened by a complex sense of responsibility. When she was with them she was with them. When she was working she was working. She'd made a studio in the glassed-in verandah on the back of the house. A gap between children suited her. He didn't fear for her, or for the children they might or might not have. They were still only thirty-one years old.

He stood up. He had promised to take Tom for a quick game of two-man cricket in the park.

When he came in, Nadine and Rose were in the drawing room, sewing, deep in one of their interminable conversations. Rose was full of plumbing and child mortality rates. "What point is there being a doctor," she was saying, "when you're just clearing up incidences of illnesses which with proper plumbing would not occur in the first place? It's like being a road sweeper in a town without rubbish bins."

Nadine enquired after various young patients by name: she ran a drawing club in Rose's waiting room on Thursday afternoons after school. When Kitty bounced into the room, she joined in the chat, drawing club being her favourite. Conversation moved on to whether or not it was too late for Little Tea that day, i.e. tea using the dolls' blue willow-pattern tea set, with slices of toast made from the tiny Hovis loaves, and slices of fairy cake cut as if the fairy cake were a full-sized cake, and the tiny pot of jam that Rose had brought back from her breakfast at the hotel in Switzerland for the children. Kitty suggested that Dr Aunt Rose should come with her into the back garden to see if the quails had laid, because if so they could make tiny fried eggs, and it could be Little High Tea.

Looking at these beautiful, beautiful women, Riley thought: Never take anything for granted.

Crossing the road to Kensington Gardens, cricket bat in hand, Tom, eleven years old, whip-thin, white-haired, blue eyes narrowed, made a declaration: he would no longer go on holiday to Locke Hill.

"Why not?" Riley asked.

"Because of *that man*."

"Which man?" Riley, ever protective, asked.

"That *father*."

Riley said nothing, letting Tom proceed — which he did, wary but determined.

"I don't want him," he said, glancing up to check for reaction. He received none, just Riley's quiet presence.

"I've been thinking about it," Tom said. "You wheel me down there and I'm always polite, but he doesn't want me, that's clear enough. You know it's true! I've had enough of all these parents who are no good and dead and so forth. I'd rather it was all kept simple. You're my father and Nadine is my mother. I may change my name. I hope you think that's fair. Because I have to insist."

How bold his look! Riley thought. But can I blame him? Actually, he rather admired him for it.

"It's absurd," Tom said, "to have parents who aren't even actually there. Even if they are there. Of course, Mummy can't help being dead, but she wasn't even there before she was dead."

"What do you mean, old boy?" Riley said.

"Going away without saying," Tom said. "Or crying at Daddy. And Daddy not wanting her. And then too much hugging."

Riley had to do some quick maths — How old had he been? Three, when his mother died? And people think children don't notice things . . . He couldn't fault the memory. That weeping, pestering woman, tricksy and difficult, always dragging at the boy.

"I know I'm meant to love them," Tom said, looking up at him. His face was white and tense. "But I don't! I think they are hateful, weak, unpleasant, unreliable and treacherous. And I might as well say so."

This boy will never be rosy and merry, Riley thought, and he was about to speak when Tom, suddenly shocked at his own forthrightness, burst out: "Sorry, sir," and turned and ran off. Riley watched him, the small figure clomping across the grass in his brown lace-ups, beneath the flat under-surface of the plane tree branches. After a few hundred yards the boy sat down swiftly, up against one of the piebald trunks, and hunched over.

People said "Life Goes On" to Tom as well. Chaps' parents, at school, usually, or beaks. He had developed his own response. "Death goes on too, you know," he would say. Quite politely.

He was muttering it now, sitting in the pilot's seat of his Gotha. Also, la mort continue, and la morte continua, mortus continuat, and der Tod whatever goes on is in German. When he ever met a foreigner, which wasn't often, he asked them to give the phrase in their language. What he really wanted was a Russian. When he wanted to think with fondness of his father, he would recall that Peter had written it out for him in Greek, both Greek letters and phonetic. But he no longer wanted to think fondly of his father.

Tom was allowing Kitty, seven years old, pink cheeked, fluffy looking, stubborn, to perch in the forward cockpit: a rusty upright cylinder on whose rim, long ago, a German machine gun had swivelled and shot its fire through the night skies. The bottom was soft with leaf mould and worms, so she sort of stood and leant and wriggled, while Tom was an emperor in the remains of the pilot's throne, with the remains of the controls before him, no longer dangling, because he, Tom Locke, had fixed them up. He had found the plane years before. In the course of a picnic, aged five or so, he had run away, scampering through incipient bluebells and old rotting conkers, and there it was. He had thought it was a ruin, overgrown with brambles, knee-deep in sludge and the knotty brown roots of ferns. But when he banged on it a deadened clunk sounded, as if the ruin wanted to let loose a loud and glorious clang but couldn't. He had climbed on a fallen tree and seen a long body with two flattened and broken wings: an iron dragonfly of massive proportions. Three big circular holes appeared along the top, into which a boy might climb. He had climbed. In front of him, controls: rusting, falling. He had reached out, closed his eyes and stared ahead, and felt the thrum of engines, and the void below, and the wide massive skies above. In the years since, he had measured it, surveyed it, identified it, run away to it, hid in it, counted the rivets on its blunt nose, dug underneath it in search of its wheels, put his foot through its rusty panels, attempted to fix the big oily bundles of engine that lay stranded among its broken wing struts. But he had never told anybody about it. Even Riley might say, It's dangerous, don't go there. Or, It's not yours, leave it alone. But someone must know it's there. You'd notice, if a plane fell out of the sky. They must all know. But that first time, he was sure, no one had been there — there were no footprints, nothing was disturbed. But someone must have been there. Unless they had jumped out with parachutes. He had always secretly thought: They might be there still. There might be skeletons.

It had occurred to him, when he was so small, that this might be where his mother had gone, and that he'd probably better not mention that. But he'd known that really mothers who have died don't go in planes, and he'd known even then that there was no point in asking his father. He had looked for the skeletons for years. He never took Kitty with him. He didn't want her to find them — to be scared, or — worse — to succeed where he'd failed.

But now she was big enough, and she could see his plane. Though the gigantic, delicate wings had fallen away, and anything removable had been taken by older trophy-hunters than he, the body of the plane lay there, an iron ghost, hollow and receptive to his purposes, demonstrative of his superiority, and of his generosity in bestowing this honour. He had something important to say to her. He was telling her, because she had a right to know, that he would not be visiting that man again, and that he expected her not to either.

"Which man?" Kitty asked, frowning, because she knew.

"Father."

Kitty raised her eyes to him and her mouth went firm.

"I'm deadly serious," Tom said. "And if you're not with me, I shan't speak to you again."

She knew he was capable of it.

"It's all right for you," Tom said. "You're a girl. You aren't meant to grow up to be like him. I don't want him, and he doesn't want me. I'm having Riley for my father and Nadine for my mother. I've told Riley. He said it's quite all right."

This was a lie. Riley had not said that. But if Kitty believed that Riley said it was all right, then it would be all right. Tom stared down at her, willing her.

"I think you should do the same," he said.

She was picking at a tiny fresh larch cone, pale green, soft and sweet.

"Where will we go, then?" she said.

"I've thought of that," said Tom. "Italy. Nadine wants to go there to see the man that writes her letters. We can make them take us there. Italy is probably marvellous."

Kitty shrugged, and threw her cone out into the woods. She didn't know what Italy was. She said, "Well, you know I want to go to Italy, but Daddy is still my father."

He looked at her bleakly. "I suppose that is your choice," he said. "But I pity you."

"I don't care," she said. "Riley is nice to everyone. I'm the only person Daddy is at all nice to."

"So what?" snapped Tom. "Riley's a good man and Peter's . . . an oaf." He could see that his calling him "Peter" upset Kitty, but he liked the distance and maturity it suggested. It was even better than "Father".

Once he had seen that he could hurt her, he didn't actually want to.

"Where would you go if you could go anywhere?" he asked her, magnanimously.

Because she was in her own trance, gazing out over blue imaginary skies of her own, Kitty said, without thinking: "To find Mummy."

"She's dead." Tom said.

"Dead people have graves," Kitty reposted.

"She was cremated," said Tom.

Kitty didn't know what that meant and wasn't going to ask.

"Are you thinking about going to heaven in this plane to find her?" he said.

She denied it.

"You want to forget about her," he said. "She wasn't nice anyway."

Kitty objected.

"She gave me away to Grandma when I was a baby," he continued. "And she did something mad to her face. I saw it. Her face couldn't move."

"Stop it." said Kitty.

"She would have given you away too!"

"No she wouldn't."

"Daddy used to hide in his study so he didn't have to look at her."

"That's not true."

"It is true. That's why he drinks whiskey and needs to go quiet. Ask him. Ask Nadine. Ask Riley!"

As if either of them would ask Riley about a face!

"She didn't like her terrible face so she died," he said.

Kitty could see the logic of that. Then she thought — "But Riley has a terrible face and he didn't die!"

"Riley is different," said Tom. "One, he's a man. Two, he's a soldier. Three, he's a hero. Riley is a superior character."

And Kitty couldn't fault him on Riley. Neither of these children had any idea that anybody had ever doubted him. They saw only what Riley was now: a heroic man, a reliable man, a successful and beloved man. That Riley was scarred and damaged and from a poor background merely added to his magnificence:

look what he had overcome! Even as a small boy riding on Riley's broad shoulders Tom had felt the strength of him, and when he slid his fingers in among the black curls under Riley's hat, and felt the strange roughness of the bare patches concealed there, he was not alarmed or repulsed. Riley published books by famous people, like Mr and Mrs Horrabin, Mr and Mrs Cole, and Mr Wells. When they came to dinner, talk was of policy and ideals, freedom and peace and education. Tom wasn't very interested, but he was proud. Whereas his actual father. Well.

Since Julia's death, Peter had hardly gone to London at all. Around 1923 he had moved into a slightly damp gamekeeper's cottage beyond the woods, where there was a small bit of garden, and no immediate neighbours. Riley's initial suspicion — that the cottage was a place for Peter to get as drunk as he needed without any interference — hadn't proved to be the case. Around the same time Peter had quietly, of his own accord, stopped drinking, as he had stopped doing almost anything else. Sober, Peter was no more sociable. He had nothing to say, and didn't listen. He didn't want to go for a walk, or to listen to music, or to see the children. Gifts of books lay unopened, food stood uneaten, messages unanswered. As Peter's responses shrivelled, so did Riley's visits. Though always regular, they became short, safe, and practical: this needs a signature; about Mrs Joyce's retirement pension arrangements; Tom must go to school/ has measles/wants to take up shooting, did Peter have an opinion?

No.

Even this kind of topic, over the years, had shrunk away.

Still, though, Nadine or Rose would periodically throw up their hands and want things to be different — let's take him for another round of doctors, perhaps they have discovered some new disease, some new test cure — vegetarianism, mentalism, psychotherapy. But Riley, Rose and Nadine all knew the horrible truth that you cannot give your life to trying to help someone who cannot help himself: whatever your effort, it won't work. So they would remind each other that things could be much worse. Peter is a bucket with a hole in it: don't keep pouring stuff in — love, hope, attention — because it will just pour straight out again. Or, Peter is a sleeping dog; let him lie.

Kitty did not know this and it could not be explained to her. She was old enough now to go about on her own, and recently Riley had seen her wandering down in the general direction of the cottage, clutching a careful bunch of bright, shiny, sticky-looking buttercups, holding them out in front of her. We all have the right to our own mistakes, Riley thought, even seven-year-olds, and how else do they learn? And perhaps I am wrong, and she will redeem him, or at least awaken him, in some way, like little Annie Ainsworth did me . . . talking of which, he needed to send her a shilling for her birthday.

But he was wary.

Well, they were going to be here most of the summer: rebellious Tom, sweet Kitty, and the realistic adults.

In view of the refusal and the buttercups, Riley thought that perhaps it was time once again to disturb the bond of silence into which he and his friend had fallen.

The room was the same as it had been since 1923, tidy and spare: a chair, a desk, a clock. On the mantelpiece, incongruous in a glass milk bottle, was the lanky bunch of buttercups. Riley saw how it would have been: Peter having no vase, Kitty embarrassed for him, and for herself for not having realised that he wouldn't, and determinedly putting it right by finding the milk bottle and making that the vase.

Peter moved very slowly, and smelt of bachelor and seclusion, of tweeds and tobacco. He made courteous moves, offering tea and a seat to his guest.

So. Riley felt a twist of nerves in his solar plexus as he spoke. "I can't help wondering," he said, "if you're going to come out of this. Ever."

Peter smiled into his tea at Riley's question. "So," he said. "No small talk."

"No," said Riley.

"I thought I might," Peter said. "After ten years. That's how long it took Odysseus, you remember — but that was one year for each year of his war, which for me meant I should have been through it by 1922 — and the thought didn't occur to me till 1925. So the equation was wrong."

"Do you still think about it?"

"Oh no," said Peter. "Hardly at all." (This was not exactly true. Instead of sleeping, he spent many of his nights in the same waking dream about it all: a long

304

complex dream involving fuel lines breaking off and flailing in the wind, himself being dragged behind something, with something important he had to do and no way off what was dragging him; Bloom's head on his shoulder; mud eating at his legs, the smells of cordite and patchouli, mixed — everything was mixed up — a feather boa on a German boy, Julia eating bacon and eggs in the waiting room of the clap clinic in Amiens, looking up and smiling at him, sweetly. The stretcher bearer with the eyebrows. And summer rain, endless summer rain, which turned into blood. Often he felt as if he was still in it, waiting for the arrival of men or of orders, behind the lines in some little village somewhere, in some Flemish parlour. And often the worst dream: somebody's weight beside him.)

"You could come out," Riley said. "The children would like it."

A long pause.

Riley sat. For a long time.

Well, I've done nothing for him for years, he thought. I might as well do nothing for him here in his company. Peter's legs were so thin now they seemed to fold up from the old armchair like a cricket's, and his shoulders were beginning to curve over. Everything about him was folding in. His fading hair, Riley noticed, was receding, leaving the start of a widow's peak.

He started to think that Peter was not going to respond at all, ever; and he began to wonder how long they would sit, and how either of them could ever break the silence, if they were ever to go back to life and reality . . .

"Do you remember being a child?" Peter asked suddenly. "Twelve or thirteen? And looking at the world for the first time and seeing — poverty, and sickness, and hunger, and war, and crime for the first time, with your young eyes, and realising the adults must all be mad? Barking mad, to let the world go on this way?"

Riley did remember. He'd been a bit younger than twelve or thirteen.

"Then as you get older, your eyes close again. It's all there, and you know that, but everybody seems to accept it, so you accept it too, and you become inured . . . Well. I have not found that happy ability to close my eyes to the real nature of humanity. I can't forget." He said it apologetically.

An intense weariness rose in Riley. He had, himself, done very well with the forgetting. There'd been no more risk. His mind was steady. He knew what he had to lose. Whether he had done well enough to feel safe to enter into this territory with Peter, he wasn't sure. The alternative was to say something facile and practical. Facile and practical, he felt, would be better, as he was going back to spend the rest of the afternoon playing cricket with the children. In fact, he had decided in favour of facile and practical years earlier, and stuck. If that made him, in Peter's terms, a barking mad adult and part of the wilful blindness, so be it. The children do not need our grief inflicted on them. They'll find their own soon enough. As Tom already has. Having been born in it.

"Life goes on," Riley said.

"How can life go on when death exists?" Peter said. "That's icing on a poisoned cake. I can't make that leap

306

into disbelief. That's why I have made my life very small. It's — easier to control. I am easier to control."

"Why do you need to be controlled?" Riley asked, though he was beginning to feel a little sick.

"Because inside I am mad with grief and loss," Peter said, mildly. "I lost my men. I have lost my peace of mind, my sleep, my manners, my — equanimity. My dignity. My wife! My children. My girlfriend, whose existence is unknown even to you. You. My ability to get anything back."

"You *can* have them back," Riley said.

"Really?" said Peter. A pause.

"Some," Riley said. "I'm here, old man."

There was a silence.

"It's getting late," Peter said. It wasn't.

"Your children," Riley said. "They're up at the house. They always want to see you." That wasn't quite true.

Peter shook his head. "And my wife . . ." he said.

"Have you ever thought," Riley said gently, "of finding someone new?"

"I married her," said Peter. "I gave my word . . . I made those promises. And I love her."

"But, Peter, she's dead. Seven years —"

"I don't seem to get things like that quite right in my mind," Peter said. "I let her down . . ."

To Riley, love was present, current, and vital. It was Nadine looking up and smiling when he came into the room, or having mended his jacket before he realised there was a hole; Kitty hugging him when he picked her up after she fell over; Tom talking to him this morning. It's a circulation of giving and receiving, a fuel, it fuels itself. Your twisting eyebeams create it when you make love; your words and kindnesses create it, and a child brings an entire new bottomless well of it. He, Riley, had been feeding from Peter and Julia's children, and Peter had been starved of it.

He wanted a big stick to stir Peter with, a great waterfall to push him under. They were both silent for a while.

"What girlfriend?" Riley asked suddenly.

A ghost of a smile passed over Peter's face. "An American girl," he said. "Eight years ago. I relieved her of the burden of my existence."

Riley's mind flicked back — the night in Soho, Christmas 1918, when he'd pulled Peter out of the Turquoisine — "The singer?" he said. "The negro girl?" The kind-eyed girl who'd called Peter honey, and told Riley he was cute. Mabel. She'd had the look of a girl who could give and receive.

"Mabel," Peter said. "Yes."

Riley waited for him to say something more on the subject.

Nothing. A little birdsong from the garden, a rustling of the breeze in the poplars.

Then Peter shifted in his chair and said, "And my peace of mind. I lost that. July the first, Purefoy. July the first, and the twenty-fifth of September."

The Somme, and Loos. The image of Mabel dissolved, and Riley's carefully peaceable mind turned, and gazed back. To all that. To that — Atmosphere? No, it was more . . . an ocean. A vast tank? . . . of some corrosive liquid, in which things look different, and move differently; sounds echo differently, your limbs are the wrong weight,

308

what should be solid has dissolved, what should be straight and strong is bending and moving — towards you? Away from you? Out from under your feet? And you have no dimension in which to consider whether it is the concrete world which is shifting, or your perception. And everything exists within this corrosive liquid: landscapes, legs, friendships, orders, appetites, sight, memory, judgement. Moving through it, your strength and the energy you are expending do not relate to the movement of your body and your limbs — not in the usual way. The focus of your mind is warped. That which you know to be true shifts and melts. In truth, you have nothing beneath your feet. But there is no truth you can rely on, and nothing to rely with.

Constant, lethal danger of death, at all times. They had breathed it, swam in it, drunk it, eaten it, been it — ferocious, insidious, perpetual danger; drowning in the constant threat — an extraordinary way to live! Immersed in danger, soaked through, inseparable. How can a man ever rinse that out of his psyche? Were we not leached and warped by that toxic bath? Our chemistry changed, our joints rusted and corroded, our hearts scorched? Like things left out in the storm then crushed forgotten in a corner, stinking, damp, stained, black with fungus, stiff with mould . . . oh it wasn't far away at all, all that . . .

By act of will he drew his mind carefully round to the present again, and staked it to the solid ground of today.

"Someone said — who was it?" Riley said, "— that only men with imagination turned neurasthenic, and that he was jolly glad he had no imagination."

"And December," said Peter. "Whatever bloody day it was in December."

"You didn't kill her," Riley said.

"Oh I know, I know," Peter said. "But then I sort of did, in other ways. Over and over."

"Please come out," said Riley. "Please."

"I don't know how you do it," Peter said. "I can't do it. I can't get away from it."

"Your children help me," Riley said.

"We both know," said Peter, "that you are a better father to my children than I ever could be."

This pinned Riley too tight between opposites. In doing right by Kitty and Tom, he couldn't but do wrong by Peter.

"You *could* be something," he said.

Peter gave him a quizzical glance, which Riley acknowledged. "We just say you're ill," he said. His jaw was aching, and the tea made him cough. He wiped his mouth. They were both aware of the quasi-irony. Though ill wasn't the word. Damaged is not ill, as he and Nadine hadn't needed to say to each other for years now.

"The thing is, Riley," Peter said, "that I wouldn't want someone like me near my children."

There's very little you can say to that. Riley dropped his head for a moment or two. Then he said, and found it useless even as he said it: "Well, if you change your mind." It was hard on all of them, keeping that door open.

Peter looked suddenly a little lost. "Interesting phrase," he said. "Change your mind. I'd love to change my mind. I'd change it to — a chrysanthemum, I think." Then: "Have you read Homer yet, Riley? It's so interesting, about soldiers. When Patroclus died, and Achilles went mad in his tent, fighting ghosts and so on — well, never mind. I don't suppose Achilles had shell shock."

"I can't think about it," Riley said. "Each man has his own way, I know . . ."

"He felt betrayed by Agamemnon, when Agamemnon took away Briseis for himself. The slave girl. Achilles' war prize? You remember. Soldiers go mad when their leaders betray them. And when their friends are killed. Don't you think?"

Riley said nothing about that.

"Who betrayed us?" Peter asked.

No helmets for the first nine months. Those home-made grenades. The great shell shortage of 1915. The utter fuck-up of the Somme — walking into gunfire. Eleven years ago. Not long. A boy's lifetime ago.

"Who did we betray?"

The same names rolled through their minds.

"We didn't kill them, Peter," Riley said. "The war killed them. Let's not let it kill us too, after all these years." A blink of an eye.

Peter laughed. "Still," he said. "Reading Homer obsessively must be better than drinking, don't you think?"

"The present exists too. You could come out and have a look at it."

"I don't really know about the present. Odysseus' ten years, you know — the long voyage home from war. I've been thinking about all that. All the places he had to stop along the way. When Circe entranced them, drugged them, and that was a long delay, with the drugs and the seductress — it makes me feel a bit better about when I was drunk all that time, and going to the brothels. I mean, if even Odysseus went through an immoral stage . . . and he spent seven years with Calypso . . . I'm just taking my time, I think. I'm probably somewhere between Scylla and Charybdis. Not much use in the real world, I know."

"Well," said Riley.

"Do you remember the Sirens?" Peter said.

"They sang," said Riley. His education had not been as detailed as Peter's.

"Do you know what they sang about?"

"Love?" Riley guessed.

"No," said Peter. "You'd think it would be that, wouldn't you? Or of some idyllic home they had all come from, and were travelling to. Each to their own Ithaca. But no — the Sirens were in a meadow of beautiful flowers, and corpses, and they sang songs of the heroic past. Of heroes of war. They sang the truth about the past. That's what it was not safe for the returning soldiers to listen to. Succumb to *that* and your ship wrecks, and your companions die. You have to sail on, sail on, into the future. Odysseus was tied to the mast, so he could hear the song and yet survive it. He is tied to the vehicle which carries him into the future, and yelling to be released, to be allowed back into the past. Arcadia — the past — is death. Do you see?"

"Not really," said Riley. "Are you tied to the mast?"

"My ship has stalled," Peter said. "It's all gone wrong. Penelope was not meant to die. She waited twenty years for him, lying and cheating to protect her son and to hold off the men who wanted to marry her. Though — you know they only spend one night together. In the whole poem. One night. Then he has to go off and placate Poseidon. Tiresias promised everything would be all right in the end, that after all that, Odysseus would have blessed peace, and his people around him. The gods wanted an amnesty — Greek is a marvellous language, Riley — do you know what 'amnesty' means? Forgetting."

"We're all here," said Riley, rather helplessly, and Peter said, with a sudden burst of bonhomie: "Well, of course you are!" And then, very quietly, "But I'm safer inside, you know. On my own."

Walking back up to the house, Riley thought, suddenly, What will happen when I go bald? Will my chin go bald? He remembered his father's hairline, and had a lurch of affection, for his father, his home, his childhood, the distance . . . My God, it was so long ago, the little house. The war was a long roll of cloud on the horizon behind him in time, cutting him off, and there were the long years since, which had, after all, been years of recovery. Back when I was a common little boy. Before I got all arty and above myself, with Sir Alfred, and my notions. He heard again his mother's scorn, and his father saying, "There's better, Riley." And so there was, Dad. Thank you.

He was glad he had talked to Peter, but he shouldn't have said "if you change your mind". He hadn't the right, really, to invite Peter in that way. Of course he hadn't the right to deny him, either; the children were Peter's. But they live with us; we feed them and clothe them and tend to them and listen to them — they have been ours, in effect, for seven years — and Nadine —

Tom, lurking in a patch of wild cherry trees, jumped out, quietly, loomed up behind Riley and spat cherry stones at the back of his head. Riley turned and tousled him, and wrestled him down a bit.

"I'm going to whittle a snake," Tom said. "I was going to say you can help me find a stick, but you can't now."

Riley just walked on. After a moment or two Tom circled back, and said: "I don't know why you take the trouble," before hurtling off again.

Riley saw it all: in the recesses of Tom's memory, drunk Peter was still shouting, smelling, lurking, unsafe, and frightening Julia and Rose. The quiet, self-emptied ghost who had retreated to the cottage had never even tried to counter that festering splinter. Part of Tom is waiting for that Peter to lurch out again, Riley thought. What does he make of the emptiness in his father's eyes?

But there is so much of Peter still there! So much thought and feeling locked away . . .

"Tom!" he called, and because it was unheard of in the family not to respond immediately to Riley's soft voice, out of respect, Tom turned back, circling, until he arrived at Riley's side.

"Your father," Riley said, and Tom looked mutinous, but Riley went on, quite quietly and firmly. "Take your hands out of your pockets, Tom. Your father was a hero in the war. As you know, I served under him; he was a magnificent officer, and performed acts of bravery and loyalty which I hope you never have to emulate. He's

314

not an . . . easy . . . man now, precisely because of the man he was in the war."

"But you're easy," said Tom.

"I'm glad you think so," said Riley, with a small smile.

"And you were — you know. Wounded."

"Not all wounds are visible, Tom. You're old enough to understand this. And if you don't understand it, you're old enough to be civil about it. I don't want to hear you being disrespectful of him. And certainly not to your sister."

"She loves him," Tom said, in as near to a sneer as he felt he could get away with.

"Of course she does," said Riley. "He's her father. And yours. And he's a good man. I wish you'd known him before —"

"I don't," said Tom.

Tom circled off again, disbelieving still, stretching his head this way and that. It's disloyal to Riley to go sucking up to Peter, Tom thought, whatever Riley says. Peter may be my father, but I shall NOT grow up to be like him. I'll work hard at my rugby this year, and get properly strong. I shall never, ever drink whisky or brandy. I shan't ever get married and have children. If I ever have to be in a war I shan't be in the Army at all, I'll be in the Navy or the RAF . . .

After a while his arms of their own accord floated up, and he was an aeroplane, soaring and wheeling across the meadows, feet stumbling over wildflowers, wind in his ears.

315

CHAPTER
TWENTY-THREE

Locke Hill, August 1927
Riley was fairly sure that Kitty didn't see the emptiness
in her father's eyes. Perhaps it wasn't there for her. She
was born after the worst of that time — though the
price she paid for that was never having her mother. The
child of peace, though, he thought, with a little smile. And
she was peaceable! Riley often read to her at bedtime,
and lately their book had been *A Little Princess*.

"Do you suppose," he asked Nadine in bed one
evening, lights out, sheet and blankets tugged round
them, nestled and entangled, "that Kitty thinks of
creeping in at night like Ram Dass with a cheerful rug,
for Peter?"

"What, to plump the pillows?" Nadine said. "To
make things right? Like Julia, all those years?"

"Yes," he said. "Like that. Does she dream of a
special bond of understanding? Does she want to make
him happy? To be special to him?"

"I hope not," Nadine said, and they were quiet for a
moment. Each feared that she did, and that she would
pour her dear self into her father, not seeing the dark
hole at the bottom.

Riley shivered suddenly.

"What is it?" she said.

"I miss him," he murmured.

"I know," she said, but she was half asleep, and didn't notice his second shiver, one of pure loneliness, of missing his friend — or rather, and he had to admit this now, the friendship they might have had. To his drowsy mind came that piece by Edward Thomas about walking all day with Robert Frost, "The Stile", from *Light and Twilight*. Peter had given a copy to Nadine, and Nadine had given it to him: dog roses, and musing oaks clustered round farmhouses, and how when your friend and you know each other well enough, thoughts come from either mind and you're not sure which. And these — friendship, and the earth — unite you with infinity and eternity — you're part of it. We're all part of it.

He and Peter should have had the kind of friendship those two poets had.

And then, the faithful and unbearable memories of other friendships lost came looming up.

He slept badly, and the following morning set out with sandwiches to walk, to clear his mind — a long walk, out into the fields, along the lanes, wherever it took him. Somewhere empty. It was going to be a hot day. The striding was good: the rhythm of feet striking earth, the walking into solitude.

The ghosts were still bothering him. August, ten years ago.

He tried to remember walking in from Zonnebeke with his face hanging off: pulling his clagged boots out of mud, duckboards, slipping, the noise and furore of battle behind him, the chaos of its margins all around him. Not knowing why he couldn't shake the flies off his face. Half a horse up a tree. Was that then? Or was it that he had remembered it on that day?

The blue sky, and Ypres two black fingers on the horizon. He tried, carefully, to walk himself through what he could remember.

Not much, really.

He had been walking for a couple of hours. The sky was beginning to burn, glowing. The day was heavy with insects and the beauty of late summer. Out here in the middle of nowhere he took his shirt off, and didn't even notice that he kept the silk handerchief round his neck, as always, something to cover his face if he — or someone else — needed it.

Bringing Peter in then, that day. July the first. Could he remember that? Tripping on roots of trees no longer there. Brambles full of dead men. Jessop shooting Dowland as he ran away, a desperate zigzagging rabbit. The revetting in the German trench.

Riley suddenly pitched himself down onto the turf of the field-side path, flattening his back against the solid ground, and stared up: leaves, sky, space beyond. It's all right. You belong. Remind yourself: I cannot do without the infinite, nor the infinite without me.

He pounded the earth beside him gently, hopelessly, with his fists. The same chill earth — follow its surface, south and east, down the cliffs, under the sea, through the floundered lands to where the unfuneralled corpses lay, organised or in shattles, making earth. Edward

318

Thomas' among them. And Jack Ainsworth's, and . . . stop it. That's a Charybdis to pull you in and down . . .

There's some link, he thought. Nature growing out of the bodies of our ancestors. Those rocks in Wiltshire, sarsens, just lying about in the fields, propped up three thousand years ago at Avebury and Stonehenge, broken to build burial mounds, barrows and barns and houses. The Valley of Dry Bones, outside Marlborough. His mind ran along the surface again, west, past London, up alongside the slow Thames a while, along the Roman road, the A4, cobbles beneath tarmac, chalk beneath cobbles. Bones. Tiny tiny flowers. The hillside where he and Nadine had first made love.

And this little moment during which we are here, to see it all, as if we were separate from it, before becoming part of it again, bones and loam and air and leaves of grass. Like poets walking and talking together all the July day, and into the English dusk.

I'm not a poet. I can't even talk clearly.

He lay there.

I'm not having it, he thought. I'm not fucking having it. He jumped up, pulled his shirt on, turned back.

He went striding down the path, through the dark dry trees. He paused a second on the doorstep, then walked in without knocking. Peter was still in the chair, doing nothing.

"Sir," Riley said, in his soft, intense voice.

"What are you talking about, Purefoy?" Peter said, frowning slightly. "What do you mean, 'sir'?"

319

"I know a bit of the *Odyssey*, sir. I read it because of
you. Not in Greek. But I read it — like Julia did,
because of you. You know where it says we're worn-out
husks, with dry haggard spirits always brooding over
our wanderings, our hearts never lifting with any joy,
because we've suffered far too much. You remember
that bit, sir?"

"Yes," said Peter. "It's what Circe told him."

"Yes, and she was fucking right, sir," Riley said.
"Excuse my French." He was staring. He swallowed, his
curious gulping little swallow.

"Come come, Riley," Peter said, and Riley said: "No.
Shut up. For all you're so quiet, sir, I know what it
sounds like inside your head. I know you think you'll
collapse if you acknowledge . . . anything . . . and
collapsing *just isn't done*. Think you'd be letting
everyone down. But you said I was in charge, sir
so . . ."

Peter wasn't looking at him. He sat like a schoolboy.

"I need you," Riley said. "I need your help. I can't
fucking bear this, not to put too fine a point on it. I
need you, for example, to come to the pub, sir, with me
and Hinchcliffe and Ermleigh. We go every Thursday,
some of the lads come along — Burgess turned up a
few weeks ago, he's an orderly now at St Mary's
Paddington; you'd never believe it. Jarvis comes
sometimes — don't think you knew him, sir, he was
with me at the Queen's. He's been working for eight
years in a cinema, projectionist, so that nobody has to
see his face. There's some lads I knew when I was a
boy . . ." Lost friendships. Friendships which should have

been and never came to be. "We have a few and we talk about the old days. Also." He swallowed again. This was a long speech for him. I can swallow. Gratitude.

The room was so quiet, so still.

In for a penny . . .

"Also," he said. "I need you to write me a book about Homer and the war. All your *Iliad* and *Odyssey* stuff. You've done all the research. We could publish next year for the tenth anniversary of the peace. It's been ten years, sir. Ten years ago this month I was walking out of Passchendaele — August twenty-first! Ten years — and every soldier I passed saved my life, sir," — Riley's eyes were full now and he began to stumble — "everyone who said, Keep your chin up, pal — don't lie down! — Lucky sod, that's a Blighty one — Oh, Lord, there's a pushload already on this train, lad, but I'll squeeze you in — Mind if I prop you in the broom cupboard — then your cousin Rose, sir — Major Gillies — Captain Fry — Nurse Blackie — Mr Tonks — Lady Scott — and then Sir Alfred — Nadine. There was Ferdinand, sir, praying at the wire. Couch, in the mud, three feet from the top of the ladder. Dowland, running back, and his brother with no legs — Captain Jessop who shot Dowland. Baker — do you remember Baker? Injected paraffin wax into his leg, died of cancer a year later — Bloom, Hall, Johnson, and Atkins, Lovall, Burdock, Knightley, Bruce, Jones. Green and Wester, Taylor and Moles, and Twyford. And Merritt . . . and everyone. Captain Harper." He gulped. Captain Harper, flying across the sky like a whirling sunflower before shattering into a flaming shell crater —

"Ainsworth," he said. "You, sir —"

He stopped. Coughed and swallowed. "Some are dead, sir, and some are not. All right? You are not fucking dead. There's three things, sir, you're going to do for me. You're coming to the pub, you're writing me a fucking book and you're coming to France where we are going to sit on Jack Ainsworth's grave and cry like fucking babies. You're going to do it because I need to do it and I'm not doing it alone and you and I are not separate, sir. We're not separate things, sir. We're the same fucking thing, sir. You're coming with me."

Riley was incoherent by the end, but Peter began to understand him. He stood up.

CHAPTER
TWENTY-FOUR

Ypres, September 1927

The two of them went. Jarvis and Ermleigh weren't up to it. Hinchcliffe got shy. Burgess said, Yeah, thanks, I don't think so. They didn't invite anyone else. So Purefoy and Locke walked alone at two in the morning, while Ypres slept around them.

It was the same, but it was different. The streets were silent, and cleaner. The cathedral was rising, half-formed, where they had last seen it in ruins. Scaffolding and piles of stone stood where rubble and detritus had been. There were plenty of prefabs, damp-looking, occupied. The Cloth Hall, as ruined as it had ever been, still stuck its two blackened fingers in the air. And ahead of them loomed the great new white arch at the Menin Gate, the biggest headstone of them all, glowing slightly. They walked on towards it, sober, clean and together.

A vast golden moon was rising, and they looked at it, with its skeins of cloud and "who, me?" face. Nobody else was there, and they were grateful for that. They did not want to be part of the show for the visitors; the sorrowing mothers, the never-got-over-it widows, the disbelievers hoping still to find their missing man, the bare-faced vultures and grief tourists. A few candles in jars stood around, along the base of the walls, their flames and shadows flickering. An owl hooted softly, somewhere out over the flat darkness to the east. A miasma hung over it, and dampness rose.

Purefoy held up their lantern; Locke lit a cigarette and looked away, out of town, down the Menin Road towards the past.

"Do you suppose it's still muddy?" he said.

Purefoy said he should think so.

"I wonder if the trenches have all fallen in."

Purefoy thought not.

"I suppose we can go and look at them," Locke said.

"Larks!" said Purefoy.

"German ones, too. They're open to the public."

"Well, we've both seen the inside of a German trench before," said Purefoy.

"Not at leisure," Locke observed, and took a last drag, and dropped his stub.

Purefoy's face was tight. Thousands and thousands of men, under the sky, in the mud, unburied, unwashed, unprayed for, unfound. Hundreds of thousands, under the sky.

We held the shit in common. It's right to hold the getting over it in common.

Peter's look was long and clear, into the darkness.

"You suggested I wasn't dead," he said. "What makes you so sure?"

Riley snorted softly. "Empirical evidence, sir," he said. "The rats haven't eaten you."

"Hmph!"

324

"But also — you haven't been exactly alive. You never expected to come home alive. And so you never have."

"Oh," said Peter. Then, "Achilles' hair . . ."

"Heel?"

"No, hair. He promised it as an offering to a river god, Sperkheios, for his safe return. But when Patroclus fell, he cut it and put it in Patroclus' hands."

"Because he didn't care any more if he got home or not."

"Mm," said Peter. Then he said, "But I didn't lose my Patroclus."

Riley smiled. "Oh, we're all Patroclus, sir. We lost ourselves and each other."

Peter thought about that. Then he said: "Drop that 'sir' rubbish, would you?"

"Force of habit," said Riley. "Something in the air."

"Ghosts of rotting friends in the air," said Peter.

"My jaw," said Riley. "Out there somewhere."

"But not your heart."

"Nope. That's right here. Thumping."

Silence.

"Lend it to me sometimes?"

"Any time you like, Locke, old boy."

Peter smiled.

They looked at the names by lamplight. Hundreds of them. Thousands of them. They went on and on. Some names they knew, and many many more that they didn't. Riley choked at the sight of them. Yards and yards of names, tidy and clean in the stone. He put his

325

finger on one or two. He pulled his coat collar round against the wind, and lit a cigarette.

After a while Peter said, "Coffee?"

"Mm," said Riley.

"Madame said she'd leave a pot on the stove for us. And to wake her if we needed anything."

"Did she? That was kind."

"Wasn't it?"

They didn't want to leave.

"Should we not do something?"

"Something symbolic, you mean?"

"Mm."

They stood in silence for a while, the two of them silhouetted, tiny under the great white arch, gazing out into the black night. Silently each man's mind ran, yet again, through his own list of names, faces, moments.

Locke was still leaning against the cold white marble wall, in the dark. Very quietly he began to whistle the "Last Post". It's a difficult tune and he couldn't make all the high notes, but it served its purpose.

Acknowledgements

My thanks to
Vanessa Branson, Robert Devereux, Charlotte Horton,
Jacqueline Shave, Emily Young, Simon Browne-
Wilkinson, Michele Lovric and Chris "Mr Bennet"
Geering, RIP, and his daughters Sophy and Lucy, in
whose houses I have written this book.

To my dear agents, old and new:
Derek Johns, Natasha Fairweather, Linda Shaughnessy
and St John Donald,
and to my editor Katie Espiner for her most acceptable faith in me as a viable project.

To Sarah Chew for the title
and to Isabel Adomakoh Young, former co-author,
perpetual first reader.

I would also like to acknowledge my debt to Jonathan
Shay, MD, PhD, Staff Psychiatrist with the US Department
of Veterans Affairs, for his books *Achilles in Vietnam:
Combat Trauma and the Undoing of Character* and
Odysseus in America: Combat Trauma and the Trials

327

of *Homecoming*, two of the most interesting books on war, damage and literature that I have read, and of great inspiration to this book and to its predecessor, *My Dear, I Wanted to Tell You*.

And I acknowledge the permission of A P Watt at United Agents on behalf of the Trustees of the Robert Graves Copyright Trust.